Praise for Christopher Greyson's

THE GIRL WHO LIVED

Winner of the Gold Medal for Best Mystery/Thriller eBook of the Year – 2018 Independent Publisher Book Awards

Winner Best Thriller – 2018 National Indie Excellence Awards

"Greyson is a master of weaving suspense and keeping the reader guessing..." – *NetGalley Review*

"The plot turns come fast and furious....Sharp characters enmeshed in a mystery that, particularly in its final lap, is a gleefully dizzy ride." – *Kirkus Reviews*

"Christopher Greyson has created a thriller on par with *The Girl on the Train*, only with more suspects, more danger, and more agony for the young heroine." – *Killer Nashville*

***

How can one woman uncover the truth when everyone's a suspect—including herself?

From the mind of *Wall Street Journal* bestselling author Christopher Greyson comes a story with twists and turns that take the reader to the edge of madness. *The Girl Who Lived* should come with a warning label: once you start reading, you won't be able to stop. Not since *Girl on the Train* and *Gone Girl* has a psychological thriller kept readers so addicted—and guessing right until the last page.

Also by Christopher Greyson:

And Then She Was Gone

Girl Jacked

Jack Knifed

Jacks Are Wild

Jack and the Giant Killer

Data Jack

Jack of Hearts

Jack Frost

Pure of Heart

THE GIRL WHO LIVED

A THRILLING SUSPENSE NOVEL

CHRISTOPHER GREYSON

GREYSON MEDIA

This book is dedicated to my daughter Laura.
She has been such a wonderful example of love, strength and creativity.
I am blessed to be part of her life.

Wednesday, April 12
Brookdale

They were coming for her, but Faith wasn't in the mood to go anywhere. Not today.

"Twenty-one. Twenty-two. Twenty-three," she mumbled, counting the white ceiling tiles for the fiftieth time that morning. Compulsively, she rubbed her hand up the back of her head, feeling the unfamiliar stubble. Since she was locked up again—and hadn't seen a mirror in weeks—she figured it looked like a crew cut now. A couple months ago she'd dyed her long, caramel-brown hair too dark, and hated it. Her radical response was to shave her head. After the novelty wore off, she knew it wouldn't make any difference. Jet-black, platinum-blond, she was the same damaged goods, no matter what the package looked like on the outside.

Unable to concentrate, Faith lost count of the tiles. *One, two . . .* "Try, try again," she muttered as she folded her hands behind her head. "Fail, fail again." *Three, four—*

A key in the lock made Faith raise her head from the stiff mattress. She scanned the room for something to throw. The room was as small as a prison cell and arranged like one. A single bed was bolted to one wall so a guard could peer through the ten-inch-square unbreakable window in the door and easily check on the occupant. A one-piece metal toilet with no lid and a small matching sink were mounted on the other wall.

The lock clicked, keys jangled, and the metal door swung open.

When Faith saw Titus filling the doorway, her shoulders slumped. Titus was built like a small mountain: six foot six and over three hundred pounds. But it wasn't his size that made her stand down. She'd taken on bigger men. No, it was the big grin on his broad face.

"Good morning, Faith." His deep voice made the toilet bowl chime like a bell struck by a hammer. His Sudanese accent was thick, but his words were slow and well enunciated. "Would you please accompany me?" He stepped into the room and held the door open with one large arm.

When Faith didn't budge, he reminded her, "You are meeting with Dr. Rodgers." And he added, "This will be a great visit for you."

Scowling, Faith stepped forward, pulling up her hospital pants as she slipped through the doorway. "When did you get psychic powers?" she snapped.

Titus's laugh echoed in the hallway. "No, not psychic—hopeful. I stay positive." As always, he spoke with conviction.

Faith lowered her head and kept walking. *Hope.* That was the last thing she was looking for. Right now, all she wanted was *out.* But Faith knew the only way out of this place was through the man she was about to see. Until he certified her "not a danger to society," she'd stay behind locked doors, peering through dirty, mesh-covered windows.

Titus stopped at the last locked door. He paused with his keycard just out of range of the door sensor. Sounding like a pharaoh issuing a decree, he said, "You will have a great visit." He swiped the card and opened the door.

Dr. Rodgers's office was the only room Faith had seen in this building that wasn't all white. Here the walls were a soft green, and a square of pale-gray carpet covered the center of the floor. Two leather chairs faced each other in the middle of the rug. This was the only room in the place where Faith didn't feel like a zoo animal on display.

Dr. Rodgers entered. Faith didn't dislike him, though not for lack of trying. His white medical coat, worn open to reveal a sedate white shirt, blue tie, and gray trousers, looked too big for his small frame and made Faith think of a child playing dress-up, and his chunky black glasses enlarged his eyes so he seemed constantly surprised or startled. He reached out to shake Faith's hand, but then seemed to think better of it and instead motioned for her to sit.

Faith remained standing—not out of defiance so much as confusion. Did he believe her or not? A lot was riding on his letting her out eventually, and she couldn't count on the fact that they didn't seem to absolutely loathe each other as a glowing recommendation on her record.

Dr. Rodgers relaxed into his seat and again gestured toward the other chair, smiling without showing his teeth.

Faith held up her hospital pants with one hand and darted toward the chair, feeling like a mouse in an open field, exposed and vulnerable. When she landed on it, she tucked both feet beneath her and stared down at the carpet, to avoid looking into his startled eyes.

Dr. Rodgers nodded at Titus, who closed and locked the door behind him.

"Do you need smaller-sized scrubs?" Dr. Rodgers asked.

Faith gave a slight shake of her head. She *did* need a smaller size, but the real problem was that they had no elastic or drawstring. Not for someone on suicide watch.

"How are you today, Faith?"

Faith shrugged. What could she say? Did the doctor want to hear that she had stopped banging her head on the wall? Titus would have already relayed that. Did he want to hear all the dark thoughts screaming through her head right now?

Dr. Rodgers sat in his chair, waiting for Faith to say something. She could imagine him in a boat out on the lake, fishing, a hint of a smile on his face. He was a patient man, kind even.

"I've been counting," Faith said.

Dr. Rodgers's smile grew. "Excellent. Counting is a wonderful coping technique. If you find yourself frustrated or anxious, pick something wherever you are and count them. Simple but effective, right?"

Faith nodded.

"Do you remember what we discussed yesterday?" Dr. Rodgers asked.

Faith nodded again.

"The police would like to ask you some questions about what happened. They're here now." Dr. Rodgers pointed toward the door behind him, the one through which he'd entered. Faith knew it led to the doctors' offices—and the outside world.

"Nobody believes me," Faith said. She didn't want to talk to anyone anyway. Not Titus, not Dr. Rodgers. She definitely didn't want to talk to the cops.

"It's okay, Faith." Dr. Rodgers put an extra dose of reassurance in his voice, but it had no effect on her.

In spite of all the sedatives in her system, Faith felt anger kick in. It was faint and low, but the spark was there, and that scared her. Questions were like gas vapors. The more someone asked her about the incident, the thicker the fumes became, and once they reached that spark of anger inside her . . . something bad might happen.

Again.

"They won't believe me." Faith pulled her legs tighter against her chest. "Besides, they already closed the case. Why do they need to talk to me?"

"Will you give them a chance? I wouldn't ask you to try this unless I believed it would help."

Faith's eyes bored into the doctor, her stare fueled not by anger but by desperation. Over the years, she'd seen countless healthcare workers, and they'd all said they wanted to help her. None had.

She closed her eyes. She'd given up hope, but she couldn't let Dr. Rodgers know that. She had to go along with him if she was to have any chance of getting out of here.

Again, she nodded.

Dr. Rodgers's leather chair creaked as he rose. He walked to the door and opened it. A woman in her mid-thirties entered, carrying a thick manila folder under one arm, and marched straight past the doctor. Her heels clicked slightly as she snapped to attention and stared at Faith.

Faith noted the woman's blond hair restrained in a tight bun, her pulled-back shoulders and thrust-out chin and chest. *Is she a cop or a soldier?*

Dr. Rodgers turned to Faith. "I'll be right back," he said, closing the door softly behind him.

The woman strode over and stood beside the chair the doctor had vacated. The creases in her dark-gray suit were so crisp, they might have been pressed with a steamroller. She stared at Faith for a moment before sitting down without offering to shake hands.

"Henryka Vasilyeva." The woman's voice was as crisp as her suit and without accent. "I need to ask you some questions."

Faith stared at Henryka and tried to look indifferent, but there was something about her gray eyes that drew Faith in. Like liquid mercury, Henryka's eyes reflected the colors in the room and gave Faith a creepy feeling, as if she were looking into a mirror.

"I talked to the cops." Faith shifted her gaze to the woman's highly polished black shoes.

"But not to me. You're aware of what today is?"

"Christmas? No, it's . . . ah, wait a minute. Tomorrow's my birthday, right? I'll be twenty-two."

"I know how old you are, Faith." Henryka waited patiently.

Faith looked everywhere but at the liquid-mercury eyes that seemed to mirror all her fears. She slapped her forehead sarcastically. "Oh—I remember! I see where you're going with this. Tomorrow's my birthday, so that means today's the day someone butchered my sister, my father, my best friend, and her mother." Faith leaned forward and held out a hand. "It's Death Day. Did you bring me a present?"

Henryka didn't flinch. "I'm sorry for your loss, but I need you to answer a few questions."

"Why? It's a closed case now, right?"

"The Marshfield PD closed *their* case, but it's still an open federal investigation. When you ran away from the cabin, you crossed into a federal park, so it's a federal case."

Faith scooted back in her chair and pulled her legs up so her heels rested on the edge of the cushion. "Federal, federal, federal. You dropped that word three times. That would make you a federal fed of federalness, right? Am I supposed to be impressed?"

Henryka glanced back at the door, then leaned closer to Faith. Her voice softened. "As I've mentioned, I'm sorry for your loss, but if you're done with your Hannibal Lecter crazy act, maybe you can stop your pity party long enough to answer some questions. The fact is, the federal case has grown cold, and cold cases don't look good to people above my pay grade. I have been assigned to determine whether we should leave this case open or accept the local police's recommendation and close it."

The woman might as well have slapped her. Faith stuck her tongue in her cheek and ran it along her gum line. She knew if the case was closed, no one would be searching for Rat Face. Gazing back into those pools of liquid metal, she saw her own eyes reflected in them like polished steel.

"Ask."

"Do you agree with the Marshfield PD's findings?"

"That my father killed his lover and her kid, who happened to be my best friend, and then stabbed my sister to death before he shot himself in the head? No. No, I don't agree with those findings. They're garbage."

Henryka jotted a note before continuing. "On the night in question, you said you saw a man in the parking lot." She opened the folder and took out a police sketch, a black-and-white drawing showing only the lower half of a man's face: pointy chin, thin nose, dirty teeth.

Faith didn't need to look at the picture. That face haunted her; she knew it better than her own. Still, seeing it again made her stomach tighten and her eyes burn. Her anger mixed with her pain only to become stronger. "That's Rat Face."

"And he's the man you think you saw again three weeks ago?"

"I *did* see him. The cops wouldn't go into the warehouse. He got away." Faith's fingers wrapped around the chair arm.

Henryka pulled out some papers and shuffled them until she got to two sheets stapled together. She read for a minute. "The official report doesn't read like that. Can you tell me what happened?"

Faith closed her eyes and tried to remember. The weeks had blurred into one long drunken haze, but that day was still clear. She still beat herself up over her failure to catch Rat Face that night. She'd been so close but . . .

"Faith?" Henryka snapped her fingers impatiently.

"I was at The Hole."

"That's the bar in Greenville Notch? You must have been there for a while. You had a BAC of point-two-one."

"A couple hours. I had a few drinks."

"A blood alcohol content of point-two-one is closing in on comatose. You had more than a few drinks."

"Whatever. I saw him leaving the bar, so I chased him."

"By chased him, you mean you stole a pickup truck and started ramming his car?"

"I didn't steal the truck. It was running."

Henryka's eyebrow rose. "You chased the car to 1080 Whiting Street. What happened then?"

"Rat Face ran into a warehouse. I couldn't get out of the truck right away—"

"Because you rammed the truck into the car, and the truck got wedged between the car and the side of the building?"

"Yeah. I had to kick out the windshield to get out. But when I got on the hood the cops were there. They pulled their guns on *me*. I tried to tell them that Rat Face was inside."

"At what point did you take the officer's gun?"

Faith shrugged. "It's kinda the cop's fault if you think about it. He didn't put me in handcuffs or anything. I kept telling them the guy who killed my sister was inside the warehouse, but none of them would listen. More cops were showing up, but none of them were watching the back."

"So, when you grabbed the officer's gun, you were merely trying to persuade them to look inside the warehouse?" Henryka's voice was heavy with sarcasm.

"I was trying to get them to catch a murderer. I knew he'd get away."

"The report showed the responding officers checked the warehouse and its perimeter and found no evidence of an intruder. The owner of the car, a retired schoolteacher, was interviewed, but *she* reported the car was stolen and she obviously didn't match your description of the rat-faced man."

"If they had just listened, we wouldn't be having this conversation. I tried to make them hear me and that got me sentenced to this pit."

Henryka's body tensed and the muscles in her jaw flexed. "No. Your actions are what got you in trouble. And it was your mother's begging and pulling every string she could that got you in here. You should've gone to prison. You're also lucky you didn't get shot."

Faith leaned forward and whispered, "I kinda don't care if I get shot. That's why they put me in the psych hospital. Suicide by cop, they call it."

"So you do want to die?"

"Every damn day. But you know what? I already have a shrink." Faith sat back and shrugged. "So why are you here if you don't believe me?"

"I'm also investigating another murder in the state park in Greenville Notch. There were similarities."

"That's why I went there." Faith stood, but Henryka held up a hand.

"Sit."

"I'm not a dog," Faith snarled.

"You stabbed your last therapist with a stylus. I'm not taking any chances. Sit."

Faith sat on the edge of the chair and glared. "Do you believe me? It was him, wasn't it? Rat Face."

Henryka scribbled a note on the back of the folder. Her writing was fast and jerky, but even upside down, the cursive script was as crisp as her suit.

"What's that say, Henry?" Faith asked.

"Don't call me that."

"Okay, Vaseline."

"It's Vasilyeva. But if it's too hard for you, Henry's fine. Are you one hundred percent certain your father didn't kill everyone in that cabin and then himself?"

"Yes." The word shot out of Faith's mouth without hesitation. When it came to that one fact, she was as certain as that the sun would come up every morning and a new, miserable day, without her sister and her best friend, would begin.

"You said the man coming out of the cabin was the same size as your father."

"It wasn't my father."

Behind Henry, Faith saw Dr. Rodgers peek through the window in the door. He was so short, she knew he must be raising himself on tiptoes to see into the room. The corners of her lips curled up and she stroked her stubbly crew cut, gestures he must have assumed meant that everything was going well, because he gave a little nod and stepped away.

"You're certain now?" Henry continued. "In your initial interview, you said that at first you believed it might have been your father."

"I told the detectives that when the guy came out of the cabin I thought it was my father, but I realized I was wrong and it wasn't him. But the cops wouldn't think about *anyone* else." Faith's fingernails dug deeply into her palm. The physical pain did little to take the edge off her frustration, but at least it was a distraction.

"Why don't you think your father killed them?" Henry asked. "The report says Mrs. Foster was ending her affair with your father. The covering detective indicated that was the trigger. Do you believe your father was having an affair with Mrs. Foster?"

"Yes."

"Did you ever see any evidence of that?"

Faith closed her eyes, recalling the last time she'd seen Emily and Anna's mother. It was late fall, and Mrs. Foster had surprised everyone by bringing her daughters to the lake. So much laughter, ricocheting off the lake—Faith, Anna, and Emily, playing hide-and-seek and horseshoes, while Mrs. Foster and Faith's father watched from the cabin. She could see her dad laughing, too, with her friends' mom.

"They spent a lot of time together," Faith said.

"If they were having an affair, why would Mrs. Foster let Anna come with her to the cabin? You said you saw Anna's bike there?"

"Emily stayed at the Fosters' cabin while Anna rode her bike and her mother went for a run," Faith said. "The detective said that Anna must have gone to my father's cabin . . . It was a surprise."

Henry tapped the pen against her jaw. "Emily Foster is Anna's sister?"

"Yes."

"I spoke with their father, Ben Foster. He said that Emily's birthday was the week before and they didn't have a party because he was out of town. Your parents had a party for you every year at the cabin. With your birthdays so close, did you ever combine your party and Emily's?"

"Once," she said. "My eleventh birthday."

Henry spoke without looking up. "Is it possible that's why Mrs. Foster and Anna went to the cabin? They wanted to surprise Emily, too?"

Faith slowly rocked back and forth and shook her head. "Maybe, but . . . my father was going alone to the cabin a lot more. So was Mrs. Foster. And my father was sleeping around with other women, too. There was Sara-Jane Bradley, that soccer mom–hooker."

Before the Reed Lake murders, everybody thought Sara-Jane was just a typical Marshfield housewife: devoted mom, preppy, pretty. Until she made headlines of her own. When Sara-Jane Bradley was arrested for running a prostitution ring out of her colonial, "Marshfield's Madam" was suddenly front-page news.

Sara-Jane was facing serious jail time, but the cops offered her a greatly reduced sentence in exchange for her complete client list, and a lot of local men were caught up in the resulting investigation. One name in particular made an already sensational story downright irresistible to the press: Faith's father, Michael Winters, the Reed Lake madman. Sara-Jane even provided dates and places of their hook-ups. According to her, he was the only client she "entertained" personally. The headline wrote itself: "The Madam and the Madman."

That story tanked what was left of Faith's life. That fall was her first year in middle school. She was at lunch when Wendy Belcher came up with three girls Faith had known in Girl Scouts. Faith had no idea what Wendy was talking about when she asked if Faith had ever been to a brothel. Then Wendy called her father a pimp and asked if her sister had worked for him, and that was the first time she had felt the Rage, as she now called it, rise up and take over her body, blazing white-hot from her sapphire eyes and setting her cheeks on fire like sparklers. Faith nearly beat Wendy to death in the middle of the crowded cafeteria. After some teachers pulled her off, they called her mother to come and get her, and that put an end to any normalcy at school, or anywhere. It also triggered her first visit to a psychiatric facility, and a long, intimate relationship with the Rage.

After that, everyone talked about her in whispers. Like father, like daughter. Fruit doesn't fall far from the tree. She's the daughter of a monster—what else do you expect? Someone even scrawled MURDERER on her locker, and she found out a group of girls had started the rumor that *she* was really the killer.

"I'm not a monster," Faith whispered to Henry. "Watkins deserved it."

"What?" Henry made another note. "Who's Watkins?"

"A doctor. The one I stabbed with the stylus. He slid his hand up my thigh." Faith wrapped her arms around her legs. "He touched other patients, too. We complained, but nothing happened."

"So you stabbed him with a stylus?"

"It sounds wrong when *you* say it." Faith put her head on her knees. "It was only his leg. He touched *my* leg, so I touched his."

Henry jotted another note.

"Why did Dr. Rodgers let me talk to you, Henry?"

Outside the office door, Faith heard Dr. Rodgers talking to a man. Their voices were muffled.

Henry glanced at her watch and stood. "My time's up."

"You didn't answer my question."

Henry cradled the folder under her left arm, regarding Faith for a moment like she was making up her mind about something. "I think Dr. Rodgers was hoping I'd tell you to forget about Rat Face. Everyone else thinks Rat Face was just some random guy waiting in a parking lot who had nothing to do with your sister's death."

"What do you think?"

Henry gave a one-shoulder shrug. "Apart from your account, there's no evidence that Rat Face even exists." She glanced around the small room. "And you're not the most reliable of witnesses."

Faith gave her the finger.

"One more question." Henry waited until Faith put her finger down before continuing. "Do you ever remember your father wearing a baseball hat?"

Like a kid flipping through the pages of a scrapbook, she ran through images of her father in her mind. No baseball cap. But it didn't matter. Faith just wanted to stop seeing the man the world believed killed her sister. Yet the tighter she closed her eyes, the faster the images came. Her father at her horse show, sitting in the stands at Kim's soccer game, his smiling face as he pushed her on the swing . . .

Faith pressed her palms against the sides of her head and started screaming.

The office door flew open. Dr. Rodgers, Titus, and two men in navy-blue suits rushed into the room.

Like a boxer against the ropes, the images rained down on Faith like blows, but she was helpless to stop them. Each one sent her head reeling until she felt like she was falling—tumbling into oblivion, welcoming the darkness and an end to the pain.

She felt Titus's strong arms around her, carrying her back to her room.

Faith stood in the doorway, gazing back and forth between Dr. Rodgers and the tan couch. Dr. Rodgers sat in his familiar brown chair and held his hand directing her to sit, but Faith's feet felt glued to the floor.

Today he wasn't smiling, and he always smiled.

"Good morning, Faith." He folded his hands in his lap. "Is everything all right?"

She shook her head and pointed at the couch. "I didn't think you shrinks did the whole couch thing anymore."

He chuckled. "I'm sorry if I left that detail out. As we discussed, as your treatment progresses, getting to the root of your emotional pain is a vital stage of healing. It's quite common that traumatic events are shut away. It's your body's way of trying to protect itself. If you're not ready—"

"I didn't say that. I didn't forget anything either. I remember it all. That's the problem."

"Have you ever shared what happened with anyone?"

Faith nodded. "The next morning. I told the detectives."

"You told them details. Facts. Have you shared your feelings with anyone?"

She wrapped her arms tighter around herself, picked a spot on the floor to stare at, and shook her head.

"May I ask you a question, Faith?"

Faith blew out a sarcastic huff. "Why do you do that?"

"Do what?" Dr. Rodgers shifted in his chair.

"Your *job* is to ask me questions. Why do you ask me if you *can*?"

"To make sure you're comfortable with what I'm doing. To show that I respect your boundaries. To please my mother." Dr. Rodgers grinned.

Faith started rocking slightly. "You smiled. You didn't smile when I came in. Why?"

Dr. Rodgers took his glasses off. "I guess our questions are related. I want to know what you recall about the night of your trauma, and that's also the reason I'm not smiling. Getting to the root of the issue is vital for recovery, but it is also painful. Today will be hard for you. Very hard. I'm concerned that you are not emotionally prepared for this."

Faith marched over to the couch and sat on the edge. "Should I lie down?"

"Before you do, you still haven't answered my question."

Faith nodded. "I need to do this." She lay down on the couch and stared at the white ceiling tiles. Her heart was pounding. *Four. Five. Six . . .* "What do I do?"

"Relax. But Faith, you can wait. If you're not ready—"

"I am. Do I just start talking?"

"Let's start with some deep breathing and visualization first. When trying to remember an event that is so traumatic, don't start with the moment the event happened. Rewind your mental clock a few minutes. What works best for some people is to pick a moment earlier in that fateful day. Try to think back to a moment on April twelfth when you were happy . . ."

Faith closed her eyes and began to take long, slow breaths. She let her mind drift back in time in pursuit of a happy moment. Just another useless therapist exercise. *Like chasing a shadow.* How could anything happy have happened on Death Day? A minute or two had passed when she landed on a thought and shuddered. Her picture of that moment was as clear as that day.

Thinking back, Faith leaned her head out the passenger-side window, letting the crisp springtime air whip her hair behind her, and shouted, "This is going to be the best weekend ever!" She whooped and waved at strangers until Kim dragged Faith back into the seat with one hand while steering the car with the other.

"Sit down, Squirt!"

"I'm so pumped you're coming out to the cabin with me tonight." For emphasis, Faith added a little drum solo on the dashboard. "I thought you were going to be totally bummed out because Tommy blew you off. You're not even a little upset?"

"Not really. You know why?"

Faith shrugged.

Kim powered down her window. The wind streamed through her long blond hair as she leaned over and yelled, "Because this is going to be the best weekend *ever*!"

Faith whooped again and they fist-bumped. She leaned to catch the wind on her face again—her skin tingled and the smell of pine grew stronger. They'd left the highway and houses behind, and the forest now ran along both sides of the car. It all begged to be explored—tall pines and open clearings, perfect spots for picnics and playing.

"Seriously." Kim slowed and turned left. "You're going to start dating soon and the number one thing you have to keep in mind is that you're special. No matter how other people treat you. So, yeah, Tommy canceled on me for the third week in a row." Kim's hands tightened on the steering wheel and then sprang open. "But this weekend isn't about him." She gave Faith's shoulder a playful nudge. "It's all about my little sister."

Faith sat up straighter, pushed back an errant strand of hair, and smiled. Special? Her? Faith never thought of herself that way. Besides her family and Anna, no one else did either. Faith tried her best to make friends, but just the idea of talking to someone she didn't know left her stammering and looking for an exit. Her father called her Spitfire, but maybe she was more like her dad—the silent type with a big heart. She wished people saw her that way, but most kids in school thought she was odd and ignored her completely. That was one of the reasons her dad started the tradition of having a party for her at Reed Lake. When she was in third grade, her mom threw a big party for Faith at their house and not one kid showed up. Faith wanted to climb into the huge rainbow piñata and die, but her father turned everything around by bringing the party out to the cabin. He probably saved her from a lifetime of therapy. Still, Faith didn't feel special.

Her older sister, though, was a rock star. Kim *was* special. Four years older, tall, blond, with the figure of a model—and, more importantly, clever, funny, and super-smart—she was Faith's own personal superhero. And if Kim said it was true, Faith was inclined to believe her.

"Should you call Mom and tell her you're staying at the cabin with us tonight?" Faith asked.

"I left a message. She's giving that speech for work tonight. I hope she'll come out after." Kimberly turned off the main road onto a dirt one.

The car rocked back and forth and up and down along the bumpy road. Faith bounced right along with it. An occasional rock pinged off the undercarriage and each time Kim winced and slowed a little more.

Faith lifted her feet and squeezed her whole frame, hugging her knees. "Maybe we can have a campfire?" She licked her lips. "Three words: Dad's super-deluxe s'mores."

Kimberly moaned with anticipation. "I can taste them now."

Faith danced in her seat. "I told you. This weekend's going to be awesome."

"It's going to be extra awesome because someone has an extra-special birthday."

"Lucky thirteen?" Faith joked. Unlike most people on the planet, she regarded thirteen as the best number of all. After all, she was born on the thirteenth.

"Well, you *will* be a teenager now. It's a big deal. That's why Mom and Dad are pulling out all the stops."

"Dad still thinks I'm five." She tapped her heels on the floorboard to watch her sneakers light up.

Kim's eyes—more ocean than sky—crinkled with laughter. "Get used to it. You'll always be his little girl. Cut him some slack, though. He thought you'd love them."

Faith tapped her shoes rapidly, the pink flashes keeping time with her rhythm. "I'm wearing them, aren't I?" Faith rolled her eyes, but she had to admit, she did kind of like them. She just wouldn't wear them where anyone from school would see her.

"That's why we shouldn't let Dad shop alone," Kim said.

"Did you let him pick out my birthday present by himself?" Images of dolls and stuffed unicorns filled her mind.

Kim gave her shoulder a playful shove. "Would I leave that awesome responsibility to him alone?"

Faith crossed her fingers and hoped, for the millionth time that week, that she was getting a new bicycle so she could ride with Anna.

Gravel crunched under the tires as Kim pulled into the camp parking lot. The sun hovered on the edge of the horizon and the sky was turning a light purple. At this time of year, the parking lot was almost deserted; it wouldn't start to fill up for several weeks yet. Kim parked her car next to their father's pickup truck. The only other car in the lot was a dark-brown sedan right next to the trailhead leading down to the cabins. At first it looked like a police car, but there was something wrong with the color.

As the two girls started walking across the lot, Kim glanced at her phone.

"He'll call." Faith bumped playfully into her taller sister.

"I know." Kim's hip shot out and knocked Faith sideways.

"Of course he'll call you." Faith stuck her tongue out. "You're like a supermodel."

Kim wrapped an arm around her sister's shoulders and gave her a squeeze. "When did you get so smart?"

"I've always been so smart." Faith hopped into the air and stomped, her sneakers sending out bright-pink stars. "You just decided to notice."

Faith was about to give Kim another shove, but Kim's hand clamped down on her shoulder. Faith gazed up at her sister, whose attention was fixed on the brown sedan. It had been backed into the space and the driver's side was closest to Faith.

And the car wasn't empty.

Someone was trying to light a cigarette. Once, twice, sparks flew from a lighter, but no flame appeared. On the third try, fire blossomed, illuminating a man's pointy chin and thin nose. He sucked on the cigarette until its end glowed. Smoke unfurled from his mouth as he turned his head in their direction and smiled. The roof of his old car cast a shadow that concealed the top of his face, but above his lecherous grin and crooked brown teeth, Faith imagined beady little eyes peering out from the darkness. *Like a rat.*

Faith recoiled and bumped into Kim.

He took a swig from a flat bottle with a picture of a full moon on the label, the liquid inside as brown as his teeth.

Kim maintained her protective grip on Faith's shoulder and guided her forward, moving quickly away from the car. "Don't look at him," she whispered. "Just keep walking."

"Should we go back to the car?" Faith asked. Cigarette smoke and alcohol wafted toward her through the half-open driver-side window.

"No. Don't worry about him." Kim's voice was steady, and it made Faith feel safe. "The world is full of creeps. Just stay right with me and we'll be with Dad before you know it."

As they walked down the familiar wide gravel path toward the lake, her sneakers glowing with each step, Faith didn't stray from her sister's side. She soon stopped worrying about the rat-faced man in the parking lot, and by the time their cabin came into view, she was breathing normally.

"Do you think we should sneak up and scare Dad?"

"No." Kim cast a nervous glance back to the parking lot. "Later."

"Hey," Faith said, "that's Anna's bike." A girl's purple bike with glittering ribbons leaned against the cabin.

They were still ten yards away from the cabin when Kim froze. "Huh?" Kim stepped in front of Faith as she tried to peer inside the cabin's window.

Faith tried to peek around her sister, but Kim turned back toward Faith and grabbed her by both shoulders. "Did Mom say anything to you about Mrs. Foster?"

The question and expression on Kim's face caught Faith off-guard. Faith's stomach tightened and churned. From the death of their beloved dog to the passing of their grandfather, it had always somehow fallen on Kim to deliver bad news to Faith. In the fading light, Kim had her bad-news face on.

"Mom didn't say anything about Mrs. Foster," Faith said.

"Did Anna say if she came out here last weekend?"

"No. Why?"

"Mom asked me." Kim started twisting the silver ring on her finger with her right hand—a sure sign that she was really nervous. Faith was even more concerned as she waited for Kim to deliver whatever news had her so upset. Instead, Kim straightened up and squared her shoulders. "Wait here a second, okay?"

"What? Why? What's going on?"

"Just do it," Kim said, already walking toward the cabin.

Faith glanced over both shoulders and saw only darkness closing in. She wanted desperately to go forward with Kim to the safety of the cabin and her father, but fear clawed at her. Each step took Kim farther away.

Kim reached the door and glanced back. The lightest part of the darkening sky was behind her, and she stood silhouetted against it, so Faith couldn't see her expression. As Kim turned back to the cabin door, it whipped open and light poured forth. A man stepped out and reached for Kim. Faith thought it was her father at first.

He wrapped his right arm around Kim's shoulders and pulled her close. He kept his head down, and his baseball cap obscured his face. In his left hand, something metal gleamed as he thrust his arm upward at Kim's chest.

Kim pushed away from the man and stepped toward Faith. Something wasn't right with her. She held her hand out in front of her and her whole arm shook, like her hand had fallen asleep and she was trying to wake it up. As she stumbled forward, Faith looked into her eyes.

Dr. Rodgers's couch began to tap against the floor with the shudders of Faith's tossing and turning. She moaned, and Dr. Rodgers leaned forward.

Kim's screams.

They weren't even human. Guttural bleats distilled from pain and terror.

Kim staggered toward Faith on wobbly legs, a large red blotch blooming on the front of her white shirt and growing bigger. Faith wanted to move, to do something, but she was frozen in place. She felt trapped in a nightmare—if she could just open her eyes, she'd wake up. But she knew her eyes were wide open.

As the man watched Kim's feeble attempt to escape, a sound as soft as the rustle of the leaves reached Faith.

He was laughing.

"Run!" Kim yelled, but it sounded like she had water in her mouth.

Fear rooted Faith's feet to the ground. She tried to scream, to call out for their father, to beg Kim to stand up straight and run to her, but the words wouldn't come. Her body wouldn't obey.

The man's head swiveled, scanning the darkness. With the light from the cabin behind him, she couldn't make out his features. Could he see her on the path? She should hide. Or run. Or—

The man dashed toward them. His feet pounded against the dirt.

"Run!" Kim screamed again. She was stumbling, hunched over and clutching her stomach. A few feet away from her, she called out. "Faith—" Her voice was cut off, and her hands dropped to her sides. Her body slumped sideways and hit the ground with a sickening thud. She turned back and grabbed at the man's feet as he tried to run past her to Faith. They crashed together and he tumbled to the ground.

"Dad! Dad!" Kim sobbed.

The man quickly got up and was closing the distance between him and Faith, still frozen in place, while her sister lay on the ground, not moving.

The shock spurred Faith into motion at last. She raced back down the path, gravel skidding beneath her feet. "Daddy! Daddy!" she called out, her voice bubbly with tears and snot. With each step, the light from her shoes cast brief pink lightning against the trees. She tripped on a root sticking up from the trail and landed hard, a rock slicing deeply into her chin, the air knocked from her lungs. Ignoring the pain, she scrambled to her feet, took two more steps—and stopped.

The sky was fully dark now, but the flash from her shoes illuminated a figure on the path ahead: the rat-faced man. When she stopped, he was once again shrouded in darkness, except for the red tip of his cigarette, glowing like a comet when he tossed it to the ground.

Faith dashed into the woods like a hunted rabbit. Branches scratched her face and tore at her clothes, but she raced onward. She scrambled over an old fieldstone wall, her forearm scraping against the rock. Someone crashed through the woods after her; light and shadow flickered all around.

My shoes! I'm showing them where I am.

Faith kicked her shoes off. Sticks and rocks jutting from the forest floor cut her feet and tore at her socks, but she didn't even feel the pain—until her foot slid sideways off a mossy rock and her ankle rolled. Pain tore up her leg.

No. No. Please. Please.

She limped forward, feeling agony with every other step. In the dim moonlight, a briar patch loomed ahead of her: taller than her head, with thorns as long as her thumb. Getting past it was her only chance of escape.

She dropped to her knees and crawled directly into the briars. When her hair got snarled on a wiry branch, she jerked her head forward with all her might. A clump of hair ripped from her scalp.

Her head poked out the other side of the thicket and bumped against a fallen tree trunk. There was a tiny bit of space underneath the trunk. She made a quick decision. She couldn't run any farther—even crawling hurt her ankle.

Careful not to make a sound, she wriggled under the fallen tree, the rough bark scraping her back as she slid in. Another jolt of pain from her ankle had her biting her bottom lip and sucking in air, but she managed not to scream.

Somewhere close by, a man swore, his voice low and muffled. "Where are you?"

Faith strained to listen.

"Don't run away." The words were just above a whisper, singsong.

"Come back and play . . ." the twisted tune continued.

He was much closer. He was humming. She couldn't make out the tune at first, but the closer he came, the clearer it became, until she recognized the melody: "Happy Birthday."

Faith felt her pants pool with warm liquid and she smelled the sharp humiliation of urine.

"Are you hiding?" sang the man.

Footsteps approached. Faith closed her eyes and pulled herself as far under the tree as she could.

"Where are you? Woods?"

The man climbed over the log. His feet hit the ground right next to her leg. A sob rose up in her throat. She clamped her mouth shut, fighting back tears; her shoulders heaved, but she didn't make a sound. She dug her nails into her arm to thwart the tears and absorb the pain her body so desperately wanted to release, and felt the sting, then the wet, warm blood instantly cooling in the night air.

She closed her eyes and pushed her face against the rotting bark, down into the cool, damp soil. Her mind swirled with images. She pictured Kim sacrificing herself so Faith could escape. But where could she go, even if she *could* run?

She wanted her father to come and save her—to scare these guys away and carry her to Kim. She pictured herself riding high on his strong shoulders out of the woods and toward their cabin. Her father had always been there when she needed him. He was her champion—he would never leave her. *Why didn't he save us? Why didn't he come?*

There were no answers, only questions that never let her alone.

Her breaths came in rapid little gulps, each one a little louder. She pressed her face harder into the ground to muffle her breathing, until her heartbeat sped up and her lungs burned. She was drowning. Dying. Kim's screams echoed in her ears.

The man's footsteps moved on, faded away, and left her in silence. Yet still Faith lay there, motionless as a corpse, until the darkness pulled her down and she no longer felt anything.

"Faith?" Dr. Rodgers's voice sounded far away. "Faith, can you tell me how you feel?"

Faith listened to her own breathing. Her chest rose and fell steadily, her heart quietly beating in her breast.

"How do you feel?" the doctor repeated.

"Dead."

Sunday, April 8

Faith stood in the lobby of Brookdale Mental Health Hospital and stared out the window while her mother, Beverly, filled out the discharge paperwork. Once she was done, Faith would be free. She closed her eyes. She'd been locked in here for a year—a year when everything was decided for her. She'd always thought that if this day ever did come, she'd rip open the doors and run screaming into the sunshine—but right now, she wanted to turn around and race through to the inner offices, down the white hallways, past all the locked doors and guards, until she was back safe in the belly of the place. This world she understood.

She twisted Kim's ring on her left hand. They hadn't allowed her to wear it during her incarceration, but now that she'd gotten it back, she found herself constantly touching the two delicate silver vines that formed the ring. The center stone, a diamond, was missing. The ring was meant to be stackable, and Kim had dreamed of getting an engagement ring that matched it one day.

Faith caressed the empty setting. She knew that would never happen; those dreams were dead, too.

Her mother put Faith's discharge papers into a folder, exchanged a few whispered words with the nurse, and walked over to Faith. They didn't hug, and they hadn't for years. It was part of her mother's dissociative disorder; at least that's what the therapists said. Faith's mother had written all about it in a book for the whole world to read. The therapists were split over the cause of the disassociation; one group believed her mother was afraid of loving and losing again, while the other camp thought the lack of love was caused by a combination of overwhelming grief and betrayal. Either way, after Kim died, Faith had lost her mother, too. In her mother's defense, she was honest about her emotions—or lack thereof.

Beverly, in her mid-fifties, boasted the same slender figure and regal bearing that she'd been known for in college. Faith had seen photos of her then, her long, flowing chestnut-brown hair pulled gracefully over her shoulders to drape over elegant dresses. She remembered her mom heading out to speak at events wearing similar gowns when Faith was ten, eleven, and twelve years old. The only signs of aging were her mom's choice to trim her hair at shoulder length and a few more wrinkles near the corners of her eyes, but Faith didn't mention those.

"Everything's signed." Faith's mother pointed at the gym bag that held all of Faith's possessions. "Can I help you with that?"

"I got it." Faith swung the bag onto her back. It was light; not much to pack. "Lead the way."

The air was warm for April. Or, at least, it seemed to be. It had been so long since she'd been outside, she wasn't sure what normal was. It was close to seventy degrees out, and everything smelled clean and fresh. Faith didn't like it; she couldn't wait to get back inside.

The headlights of a new blue BMW 7 Series flashed, and its trunk opened. "Thad wanted to come—" Faith's mother began.

"But something came up? What?" Faith dumped the bag in the trunk next to a brown shopping bag. "Let's see, stepdaughter getting out of the loony bin, or golf? I'd pick golf, too."

"No. I told him not to come. I believed it would be best if you and I talked first—alone. From your reaction, I think I made the right call."

Faith got into the passenger seat of the luxury sedan and made a face. "Looks like your book's doing well."

Her mother slipped into the driver's seat but didn't start the engine. "Honey, I never imagined I could write a book at all, let alone that it would be a bestseller. And I didn't write *The Girl Who Lived* for sales. It was part of my therapy."

"How does writing about *my* life constitute *your* therapy?"

"Dr. Melding thought it would be an outlet for releasing my feelings. I was having an issue expressing myself in therapy."

"Maybe that's because your therapist works for you."

Faith's mother exhaled and started the engine. "He doesn't work for me. He's a partner. For now."

"For now?" Faith tried not to look at Brookdale in the side mirror as they drove out of the parking lot, or at her own face. With her hair still pretty short, just below her ears now, her face and eyes seemed exposed. She looked younger, not older, than before. "Isn't he the guy you're making me see?"

"Yes, Dr. Melding will be your therapist, and he's excellent." Beverly tapped her thumbs on the steering wheel. "In fact, I'm selling him my half of the practice."

"When? Why now?"

"It's planned for the fall. I just have to get my ducks in a row first."

"But why now? Are you—and Thad—going to move?"

Her mother's eyes glittered with the chance to elaborate on her plans and prospects. "I should have done it a long time ago. And we're not sure. Thad's talking about building a home in the mountains."

They rode in silence for several minutes. *What am I supposed to do now?* Any hope Faith might have felt about being free and an adult, about trying to move on from the past or forge a new future, suddenly seemed like a hallucination or something someone else had dreamed up for her. After the killings, Faith wanted to move—*needed* to move, so Faith's mother moved them to her childhood home, on the other side of Marshfield. Faith's grandfather had passed away two years earlier, and her grandmother was grateful to not be alone. Staying in Marshfield wasn't what Faith had had in mind at all. She'd wanted to move out of the state at least, and preferably to a different planet. But her mother had had one main reason for staying in Marshfield: her practice. And that had always been more important to her than her daughter's sanity. Now that Faith needed something to hold onto, someplace where she could heal and call home, her mother was locking her out again.

After a few more miles, Beverly spoke. "Are you sure I can't convince you to stay with me and Thad?"

Faith turned from the window to reply that she'd rather eat sand, but she just shook her head instead.

"We got you a small place. And a car. It's used, but you'll need one to go to a job. I know several places that will hire you. You just need to walk in. And I got you this." She reached into her purse, pulled out a smartphone, and handed it to Faith. "Your schedule is on it. You have AA on Sundays—yes, that includes today—Tuesdays, and Thursdays. I set up a temporary sponsor for you. Her name is Amanda Hill. Her contact information is in the phone. On Mondays, Wednesdays, and Fridays you have survivors' group meetings. Your appointments for Dr. Melding are in there, too, as well as your meetings with your probation officer—uh, Barbara Finney. All of the meetings are part of your probation. You'll have to have a form signed to prove you went. You can't miss any without a doctor's note." She pulled out an envelope from her purse and held it out toward her daughter. "A little cash—for now. I'll give you a couple of weeks to get settled, but after that I expect you to earn your own money."

Faith knew her mother was expecting an answer, but after so many years of being escorted everywhere she went, in and out of institutions, the thought of working, of managing appointments, even just getting herself where she needed to be . . . it was overwhelming. She'd been committed to her first mental hospital at thirteen. She hadn't even finished high school, expelled in her junior year. She'd bounced in and out of psychiatric hospitals, never held a job, never paid a bill, never owned a car—though she did learn to drive. Her teenage years had passed in a haze of anger, alcohol, and trouble with the law. Brookdale had been hell—a secure mental-health hospital one step removed from prison—but it had also taken care of her. In a way, it was home.

Now she felt like she'd walked out of a dark cave only to step right off a cliff. She didn't know which she feared more: the darkness behind her or the fall ahead.

"No drinking. No drugs. Is that one hundred and ten percent clear?"

Faith nodded. *So, this is freedom?*

With each mile closer to Marshfield, Faith's heartbeat raced faster. Her grandmother had never been fond of the cabin, or of

Marshfield. She called it a "backwater"—and Faith got the feeling her own mom felt the same way, even though she, like Dad, had grown up here.

When she was little, Faith had loved Marshfield. All of it: the lake, the cabin, the town. It wasn't so small everyone knew everyone else's business, but it wasn't a big city, either. You could probably walk from one side to the other in a couple of hours. As far as Faith had been concerned, it was just right.

After that night at the cabin, she never wanted to come back here, but it seemed inevitable. Somehow fate would make her go back to the cabin. Deep down she knew that someday, like a piece of trash swept along the river, she'd be drawn back and spat out here.

As familiar places flickered past, she saw them as they were now, and also how they had once been. The ice cream stand next to the field full of cows, its bright flags flapping in the wind. But the cows were gone, the field under construction. The flags that used to be purple and pink polka-dots were now red and white, and the place was called The Healthy Cow. Faith remembered it as The Crazy Cow.

Kim had called it The Smelly Cow.

They passed the soccer field. The whole family used to go to every one of Kim's games. They would all wear bright blue and yellow and cheer her on from the stands that now sat rusting in tall grass. The old brick elementary school, at least, hadn't changed at all. Faith still remembered her first day there. After school, Kim met her outside, and Faith was so excited she tripped down the stairs. Billy Marsden laughed—until Kim picked him up by his curly red hair and shook him.

How would her life have turned out if her protector had lived? Faith watched the school fade into the distance in the rearview mirror, leaned against the door, and stared at her lap for the rest of the trip.

Downtown, Faith's mother parked in front of a laundromat. She reached for Faith's hand, but Faith drew back.

Her mother sighed. "I'm sorry about the past. There's nothing I can do to change it, but I can try to make the future better. You're almost twenty-three; you have your whole life ahead of you. This can be your second chance."

"I think it's my seventy-second chance, and my last one." Faith knew if she blew this opportunity, she'd be locked up again—and there was no guarantee she'd ever get out.

Faith's mother grabbed her wrist before she could reach for the door handle. "Then make it count. You can do this, Faith. I know you can."

Faith opened the door and got out. "Yes, well, I'm sure your plans will all work out, just like they always do." Sarcasm, the weapon of the weak. Any promise she could muster would sound as hollow as she felt inside. She'd promised her mother and herself she'd change so many times that she'd lost count. Beverly looked as if she was about to frame a retort, but just sighed.

Outside the car, Faith felt disoriented and a little dizzy. She was officially back in Marshfield. And legally she was trapped here—she couldn't leave without violating her probation. If she hadn't agreed to those terms, she'd still be locked away.

Her mother reached for the gym bag, but Faith said, "I got that," yanked the bag out of the trunk, and swung it over her shoulder.

Her mother reached back into the trunk and picked up a brown-paper shopping bag. "Emergency supplies." She smiled. "I got a few things before I came to get you. But if I missed anything important, there's a little supermarket around the corner." She pointed left. "And your apartment's upstairs."

Faith followed her mother to the side of the laundromat. A narrow wooden staircase led up to a small balcony that ran along the front of the building, a single door leading inside.

Faith's mother took out a key and opened it. "This is your place."

The apartment was tiny, but it was huge compared to what Faith was used to. A single room served as bedroom, kitchen, and living room, and an open door on one wall revealed a tiny bathroom. There was no TV.

Her mother set the grocery bag down on the lone table. Beside it was one chair and one stool. She adjusted the chair so it was tucked under the table. "Are you sure you don't want to come stay with us?"

Just the thought of living with her mother again made Faith break into a sweat. "No. But I'm guessing you picked the smallest, lousiest apartment you could find, hoping I would break down and move in with you? Be careful or I'll tell Dr. Melding, and they'll take away your therapy license."

Her mother smiled but didn't laugh. Faith couldn't remember the last time she'd heard her mother laugh.

"I got you some bed linens and toiletries. Thad helped me pick them out."

Faith bit her tongue. She hated Thad, even though the only thing he had ever done to her was marry her mother. Maybe it was because he did so only two years after her father and sister had died.

Died. The word echoed in Faith's head. No. They didn't *die.* "Die" meant you had cancer or a heart attack or something. *Killed. Murdered. Butchered . . .*

"Faith?"

The concern in her mother's voice made Faith open her eyes. Her hands were balled into tight fists at her sides. "I'm fine." She walked into the kitchen, eager to distance herself from the conversation. She opened a cabinet, revealing some mismatched glasses, and filled one at the sink.

"I spoke with Tommy Carson before coming to pick you up," her mother said.

"You went to him? Why? You couldn't stand him when he was dating Kim." Faith chugged the water and wiped the back of her mouth with her hand.

"I didn't dislike Tommy. I just didn't think he was the best choice for Kim."

"Why did you talk to him now?"

"He wants to help."

"Ten years too late, isn't it?"

Faith's mother gave her a disapproving look. "That's not fair. It wasn't his fault." She tapped her hand on the wooden chair as she spoke.

"He broke the date with Kim. If he hadn't, she never would have gone to the lake that night," Faith snapped, exasperated at having to spell it out.

"You and your father would still have gone."

The words hung in the air. Faith shoved her glass into the sink. "So?" she said in an even, measured tone.

"Faith, your father—"

"Was an ordinary man who snapped. Blah, blah, blah. I don't want to talk about it, Mom."

"You need to get your feelings about him out."

Faith wanted to say, *Maybe I'll write a book.* She settled on, "I'll talk to Dr. Melding about it." When her mother opened her mouth, Faith held up a hand. "You agreed that you wouldn't try to be my therapist."

"I'm not saying these things as a therapist. I'm saying them as a mother."

"But you're still a therapist, so stop it."

"One last question." Her mother folded her hands. "Are you sure you don't want to at least come with me and get something to eat?"

"Not right now." Right now, Faith wanted to hide under the covers. "I think I'm gonna need some time to get used to everything. And . . . " She swallowed. "I want to reach out to Emily Foster."

"Faith, I . . . " Her mother stared down at the table, her face pinched from the struggle to find the right words. "You know, I've spoken with Mr. Foster a few times. It's been awkward trying to stay in touch with him over the years."

Faith wanted to say, *Awkward sounds like a hell of an understatement considering you think your husband slept with his wife and then killed her and his daughter.* She pretended to be interested in the floor.

"Emily's gone," her mother blurted out.

"Gone? Where?"

"She hanged herself. Three months ago."

No, no, not Emily . . . Faith reeled as if she'd been struck.

She and Emily had avoided talking to one another for years after the attack. Every time Faith looked at Emily, she saw Anna. So Faith assumed that every time Emily looked at her, she saw the man she thought had killed her mother and sister.

But that changed when Emily and Faith were forced together. Six years ago, Emily tried to overdose and wound up at the same mental hospital as Faith, a place for troubled teens. Not Brookdale—that was later. Faith didn't remember the name of the place, but they were both there for the same reason: attempted suicide. Faith had jumped off a bridge, but some Boy

Scouts at a summer camp dragged her out of the river and gave her CPR. *Stupid Scouts.*

Faith remembered little about the hospital. But the memory of reconnecting with Emily coursed through her like a strong river current. They had talked. It had been . . . well, "nice" wasn't the right word. But Emily understood. With her, Faith didn't feel alone.

Faith's mother stood silently, hands folded, her face a neutral mask. Faith pictured her mother in her office, tablet at the ready, waiting for a patient to express how they felt. It was the therapist in her. She might try to shut it off, but she couldn't.

"Emily wrote to me at the beginning of December," Faith said. "She said she was getting better."

"I'm sorry, honey. She must have suffered a setback. That's why it's so important for you to work your program."

"I bet Emily's therapist said that to her, too."

Her mother moved closer.

Faith just stood where she was. "I need to get the apartment set up."

"Are you sure you don't want to come home with me?"

Faith shook her head.

Her mother put a set of keys on the table. "Marshfield is so small, I don't think you really need a car, but Thad insisted. There's a dark-blue Camry parked out back. It's old, but it was well maintained. It's yours now."

Faith nodded. Part of her brain was trying to process what her mother was saying and doing for her, but her mind kept tripping over her heart. It hurt.

"If you need anything, please reach out. If not to me, someone." Faith's mother walked to the door and stopped. "You need to talk to Dr. Melding. And no drinking. If you do . . . " Her shoulders straightened. Faith expected her to continue her lecture, but instead she just opened the door and said, "You can do this."

For an instant, Faith wanted to run to her mother, wrap her arms around her waist, and cry. It was a glimmer of her old self. But that little light had long ago been swallowed up by the dark void inside her. The dead space no feelings escaped from.

"Thanks," Faith mumbled. It was the best she could do.

Her mother closed the door behind her, and Faith felt the familiar weight of claustrophobia press in on her. She'd been locked up so many times, she figured she ought to be over it by now, but she wasn't. She felt trapped, yet she feared going outside just as much. *I'm in hell wherever I go.*

She walked over to the bed. It was hardly more than a cot, with a pillow, a flowered bedspread, and a folded afghan. Faith recognized the afghan: her grandmother had made it. Both she and Kim had had afghans from their grandmother. Faith snatched it off the bed and shoved it in a dresser drawer. *Out of sight, out of mind.*

Faith paced. All she could think of was Emily—hanging.

She grabbed her gym bag and unpacked everything. It didn't take long; she didn't have many clothes. No jacket, just a sweat top. One pair of shoes. But she found a pair of running shoes at the foot of the bed, no doubt left for her by her mother. Faith's hands shook as she laced them.

Go for a run. Don't think. Get up and go. Get fresh air. She tried to give herself a pep talk, but when she yanked open the front door of her apartment, the voice in her head wasn't hers. It was Kim's.

RUN!

Faith glanced at her new phone as she arrived at the church. Only five past seven. Her meeting might not have started yet, but she hoped it had—the last thing she wanted was to arrive early.

She stopped in front of the doors leading into the church's boxy annex. She'd been to so many of these AA meetings, she could see it all: there would be a chest-high, dark-wood podium that leaned slightly from the scores of ex-drunks clinging to it as they related their tales of woe over the years. In front of that, interspersed among metal poles that supported the ceiling, would be rows of folding chairs—probably those old sheet-metal chairs built from tanks melted down after WWII. Her butt was in for a beating. Along the back wall, there'd be the bikers who felt too cool to sit, the old-timers who were tired of sitting, and the drifters who felt that if they sat they'd be admitting to a problem, so they stood white-knuckled against the wall, occasionally smacking the back of their head on the bricks.

There would also be a table with coffee, and since caffeine was an acceptable addiction, it flowed freely. Because this was a small town, there might even be stale cookies. Faith's stomach grumbled; she should've accepted her mother's offer to get dinner.

Taking a deep breath, she slipped through the doors. The room was laid out exactly as she had guessed. Better yet, the meeting was already in full swing; some guy was giving his story at the front. His shoulders shook, along with the old podium he gripped with both hands.

Faith headed for the back wall, but noticed several faces had a look that screamed *Do you need me to be your sponsor?* so she quickly changed course toward the nearest seat in the last row. The chair was as warm and comfortable as a marble tombstone, but Faith didn't care. She curled into her turtle-under-attack position—crossed ankles, legs pulled in, arms wrapped around her waist, her chin tucked into her chest. She could survive most meetings, therapy sessions, and counseling appointments hidden in her shell. If anyone came too close, she shot them a glare, accompanied if necessary by a snarl, and they'd usually back off.

As the sad man continued his story, Faith spotted the table off to one side. No tablecloth. She frowned. If someone went to the trouble of laying out a tablecloth, there might be cookies to go with the coffee. But no tablecloth? Forget the cookies. No chance. The brown box next to the bottles of powered creamer had to be for stirrers.

Faith hated AA, and especially on Sundays, when everyone seemed unconcerned how long the meeting dragged on. She knew it helped a lot of people, but not her. For her, it was a trigger, and by the end of a meeting she craved alcohol so badly she'd drink mouthwash. No matter how many therapists she told that to, they all dismissed it. Except Dr. Rodgers. He was the only one who'd understood, but he'd still gone along with the judge and made AA a condition of her release.

The man speaking at the podium lifted his chin. His smile was an addict's grin, a mix of wonder and unbridled desire, and Faith knew he was now talking about his first drink. She knew this even though she'd mostly tuned him out, because he was talking with more fondness than a man would talk about his first love or a woman about her firstborn, going on about how wonderful it smelled, how smoothly it went down, how good it felt. He licked his lips, and Faith did, too. She'd been in the room less than five minutes and already she could taste whiskey on her tongue.

She made it through one more speaker, but after fifteen minutes she slipped out of her chair and joined the white-knuckles in the back. No one said anything to her. That was the only thing about AA she did like: people left you the hell alone. Of course, there was always that one guy who wouldn't stop talking if you talked to him first, and there might be one or two do-gooders who earned their gold star for the day by asking everybody how they were feeling. But for the most part, everyone there was too busy fighting their own demons to bother anyone else.

Break time must have been approaching because cigarettes and lighters appeared from pockets all over the room. A couple of people shifted over to get close to the door.

"Do you have a smoke?" the woman next to Faith whispered. She was bone-thin, painfully so.

Faith shook her head. She'd quit in the hospital. Being in lockdown for a few weeks had helped. She tried not to stare at the woman. Despite years of witnessing drugs, alcohol, and mental illness destroy people, she was still shocked by the physical toll. Faith had seen men so yellow from cirrhosis they looked like they'd been colored in with a crayon. She'd met anorexic girls as thin as concentration camp survivors, and food addicts so far gone they couldn't walk. But one look at the woman next to her—protruding collarbones, deep-set eyes, pale skin—and Faith knew.

Dead woman walking.

"I'm trying to find Amanda," Faith whispered. "Do you know her?"

The woman smiled and nodded. She was missing some teeth and seemed embarrassed by it, tilting her head away slightly and trying to cover the gaps. She scanned around the room and pointed. "First row. The little brunette."

Faith groaned internally. The brunette was front and center, in the seat closest to the podium. *Figures Mom picked her.* Some sponsors preferred the person they were sponsoring to sit next to them in meetings, but Faith would rather light herself on fire than sit in the front row.

The thin woman tapped Faith on the shoulder and held out a greasy folded paper napkin with two sugar cookies inside. "They had some at the six o'clock meeting."

Be careful what you wish for, Faith thought, remembering her craving just a moment ago. She forced a neutral expression onto her face as the woman's outstretched hand trembled, and Faith realized she had to take the dubious gift.

"Jane." The woman gave a slight bow of her head.

"Faith." She bravely bit into one of the cookies—*Not bad!*—and ceremoniously handed the other one back to Jane.

Jane carefully folded the napkin around it and put it back into her pocket. "I'll save mine for later." She smiled like a little girl misbehaving.

"Good idea."

Faith was rescued from further conversation by the official announcement of the break. As everyone headed outside for their smoke, she cut through the crowd like a salmon swimming upstream, heading straight for Amanda Hill.

Amanda was talking to the moderator of the meeting, so Faith studied her while waiting. Amanda was a tad under five feet tall, yet wore flats. Probably late forties. A thick frame, wedged into a black skirt and loose-fitting top. Faith couldn't tell if her hair was heavily processed or if she was wearing a wig. Either way, there was so much hairspray it looked shellacked. *She'd better steer clear of the smokers—her hair helmet would light up like a sparkler.*

After Amanda had finished speaking with the moderator, Faith cleared her throat. "Excuse me?"

With a frown, Amanda held up her right hand, index finger raised, the way a mother would silence an interrupting child. With her other hand she fished around in her pocketbook and finally yanked out an oversize makeup mirror.

Faith thought about holding up her own hand with a different finger raised, but decided against it—she needed to get her paper signed for her probation officer.

Amanda wiped the corners of her mouth with her index finger and thumb, wet her lips with a loud smack, and closed the mirror with a snap. Only then did she turn to Faith, crossing her plump arms and shifting her weight over one hip. "Yes?"

"Are you Amanda? I'm trying to find my temporary sponsor."

"You must be Faith Winters," Amanda said loudly.

The people left in the room turned to stare. Even here, where everyone was assumed to have hit rock bottom, Faith was an outcast. Faith cringed. So much for anonymity. "My mother said you'd agreed to be my temporary—"

"Yes, I'll be your sponsor. I just adore your mother. After all that poor woman has been through, it's the least I can do."

Amanda stared pointedly at her watch. "Did you have a problem finding the church?"

"No."

Amanda waited silently, obviously expecting Faith to explain further.

"I was, like, a couple of minutes late. I stood in the back."

"I didn't see you." Amanda shifted her weight to her other hip.

Faith felt the cookie fracture as her fingers tightened around it. "Ask Jane." Faith pointed toward the back of the room.

"Jane? I'd just as soon ask the moon. Her mind is gone. I'll let this one slide, but I expect you to be on time for meetings from now on. Your mother entrusted this responsibility to me. I know how you've felt betrayed by those closest to you, and how that put your feet on the path to rebellion."

The cookie turned to dust as Faith made a fist. Amanda was quoting directly from chapter 6 of *The Girl Who Lived*. This complete stranger was regurgitating facts about Faith's life that should never have been made public. But at this point Faith had already been emotionally stripped naked and paraded on the bestseller list in front of millions. What did one more stranger's opinion matter?

"Do you have the paper?" Amanda waved her hand under Faith's chin, and Faith realized she was asking for the second time.

Faith's right hand was filled with cookie crumbs, so she awkwardly reached into the right pocket of her sweatpants with her left hand to pull out the form.

Amanda took the paper and pointed to the front row of chairs. "Sit next to me. I'll sign this when the meeting's done."

"I'm standing at the back."

Amanda's eyes narrowed. "I don't think that's wise. You'll get more out of the meetings if you sit up front with me."

"I can't sit." Faith exhaled, trying to stop herself from getting upset. "I have hemorrhoids," she lied. "Seriously. They're the size of a grapefruit."

Amanda's face twisted in disgust. "Really?"

Faith no longer cared what people thought of her. There's a benefit, after all, in being publicly humiliated and misunderstood—desensitization. And, if you're lucky, a sense of humor.

"Yeah. You want to see? We can go to the bathroom, or I can drop my pants right here." She stuck her thumbs under the waistband.

Amanda took a step back and shook her hands. "No!" A few people turned and looked. "Fine. Go stand at the wall."

Faith hurried to the safety of the shadows. Along the way, she emptied the crumbs in the trash bin. When she got to the very back of the room, she pressed her back against the bricks, crossed her ankles and wrists, and tried to tune out the world, like an honor guard, frozen in position. She found a flower pattern along the top of the walls, and started counting the petals.

Another speaker headed to the podium, and Jane came back from the coffee table carrying a cup with both hands. *Sixteen, seventeen . . . Please go away!*

Jane stopped beside Faith but kept her gaze on the floor. "You should come to the morning meeting," Jane whispered.

"I'm not a morning person."

Jane tipped her head toward the front of the room. "Neither is Amanda. Was that a form for probation you needed her to sign?" She tucked her chin down and cast Faith a nervous glance.

"Yeah."

"You can have the meeting moderator sign it. Amanda works in the morning, so she won't be at the meeting."

A smile formed on Faith's face. *Avoid Amanda? It's the perfect out.*

"Amanda was my court-appointed sponsor. I made the mistake of dropping her. She'll try to make your life hell if you do that."

"Did she do that to you?"

"Amanda told the judge I wasn't working my program and made coming to meetings even more miserable by *making* me share my story." Jane had a haunted look. "My life was already hell."

Faith knew the feeling. She cast her eyes at the floor and counted the tiny cookie crumbs as they dropped from Jane's clenched hand.

Faith hurried down the rickety apartment steps, clutching her new purse—another "essential" left in the apartment by her mother. After AA, she'd gone for another run, then done a full-core workout in her apartment, but nothing had helped. As she leapt onto the sidewalk, she told herself she was just going for a long walk, but she knew that was a lie. She was going for a very short walk—to O'Lindey's, a little Irish bar a block away that she noticed coming back from AA.

A voice in her head was begging her not to go, but another, stronger voice urged her to hurry. It was almost midnight, and she had to do what she had to do. Her brain was on fire and this was the only way to drown the flames.

She'd always thought that when she got out of Brookdale, she'd meet with Emily and they'd get through this together. But now . . .

Faith pictured Emily standing on a chair, eyes closed, beads of sweat rolling down her temples, a noose around her neck, stepping forward. Faith wanted to shout and beg Emily to stop, but she knew if she'd been there, she'd have pulled over another chair and unwound a length of rope for herself. Maybe neither of them was ever going to make it—maybe if they had banded together, the result was the same. They both die.

Like humidity rising before a thunderstorm, cold sweat prickled her skin as a panic attack threatened to sweep in. She ripped open the door to O'Lindey's and stomped inside. A little bell chimed, and every patron in the grimy, dim tavern turned to stare at the only woman in the room. When the door clicked shut behind her, she focused her attention on the bartender, a gangly man in his late fifties. His large eyes had a yellowish hue, and so did his pale skin. He placed a dirty elbow on the bar and trained his jaundiced gaze on Faith.

"Six shots of Pale Night whiskey." Faith reached into her purse and grabbed two twenties. It was the first time she'd ordered six; before it was always five.

He didn't move. "Two-shot maximum."

"I'm meeting some friends tonight. They're for them." She slapped the bills on the wood and met his disinterested gaze with a fiery stare. *I dare you to say no again.*

He shifted his eyes and pushed away from the bar. Moving at sloth speed, he managed to line up six shots. As the ghoulish bartender filled each glass, Faith pressed her hand flat against the counter to keep her fingers from quivering. The mere sight of the whiskey struck her like a hit of crack, and her mouth watered. She wet her lips and swallowed. When the aroma drifted up to her nose, she pictured the rat-faced man. As his crooked brown teeth slowly came into focus, she stopped seeing Emily's feet twitching inches above the floor.

The bartender moved away, and Faith raised the first shot to her lips.

"Here's to the dead," she whispered. "Kimberly Winters."

The alcohol burned her throat and warmed her stomach, like a signal fire: relief was coming.

"Anna Foster." Faith drained the second shot.

She paused, letting the liquid heat spread through her body, and glanced up once, but when she caught her reflection in the huge mirror behind the bar silently condemning her actions, she quickly looked away and got back to business.

"Jessica Foster." Faith drained the third shot and inhaled sharply through her nose.

It had been a year since Faith had had a drink. They were hitting her hard, each one a solid blow. She didn't weigh much, and she hadn't eaten for hours. A bowl of peanuts close by was tempting, but just as she was reaching for a few of those salty, toasty, Heaven-sent little nuggets, she saw the bartender scratch his armpit inside his shirt and grab a handful. *No thanks.*

The fourth shot awaited. *Michael Winters,* she thought. She couldn't even say her father's name aloud; his betrayal cut too deep. She couldn't help it; her mind raced through all the old, old questions: Had the murders been caused by his affairs? A husband seeking revenge? Her father's infidelities were bad enough, but the possibility that he was responsible for this hell was beyond her pain threshold. What had he done? Before the murders, he was her hero. Now she wanted to forget he ever existed. The faces around her all showed deep awareness of her every action, though seeming not to. Any one of the older men, with their normal abnormalities, could be her father. *But no. Michael Winters was my father.* She drained the shot and slammed it down, and the three empty glasses hopped into the air. One wobbled back and forth before tipping over and dribbling a tear of brown liquid down the glass and onto the wood.

She wiped the whiskey off her lips with the back of her hand, looked up at the mirror, and forced her features into a fourth-shot semblance of clear-eyed defiance. This would be a good time to remember why she was here. She inhaled slowly and drank in the aroma. Again she pictured the rat-faced man. *That's why I'm here.* Numbing the pain was just a bonus—she was looking for him.

"Last call in twenty minutes!"

Faith forced her head up and scanned the crummy little bar. Most of the drunks had staggered off. Three young guys jostled each other in the corner, and two older men sat at opposite ends of the bar. One was short, fat, and bald; the other looked like Thad, twenty years younger—close-cropped hair, two-day beard, jeans, sneakers. She got a glimpse of his mouth and frowned. She shook her head and the lights blurred.

Not him. He's got good teeth.

Rat Face wasn't here.

She glanced back at the three young men laughing in the corner; they were only boys, really. Were they even old enough to be in here? The truth was, they were about her age, but she felt old inside now, much older than nearly twenty-three. The last ten years had aged her. She stroked her left arm, fingertips tracing down the four long, self-inflicted scars along her forearm. A spiderwebbed crescent ran across the first two knuckles of her right hand. She didn't remember punching the drunk in the mouth after he grabbed her, but the police said she had, and the scar on her hand was proof enough for her.

No more fighting. Dr. Rodgers's warning echoed from somewhere in her mental fog. She pictured his kind eyes, made larger by his thick glasses, and twisted Kim's ring on her left hand. Looking around the room for a clock, she made the mistake of meeting the gaze of the tallest of the three boys. She turned away, but the damage was done—a split second of eye contact was all the encouragement he needed. He puffed out his chest, rolled back his shoulders, and strode over.

Getting ready to mutter a quick rejection, Faith ran her tongue across her teeth. They felt thick and coated. She tasted bile mixed with the liquor.

"Hey." The kid tried his best to pull off the good-old-boy romantic lead, planting one hand on the bar and one cowboy boot on the rail.

"What?" Her eyes locked on his now. As she gazed into the young man's baby blues, she saw more than hesitation—she saw fear. Everyone seemed to get that reaction lately when they looked at her.

He swallowed. Faith didn't know if it was the booze or the razzing he'd get from his friends if he chickened out now, but he kept at it. "My buddies and I had a bet going." He pointed at the empty shot glasses. "What're they for?"

Really? Sure you're ready for that? Faith rubbed a palm against her eye hard, as if to clear her vision, then laughed. A drunken chuckle at first, it grew until she had to tip her head back and roar at the ceiling to give it full voice.

The boy glanced back at his friends. He seemed nervous, but they didn't. They should have been. Faith's laugh could change direction like the winter wind. One moment she was laughing along with you, the next she had veered into hysteria or tears. Right now, her laugh was the type that often echoes down the halls of asylums.

"So, you want to know about the shot glasses." She wiped both hands down her face.

The two other boys came over to back up their friend.

"I bet that's how many years you were married," one suggested. His weird half-grin pushed up one side of his pockmarked face. Faith suspected he'd killed bugs with a magnifying glass as a kid and enjoyed it.

"I think you lost your job," said the other, a chubby boy in a Red Sox shirt, "and that's how many years you worked there."

Faith reached down and straightened up the glass that had fallen over. "Nope and nope." She let her head roll to the side. "What do you think, Cowboy?"

He lowered his voice, trying to sound sexy. "I think they're for past lovers."

His friends snickered.

"So, what're they for?" Pockface asked.

"Thursday is April twelfth. Death Day." Faith grabbed the empty shot glass on the left and turned it upside down. "This one's for Kimberly Winters." She flipped over the next glass and the next. "Anna Foster. Jessica Foster."

The bartender's head shot up, his yellowish eyes wide.

Number four. She forced herself to say the name aloud. "Michael Winters."

Red Sox took a step back and bumped into the bar stool behind him.

Pockface turned to the bartender and his stumbling friend. "What's she talking about?"

Faith stared at Red Sox. He knew who she was—the expression on his face confirmed it. He was giving her that look: a mix of pity, morbid curiosity, and terror. She hated that look.

"One for each of the girls." Red Sox's voice was faint; she almost didn't hear it.

"Huh?" Pockface lifted his eyebrows, compressing several pockmarks into a confused, wavy line across his forehead.

"The murders at Reed Lake," the bartender muttered.

"My dad knew the Fosters," Red Sox said.

"My sister shouldn't have been there," Faith said. "She was there because of me. Kim opened the door, and—" She mimicked a stabbing motion.

Red Sox took another couple of steps back.

"But that was all the victims," said Red Sox. "Four. You've got two more shots. Who are they for?"

Faith held up shot number five. "Emily Foster. Anna's sister. Mrs. Foster had brought her two daughters up to the lake that night. Mrs. Foster and Anna went to my father's cabin. Emily stayed back in their own cabin but was close enough to hear the screams. She hid under the bed." Faith emptied the shot. "Emily hanged herself three months ago." She stared at the horrified faces of the boys; they seemed even younger now. "But she died that night. It just took her ten years to realize it."

"Who's the other shot for?" Cowboy asked quietly.

Faith broke into a slow, thin smile that offered little warmth, like a cloud-filtered sunrise on a frigid winter morning. Her eyes—empty and cold—drained the smile of emotion.

"This one?" Faith raised the glass. "It's for me. Here's to the dead."

The empty glass rang out with the finality of a judge's gavel when she slammed it down, the echo resonating throughout the room. The bartender stepped backward until he bumped into the back counter and the liquor bottles on the shelves rattled like frightened birds.

"We're closing." He flashed the lights, his face pale and his hand trembling.

"But it ain't one o'clock yet," the man at the far end of the bar objected. "We ain't had last call."

"We're closing."

The boys shuffled away.

Faith gazed at the line of shot glasses spread out in front of her like little tombstones. She thought about hurling them against the wooden floor and watching them shatter. But she resisted the urge. She didn't need to get arrested again. As she slid off the bar stool, the room seemed to tilt in the opposite direction. She clamped her eyes closed and grabbed the bar to find her balance, but in that moment of darkness, screams from that night echoed inside her mind. She gasped and jerked forward, bumping into the stool next to her. The last-minute lingerers stared as the stool scraped to a halt.

She shouldn't have talked to those boys. Ten years, and the pain was still fresh. Raw.

Faith grabbed her purse and stumbled toward the door. The little bell over the door chimed once more as she shoved it open, the cool night air filling her lungs. She shuffled down the sidewalk, lurching in a zigzag pattern. Only a couple of cars drove along the quiet street. All the stores were closed. Faith caught her reflection in the window of a hardware store and stopped. She saw the ghost of her father in her high cheekbones and Roman nose, and her intense blue eyes were identical to his—the kind of vivid blue you see in the middle of a lightning bolt or inside the hottest flames of a campfire. It was her reflection, but her father stared back at her.

She glared at the ghost and snarled. *I can't deal with you. I can't deal with what you did.* Drunken tears were coming now. *And I can't deal with what happened . . .*

She spun around, steadied herself against a streetlight, and wiped snotty tears with the back of her hand. She was unzipping her purse, hoping to find a tissue, when a dark-brown sedan drove past. The driver only glanced at her for an instant, but at that moment her brain flashed and her body froze.

Crooked brown teeth. Weak chin. Rat-thin nose.

The face that haunted her in a thousand nightmares and tormented her whenever she closed her eyes. She couldn't draw stick figures, but she could sketch him flawlessly. She even drew his face once on a bathroom wall, using her own blood, after she slit her wrists. But this demon was flesh-and-blood, passing mere feet from her, where a moment later she suddenly ejected the contents of her stomach.

Her body's instant reaction took her by surprise. She thought she'd reduced the fear, maybe even eliminated it. For ten years, she'd beaten herself up for her cowardice that night. She'd run away and let her sister die, and since then she'd sworn that if given the chance she wouldn't repeat her sin.

"STOP!" she shrieked like a banshee unleashed from hell as she dashed into the street.

The sedan's brake lights glowed an angry red, and the car stopped.

As Faith rushed toward it, she stumbled into the path of a van coming from the opposite direction. The driver slammed on his brakes and laid on the horn, the tires squealed, and the van skidded to a stop inches from Faith.

Rat Face grabbed his side mirror and angled it to look at her. In the light from the streetlamp, she could see his brown hair. It was him. The man she'd chased for so long was twenty feet away.

She screamed again, a feral yell of pain and rage that needed no words. Her intent was clear enough. She was going to drag him from his car and rip him to shreds with her bare hands.

The sedan shot forward and sped away.

Faith chased the car down the middle of the street. As it drew away from her, she flung her purse after it, but even if she'd been sober, she couldn't have caught up to a speeding car. Up ahead, it took a right and disappeared behind the building.

"No!" Her hands pressed into her skull, and her fingernails dug at her flesh.

Down the block behind her, blue police lights flicked on.

She raced toward them, waving her arms wildly.

The cruiser skidded to a stop, and the policeman jumped out, concern etched on his face, one hand on his gun and the other on his radio. "Faith?" It took her a second to recognize Kim's old boyfriend—Tommy.

"It's him!" Faith jammed her arm in the direction the sedan had gone. "Don't stop. Go! Go!"

"Faith . . ." Tommy looked hesitantly at the radio in his hand.

"A brown car. Four doors." She closed her eyes, grimaced, and slammed her hand into her head. "I didn't get the plate. Stupid. Stupid!" Her eyes opened, and she swayed like a sailor on the deck of a ship. "Go! He's getting away!"

Tommy took his hand off his radio, his lips pressing together and his shoulders rounding. *He doesn't believe me!*

"Tommy!" Faith rushed over to him. "It was him. I know it. I know it." She grabbed the fabric of his policeman's uniform in her fists.

"You're drunk." Tommy's voice was a mixture of disappointment and pity.

"Don't do this, Tommy. Get him. Please." Faith tried to shake him, but it was like pushing against a tree. "It was him." Her anger flashed. Of all the people in Marshfield, she needed the help of Tommy Carson.

Tommy grabbed her hands and pulled them off his shirt, his gaze shifting to the silver ring on her hand. He stiffened and his eyes widened in recognition. Releasing his grip, he stepped back. "Let's get out of the road. Step over there, on the grass, and we'll talk."

Faith started to protest, but then she turned on her heel and stomped to the sidewalk. Like a caged lion, she paced back and forth, glaring in the direction her prey had fled. Each second she waited, her chances of catching Rat Face plummeted. She bitterly watched Tommy get into the cruiser, pull it over to the curb, dutifully shut off the lights, and slowly walk over to her.

"You let him get away." She tasted vomit in her mouth, and spit.

Tommy unscrewed the cap of a water bottle and held it out to her. "The last time you were drunk and thought you saw him, you got put away for a year, and that was getting off easy. You just got out. Are you in that much of a hurry to go back?"

"I saw him in Greenville Notch, too." She pushed his hand away and water from the bottle splashed the ground. "It was him, Tommy."

"Drink this."

She pulled the bottle from his hands. "He's getting away. If you're not going after him, call a cop who will."

"I'm not calling it in."

At that moment, Faith wanted to kill him. Rat Face was once again disappearing into the night, and it was Tommy's fault. She was about to rip into him, but Tommy took out his cell phone and dialed a number.

Faith took a sip of water, swirled it around her mouth, and spit.

"Mark? Listen, I need a solid. Do not call it in, but I need you to be on the lookout for a brown four-door sedan. It's headed from downtown, west toward Hingham. You are? Then he should be coming your way." Tommy turned back to Faith. "Do you remember anything else about the car?"

Faith squeezed her eyes shut. "One white tire on the back. Driver's side. The stripe thing. It was white."

"One whitewall on the rear driver's side," Tommy said. "No, totally under the radar. I owe you. I'll explain later."

After he ended the call, Faith said, "You should go, too."

"I need to look after you."

Her anger softened. She knew Tommy had loved her sister, and the faint echo of that caring still rang in his voice. "I'm not crazy."

"But you're drunk."

She lifted her chin. "So?"

Tommy ran his hand through his short brown hair. "You just got released from a mental hospital. You're lucky it wasn't jail. Your mother said you were working your program. You're not supposed to drink." Tommy folded his arms across his broad chest. He had always been in shape in high school, and he'd bulked up since then.

"There's no law against it."

"There is for drunk and disorderly. You've been arrested for it, what, six times?"

"I'm not disorderly."

"What do you call running down the middle of the street screaming at the top of your lungs?"

"BUT I SAW HIM!" she yelled.

In the awkward silence that followed her outburst, a car drove by, its tires crunching something in the road. Tommy turned his head.

"Damn it!" Faith stumbled forward and Tommy grabbed her arm.

"Get back on the sidewalk."

She thrust a hand out. "My purse."

"I got it." Tommy snapped his flashlight on, retrieved the purse, and handed it to her.

Faith peered inside. Her pill case was crushed, but her new phone looked okay.

Tommy was staring at her hand, and she realized his focus was once again on her ring.

"She'd have wanted you to have it." He cleared his throat and tilted his head toward the cruiser. "Let me take you home."

"I'm fine." She started to walk in the direction Rat Face had taken.

Tommy stepped in front of her. "I take you home or to the police station."

Faith looked everywhere but at Tommy, rage beginning to bubble up. Her lip twitched, and she drew in a jagged breath, trying to remind herself it wasn't his fault. But if he hadn't blown Kim off that night . . .

Tommy opened the back door of the cruiser and pointed inside. "Your call, Faith."

She stared into the blackness where the brown sedan had gone. The keys were dangling from the ignition of the still-running police cruiser. The idea of dashing to the driver's side, jumping in, and chasing after Rat Face herself flickered brightly but briefly. Tommy was too strong and too fast. She'd never get past him.

"It was him." Her voice sounded foreign; the hard edge was gone.

"I'm sure you think you saw him."

Faith slid into the car seat, the adrenaline fueling her system had vanished—and with it, her resolve. Was it really him?

Monday, April 9

J effrey swerved across the double-yellow line as he struggled to yank his phone out of his pocket, then veered back into his lane and wiped his hand down his thin nose and over his weak chin. His thumb left greasy smudges as he punched in the number.

Damn it. Damn it. Damn it, he chanted as he waited. Finally, someone on the other end picked up. "This is bad. This is really bad, man."

"Jeff?" a man responded. "What—"

"She saw me. She looked right at me. Tried to chase me down."

"Back up, buddy. Wh—"

"You said she was locked up. She wasn't supposed to be in Marshfield."

"Chill out and tell me what the hell happened."

Jeffrey sat up straighter as a police cruiser drove toward him. He lowered his phone and kept his eyes focused on the road until the car passed.

"Hello? Jeff, are you there?"

"Yeah, I'm here. It was the girl. She saw me."

"What girl? The one from the Charlie Horse?"

"No. The girl from the cabin. The girl who lived."

Silence on the other end of the phone. Jeffrey checked his rearview mirror. The cruiser had rounded the corner and was nowhere in sight.

The silence stretched on as he sped down the street, apprehension growing as he waited. Jeffrey imagined him glaring down at his own phone, eyes inflamed, the tendons in his neck taut—a beast about to charge. Finally, he heard something—something smashing, followed by a string of screamed profanities.

This is bad. This is so bad.

"Why did you have to come back?!" the other man shouted. "I told you. I *told* you this would happen."

"*You* turn down a free house," Jeffrey snapped back. "You didn't have to move. She didn't see *you*. You didn't have the cops looking for you."

"You shoulda sold the house and moved. I told you that after she saw you in Greenville Notch. Move to California, go to Vegas. But did you listen? No! I was so stupid to let you come back."

"My mother was dying. I hadn't seen her—"

"She's dead now, but you're still here."

"You told me I could stay! Where was I supposed to go with no money?"

"For a couple of weeks, not four months. I gave you a job so you could get some cash and leave." A huge sigh rattled through the phone's tiny speaker. "Are you sure she saw you?"

Jeffrey pictured the girl flinging her purse after him and running down the middle of the street. "Yeah, I'm sure."

Another stream of profanities. "You've got to leave town *now*."

"Now? No way. I can't."

"*What* did you just say?"

Jeffrey was afraid to answer. This was the last person Jeffrey wanted to make angry, and he'd already overstepped by getting into a shouting match with him.

The voice changed. The tone. "Jeff. What did you just say?" It was the same man speaking, but he sounded so calm he could have been ordering a sandwich. "Please, repeat what you said."

Jeffrey pulled up to the garage, stopped the car, and rested his forehead on the steering wheel. He was shaking. The police he could deal with, but the man on the other end of the phone . . .

"I'm just . . . I'm saying that I can't move because I don't have the money. I'm putting my mom's house on the market. I can't just walk away from that money, man. It's all I got."

"Don't worry, Jeffrey." The voice was smooth and soothing, like a parent comforting a child. "I'll figure it out. Why don't you take this week off?"

"Really?"

"Take the week, but don't go anywhere for anything." Each word sounded hard around the edges. "Do you understand me?"

Jeffrey winced. "Yeah. I won't. I get it."

"You sound upset still. Don't be. Are you upset?"

He wiped the sweat off his forehead with the back of his hand. "No, man. I'm cool."

"Good. There's no reason to worry. I got this."

The phone disconnected.

Jeffrey pulled the car into the garage and dragged a tarp over it. If he hadn't been so occupied, he might have marveled at how the brain can delegate thousands of tiny mechanical motions to the body while it amuses itself by churning out an incessant silent soundtrack. *This is really bad. This is so, so bad...*

Faith's temples were thudding like a bass drum; then she realized someone was knocking on the door. She groaned, pulled the pillow over her head, and rolled over.

Great. Just great.

The knocking continued and grew louder, faster.

She dragged herself out of bed and plodded to the kitchen sink. Jamming the lever up, she tilted her head to one side and drank directly from the running faucet. The door shook with each blow.

"Hold on!" Only two people would just drop by, and she didn't want to see either of them. And she definitely didn't want to explain why she was hungover. She wiped her mouth and felt the scar on her chin—another reminder of that night in the woods. She breathed into her hand to smell her breath. *I stink like a brewery.*

The pounding continued.

"One second!" Faith grabbed a jar of peanut butter off the counter. She stuck a finger in it, scooped out a blob, and smeared it over her teeth and around her mouth to try to mask the odor of whiskey. Smacking her lips, she thought about changing the clothes she'd passed out in, but there wasn't enough time. Her mother or probation officer would only wait so long.

She yanked opened the door and stepped back for the unpleasant surprise.

Henryka Vasilyeva stood in the doorway, as polished as ever. She leaned forward until Faith could see herself clearly in the reflection of Henryka's mirrored sunglasses, just above Henryka's tight-lipped scowl. Faith looked as bad as she felt; matted hair, mauve semicircles under her eyes.

"Don't tell me I just drove all the way here because you went on a bender last night," Henry said.

"What? No." Faith shook her head. Big mistake. *Wow, I didn't know the Tilt-A-Whirl was open this early.* She hoped it wasn't obvious that she was grabbing the door for support.

Henry removed her glasses and held them out between her thumb and index finger. "Do you happen to remember calling me at two this morning?" To her credit, she didn't pause long enough to make Faith provide the answer they both knew beyond a shadow of a doubt. "You said you found Rat Face, but I didn't know that you'd been drinking. I was under the impression that you'd just been released from a mental hospital, what, ten hours earlier? I figured you could make it at least twenty-four hours."

Faith feigned shocked indignation. "I haven't been drinking."

Henry walked away, toward the stairs.

"Wait, where are you going? I did see him! I swear it. He was driving a brown sedan."

Henry stopped. "You lie to me again, about anything, and I'm gone. Do you understand?"

"Yes," Faith mumbled.

"Did you drink?"

If she admitted it and Henry informed on her, she'd be locked up before sundown, but Faith had no choice but to trust her. "Yes."

"How many drinks?" Henry asked loudly.

A middle-aged woman walking her dog stopped and gawked at Faith.

"Can we have this discussion inside?" Faith said, motioning for Henry to come in from the balcony.

Henry seemed to take forever to make up her mind whether to continue the conversation. Finally, she exhaled loudly, muttered something under her breath, walked past Faith into the apartment, and scanned the entire place with one swivel of her head.

Faith shut the door after them, sat in the chair, and motioned for Henry to take the stool, but Henry remained standing and at attention—feet shoulder-width apart, shoulders back.

"How many drinks did you have?"

"Six shots of whiskey."

"How long in between?"

"I got there—the little place on the corner, O'Lindey's—a little after midnight and left just before closing at one. I came out of the bar and Rat Face was driving a brown sedan. He definitely saw me, and I saw him. It happened really fast; he drove off and I didn't have time to get the plate or . . ." She stopped.

"Catch your breath," Henry said, almost kindly.

"The rear driver-side tire was a . . . it had a white stripe around it."

"A whitewall?"

"That's it."

"You spoke with the police." Henry popped her sunglasses into one pocket and took a pen and notebook out of another. "Which officer?"

She didn't want to mention Tommy or his help, but her mind was still groggy and she couldn't think of an excuse.

"I know you spoke to an officer. You just retold it sounding like a cop. Did they put out a BOLO for the car?"

"A what?"

"A BOLO is a Be On the Look-Out alert. What happened when the officer called it in?"

Faith swallowed. *Oh, crap.* "Well . . . he didn't."

Henry's pen stopped. Her cursive script looked like calligraphy on the page. "So, you're saying you saw Rat Face, but when you spoke to a police officer, for some reason he didn't report it?"

"Yes."

Henry closed the notebook with a snap. "Don't call me," she said, and headed for the door.

"What? Why?" Faith asked, following. "Why the hell are you leaving?"

"I warned you." Henry spun around, and Faith almost crashed into her. Henry's steely eyes narrowed as she leaned toward Faith, a vein in her neck throbbing as she clenched her jaw. "You wake me up at two o'clock in the morning, I drop everything and drive here first thing, and now you want me to believe that a police officer didn't follow procedure and call in a report? I'm guessing there *was* no rat-faced man and therefore there was no conversation with any policeman—"

"No. You're wrong. He didn't want . . . the policeman didn't want to call it in because it was me and I'd been drinking."

"You're full of it, Faith. Do you know the police chief is not only a fan of your mother's book, he's also listed as an official consultant?"

"Trust me, I know everything about that book. So what?"

"So what?" Henry looked like she was about to burst a pipe. "So, you don't seem to know *anything* about the book that the cops are going to follow *to the letter* when it comes to you. Every cop who wants to keep his job is going to proceed strictly by that book, if only to cover his own ass, because the reporters are going to be all over any story about you like stink on a monkey. You haven't figured out why your mother gave you a nice car, a nice apartment, and a new phone, but no TV?"

Faith shook her head.

"Because you're all over the news. Well, 'the girl who lived' is, anyway. With the tenth anniversary coming up and a new TV special, if you *did* watch TV, now would be a good time to switch to books."

Faith pressed her palms against her eyes. She wanted to run again. Go up to the mountains, find a cave, crawl in, and die.

"*If* you saw Rat Face, and *if* you told the police, the only reason a cop wouldn't call it in is if"—Henry flashed the briefest of victory smiles—"he was looking out for you. You reported it to Tommy Carson, didn't you?"

She couldn't tell on Tommy, but she didn't want to lie to Henry either. "Who?"

"Officer Carson was your sister's boyfriend at the time of the murders. He was also a suspect."

"What? Tommy wasn't a suspect."

Henry sat down on the stool and pointed to the chair. "Everyone's a suspect, Faith. And when it comes to murder victims, the spouse or boyfriend is always number one. So— you're saying you told Officer Carson, but he didn't call it in?"

"He called another policeman."

Henry raised an eyebrow. "You're telling me he used his radio to—"

"No. He didn't want it to be official so I wouldn't get jammed up if I was wrong. He used his cell phone. He asked the other cop to keep an eye out for the car. Look, um, I really don't want Tommy to get in trouble. I'll say I didn't even see the guy if that happens."

"Did either he or the other officer find the car?"

"I . . . well, he hasn't contacted me, so . . . I guess not."

Henry glanced up from the notepad and paused. "You look like hell, Faith. You do realize you're killing yourself slowly, right?"

A number of responses passed through Faith's mind. Most included profanity, and one involved throwing something. But she bit her tongue and kept her hands at her sides.

"Have you given any thought to what happens if I catch this guy?" Henry asked.

The truth was, she hadn't.

"Obviously not. Let me put it this way. You're called 'the girl who lived,' right? That means you're the only one alive who saw the guy. That means you're the only one who can pick him out of a lineup. *If* I catch him, it'll be up to you to put him away. Now, ten years of drug and alcohol abuse and frequent flyer miles on the mental hospital express don't exactly lend credibility to your testimony, but still, the DA might—*might*—get a jury to believe you. That's *if* you're sober and alive. If you go back to drinking—you can forget about it. I could find the guy and you could swear up and down that he's the one, and he'd still walk. So, I'm going to ask you again. Do you want to catch this guy or not?"

"Yes. I do."

"Then, no more drinking."

Their eyes locked, steel against sapphire. "Okay," Faith whispered.

Henry paused again, as if considering whether to believe this, then nodded. "You're sure you saw him?"

"I'm sure."

"Then I may have you come in and talk to the sketch artist."

Faith shook her head. "It wouldn't do any good. Weak chin. Rat face. That's all I saw. You already have the sketch."

"You saw the driver, but you didn't get a full look at his face?" She tapped the pen against the notepad. "You didn't see his eyes *again*?"

Faith exhaled slowly. "I didn't see his eyes because they were in shadow. He was driving. That was the same way I saw him that night at the campground."

"But you saw him on the path later. Right?"

"He was in silhouette then. I didn't see any details."

Henry sighed. "So. I'm looking for a brown four-door sedan with a whitewall tire. I want to help, Faith, but it's not a lot to go on."

"I know it was him."

"You've made that claim before," Henry said.

Faith bit her cheek. "Yes, I saw him that time, too! I'm positive. I just spent a year in an asylum because of that. I know what I saw. Rat Face ran into that warehouse."

Henry took a deep breath. "Just tell me what you remember about the car. The make? Any damage, bumper sticker? Anything?"

Shame and anger churned in Faith. She hadn't noticed anything else because she'd been drinking. "I just—I saw his face and I . . . I just locked in on it."

Henry closed her notebook. "I want you to come down to the station and look over some car books."

Faith hesitated. Henry might as well have asked her to have tea with the Devil. She'd rather go to the morgue than the police station. "Can't you bring them here?"

"Do I look like I have time to adjust my schedule for you?"

"I wasn't asking that." Faith twisted the ring on her left hand. "I hate the police station."

"I'll see what I can do." Henry glanced down at Faith's hand. "What happened to the stone?"

"It fell out that night." Faith traced the damaged centerpiece, where the diamond was missing. The silver vines that had cupped it were bent and misshapen. "You're not going to say anything about Tommy?"

Henry walked to the door. "Not right now."

Faith jammed her hands into her pockets and cleared her throat. She didn't look at Henry directly—it was like trying to bring opposing magnets together, and her eyes turned away. "Thank you for coming out."

"I was coming to Marshfield anyway. The ten-year anniversary is this week, and . . . Listen, Faith. We need to close the case. With all the attention around the ten-year anniversary, my supervisor thinks now is the time."

"But I saw the guy."

"Then you'd better start praying we find him, and fast. We have less than a week."

Faith shut the shower off and tried to will the pool of soapy water at her feet to go down. Even though the drain was open, the two inches of water at the bottom of the tub refused to form the little funnel she had always loved to watch as a kid. Finally, she decided to get out, but even after she'd dried off and wrapped a towel around her hair, when she checked the tub, the water level remained about two inches high. Right where she left it.

Great. Just like my life. Stagnant.

She pulled on a pair of jeans and a baggy T-shirt, and tossed a sweatshirt over it. Her phone beeped and vibrated on the kitchen table with a text message from Tommy—DIDN'T FIND THE CAR. NEITHER DID OTHER GUY. WE'LL KEEP AN EYE OUT FOR IT. The words hit a nerve, and Faith's right hand came down hard on the table with a sharp smack. Keeping an eye out for Rat Face wasn't good enough. She was done waiting. All these years other people would say they were searching but never found him. Those days were over.

She grabbed her keys and headed out to the back of the building in search of the Camry. She hadn't needed it till now because both the meeting and the bar were within walking distance. She found the car as soon as she rounded the corner, and Faith had to admit, it was in better shape than she'd expected. The dark-blue paint was a little faded, but there were no dents or rust, and the inside proved to be immaculately clean. Faith slid the key into the ignition, but hesitated before starting it. Her first car. Okay, technically it was in her mother's name, but still, for now it was hers. And she hadn't driven in years. Sitting in the driver's seat of her own car felt strange. *Too many years locked up, told when to eat, when to sleep, where to go, where not to go . . .*

Now she could go wherever she wanted, cruise all the way to the coast to feel the ocean breeze or drive into the mountains to watch a sunset from on high. Realizing she was free poured panic into her muscles like water into concrete. She stiffened and froze, like a small child standing on the front porch steps, afraid to go down into the vast, teeming metropolis.

She locked the car doors and slumped in the seat. Glancing up at her apartment, she imagined herself walking back in, calling off her search, retreating to her sanctuary, and getting under the covers. Her hand seized the door handle. Either choice led to pain. She could go upstairs, pace the floor, and think about jumping off the roof, or she could try to face the demons lurking in a world that felt suddenly overwhelming.

A red pickup truck drove past. A yellow Bug zipped down the street after it, riding the rear bumper all the way to the stoplight. Faith was tempted to sit there and wait. Maybe lightning would strike a third time and Rat Face would just happen to drive by in his brown sedan. Or she could take matters into her own hands. Because Faith didn't need to feel an ocean breeze or watch a sunset or jump off the roof just yet. She needed only one thing—to find Rat Face.

She turned the key, goosed the gas, and pulled away from the curb like she'd been doing it all her life.

It was almost eight in the evening when Faith pulled in front of the redbrick school building. She couldn't resist parking behind the locksmith's van topped by a magician statue triumphantly holding a magic wand in one hand and a key in the other.

She had driven around Marshfield for two hours searching for the brown sedan and Rat Face.

Nothing.

Had she expected him to be standing around, waiting for her to find him? Yeah. She *had* expected that. Somehow, she'd allowed herself to believe she could choose to control her life. She'd bought into the hope that fate was something she could direct, or that would at least step aside and let her steer for once. She, of all people, should've known better. And now she was forced to attend yet another group.

She loathed groups. She'd been to hundreds of them, maybe. She tried to do the math in her head. Thousands? She groaned. Regardless, she didn't have a choice. The judge had made the decision for her, and that probation stipulation was a gun to her head, forcing her out of the car and marching her up the granite steps.

The heavy door opened to reveal a school built in the 1940s. A combination of mustiness and Lysol led to the inevitable conclusion that someone had mated an old library and a hospital. Polished wooden floors stretched off in three directions. *Where am I supposed to go now?* A small sign on a metal stand pointed the way to SSG: Survivors' Support Group.

Faith indignantly huffed and puffed her way past the signs, down the halls, and through a set of double doors, to find herself in the school's combination gymnasium-auditorium, with a raised stage at the far end and a ring of folding chairs in the center. A small table to the left of the door held a stack of name badges and black markers in a cup. A sheet next to the badges read, *Use your first name if you want, but it's not required.*

Faith left the badges alone altogether.

Seven people sat in the circle of chairs, and a little old lady sat a dozen feet away, removed from the group, next to the stage. She was knitting, a trail of yarn stretching down to a wicker basket beside her. A man—Brian, according to his name tag—was rocking back and forth and speaking rapidly to the group.

"—and they just don't stop," he was saying. "It's like I close my eyes and *boom!* I'm in another nightmare. All week. I mean *all* week. I haven't slept. I—"

He stopped talking when Faith took her seat.

Faith focused on the floor and assumed her attacked-turtle position: head tucked into her chest, arms and legs crossed.

"Brian? Go on," said a young man whose name tag read *Robert.* He was around Faith's age, with chocolate-brown hair and coffee-colored eyes. "You were talking about your nightmares?"

He's the group leader. He was dressed in rumpled khakis and a well-worn shirt with the sleeves rolled up. *Harmless geek,* she decided. She'd have to get him to sign the form for her probation officer.

"Yeah." Brian sat back in his seat and crossed his arms. "I just ... I just want some sleep. It's like ... haven't I been through enough? After all this crap, all I want is one good night's sleep."

"They say that's common." The woman sitting next to Brian looked like she'd come straight from work, dressed in hospital scrubs with her ebony hair pulled back in a tight bun. She pointed to herself with a slender hand. "I still have them, too. Nightmares. They're not as bad now because I work out. I run. On days I don't, I get them. You have to find something that works for you." Her high cheekbones accentuated her big brown eyes, which stared at him intently.

Brian nodded. He seemed to have run out of steam and slumped back in his chair.

Robert steepled his fingers as his eyes briefly landed on each person of the little group, like a teacher searching the class for a volunteer.

A thirty-something man with a neatly trimmed beard raised his hand. "Hi." His voice cracked, and he coughed. "I'm Adam. I, uh—I haven't been in a while."

"It's almost been a month," said an older man with close-cropped white hair. Faith guessed he was close to seventy. He sat ramrod straight with both feet flat on the floor and his hands on his thighs.

"Yeah, well," Adam continued, "the anniversary of my incident is coming up again."

"Anniversaries tend to do that," Brian muttered.

Adam chuckled nervously. "Yeah. Well, I haven't shared before and—and I guess now's the time. I'll be quick, but I want to know if it's okay?" He looked to Robert.

"Certainly. You should be able to share anytime." Robert turned to Faith. "As part of the group, we encourage members to share their experience. Those events can be . . . " He seemed to be searching for the right word.

"I've been around. He can talk." Faith spoke to her feet and didn't meet anyone's eyes.

Adam nodded. "Well. I was six and my family was on a trip out to California. We got caught in a storm. My brother and I—Nathan, his name was Nathan; he was five—we were playing in the back seat, but it kept raining, and the more we drove, the more freaked out my parents got."

Adam reached down, picked up the water bottle next to his chair, and took a long sip before continuing.

"My dad was driving. We hit this huge puddle and the car stalled. He kept trying to start it, but then . . . the water came. It wasn't a gradual little rising of rainwater—it was a wall of water, a flash flood. It hit, and the whole car moved like we got smashed by a train. It pushed us all the way across the road, and then the road disappeared—it was underwater. My mom started crying. My dad told us we needed to get out and it was going to be okay, we just needed to hold onto each other, no matter what. He climbed out the window, and my mom handed Nathan out first, then me. Then another wave hit and swept us off the roof. It pulled the three of us away from the car and away from my mom. My mom was screaming and Nathan was crying, but I just . . . I just . . . I couldn't say anything. It was so weird. One minute we were in the car, and the next we were in a river that had been the street."

Adam's eyes were unfocused, as if he was looking at something no one else could see; something he wished he couldn't see either.

Faith knew the feeling. She was staring at him as he spoke, like a witness to an accident. She knew what was about to happen but couldn't look away.

"My dad was coughing and spitting up water. He was trying to swim while holding onto me and Nathan, but his head kept going under the water. I knew he was drowning and I thought we were all going to die." Adam closed his eyes and hung his head. "But my dad . . . he let go of Nathan. He just opened his arm and let the river take Nathan away. It made no sense—none of it did. He said to hold onto each other *no matter what*, but he let go of Nathan . . . "

Adam lifted his head and looked around at the other members of the group as if searching their faces for the answer. Faith forced herself to meet his haunted gaze.

"Dad and I made it to a tree and waited for the water to go down. Dad wanted to find the car, but it was nowhere in sight. I don't remember much after that. They found my mom in the morning. She never made it out of the car. They didn't find Nathan for four days. I guess the hardest part for me is the why. Why me? Why didn't my dad let go of *me*? I asked him once. He didn't say anything. I guess I'll never know." Adam cleared his throat again and took another swig of water.

"Thank you for sharing," Robert said. "*Why* is one of the biggest questions we, as survivors, face."

Faith didn't mean to, but a sarcastic huff escaped out of her mouth. She coughed in an effort to disguise it, but given the looks from the rest of the group, it didn't work.

"Would you like to contribute?" Robert asked.

The words hung in the air. Everyone's gaze focused on her. Her hangover was still using her head as a piñata, and the gym's bright overhead lights were shooting spikes into her eyes.

"Faith," she said. "I didn't mean to offend anyone. Sorry." She held up a hand and forced her mouth closed.

"You don't have to worry about that." The older man leveled his gaze at her, and she couldn't help but think of her old family doctor sitting on a stool and telling her to take her medicine. "You got something to say, best thing is to say it. Some of us survivors are a pretty bitter lot."

Faith's skin crawled. She never should have opened her mouth, but now that she had, the only way to get everyone to stop looking at her was to say something.

"Survivor?" Another snort erupted. "That title's a riot." She pressed her thumb down hard against the back of her other hand. "You'd figure a group of *survivors* would be high-fiving each other or something, but it doesn't work that way, does it? Instead, it sucks. Yeah, we survived—but for what? It's like a guy who survives a fall from an airplane with no parachute. Yeah, he *survived*, but he's so busted up he'll never be okay. Everything inside him is broken. He'll never be right. And we call him a *survivor*. It's a joke. His whole life is one big walking nightmare. Just like ours."

"Not mine," said the woman in hospital scrubs. "You said *our* lives, but you should've said *your* life is a nightmare. You don't speak for me."

Her voice was even and without malice, but Faith bristled.

Robert seemed to pick up on it. "That's correct, Nyah, but since it's Faith's first time here I want to thank her for sharing. And she raised an important question. What are our lives like after our incident? That's something I think we need to touch on."

The conversation moved away from Faith, and she breathed a sigh of relief. She tucked her chin into her chest and sat as silent as a mummy for the next twenty minutes.

Finally, Robert placed his hands on his thighs and said, "Why don't we take a fifteen-minute break, okay?"

No one needed any encouragement. Everyone besides Robert headed for the side door—to smoke, of course. Most survivors smoked. Hell, if they could, most of them would walk around 24/7 with an intravenous drip of their drug of choice. Faith was surprised she hadn't seen any of these people at the AA meeting.

Robert held out his hand to her. "Welcome."

Faith nodded but didn't shake his hand.

"There's coffee over there." Robert pointed. He leaned forward and whispered, "It's decaf. Some of us have issues sleeping." He fumbled in his pocket and handed her a business card that looked like he had printed it himself. It listed only the address of the school and a phone number. "We try to keep anonymity, but if there's inclement weather or the meeting gets changed, I keep an email list of members to let them know. Would you like me to put you on it?"

"No, thanks." Faith put the card in her pocket.

"Robert?" Adam called out from the side entrance. "Gus and Brian are arguing politics again."

"Excuse me." Robert left Faith alone and crossed the room.

Adam didn't follow Robert. Instead he walked over to Faith. "Hey. Welcome."

Faith nodded. "Sorry again for the sarcasm."

Adam waved his hand dismissively. "Don't worry about it. You should hear Gus—that's the older gentleman. He flings buckets of sarcasm when he gets down. Not to imply that you're down," he added. "You want a cup of coffee?"

"No, thanks."

"How about you, Mrs. H.?" Adam called over to the old woman sitting by herself, knitting. "You want a cup of coffee?"

The old woman shook her head and smiled politely.

"What's with her?" Faith asked. "Why don't you let her play in your reindeer games?"

"Mrs. Henderson likes to listen. She actually started the group after her son died."

The old woman glanced up, smiled, and waved Faith over.

Oh, great. Faith had already far exceeded her talking quota and her stomach was doing flip-flops trying to recover from the booze. The last thing she wanted to do was talk to more people, no matter how old and sweet they looked. She pretended not to notice the invite.

"Nice meeting you," Adam said. "Thanks for sharing, Faith. You gave me a lot to think about." He headed for the coffee.

Mrs. Henderson waved Faith over again. Her arm was stretched as high as it could go and she looked like she might fall off the chair if she kept it up. Maybe it was that, or because she reminded Faith of her grandmother, but Faith felt drawn to her. She started twisting her ring and walked over.

"Welcome." The old woman neatly folded her knitting in her lap. "I'm Mrs. Henderson. Nice to meet you, Faith."

"Hi." Faith leaned against the side of the stage. "Were you bad or something? Are you in time-out?"

Mrs. Henderson covered her mouth with her hand and laughed politely. "Oh, no. I prefer to listen."

"They don't make you share? What's your secret?"

"Oh, no secret. For some people, it helps to talk. For me, it does me good to listen. Sometimes that helps you forget about yourself."

"Sometimes?"

Mrs. Henderson nodded. "It only works sometimes to fix the pain. Sometimes you need to do something."

"Like what?"

"Ask for help."

That was Faith's signal to end the conversation. "Thanks, but I've got a sponsor."

"Oh, I wasn't talking about a sponsor." Mrs. Henderson shook her head. "You need some faith, Faith. You need to believe it will get better." She closed her eyes and turned her head slightly like she was listening to someone talk to her. She nodded twice and pursed her lips.

Faith shifted uncomfortably. She was used to being around people who acted strangely, but right now the little hairs on the back of her neck were tingling.

Mrs. Henderson's eyes snapped open, and her hand shot out and grabbed Faith's wrist. "I was so worried about you."

Faith tried to pull her hand away, but the old woman's grip tightened on her arm.

"I've been praying for you since you lost your father and Kimberly." Mrs. Henderson pulled Faith closer and her hazel eyes locked on Faith's. "And after your scare the other night, I've redoubled my efforts. But don't worry, he'll find the man you saw." Mrs. Henderson let go of Faith's wrist and smiled.

Even though she was free from Mrs. Henderson's grip, Faith found herself unwilling to lean away. She stared at the old woman's confident face and had to know the reason for her certainty. "Who will?"

"My son."

Faith was about to ask if her son was a policeman when she remembered that Adam had said her son had died. Like a koi fish, her mouth opened and closed but nothing came out. *Get it together and get out of here.* "Okay . . . Nice meeting you."

"I'll let him know that we talked." Mrs. Henderson picked up her knitting.

Faith hurried away. She often talked to people who weren't all there mentally, but Mrs. Henderson had caught her off-guard. And after spending ten years in and out of institutions, Faith had had her fill of insanity.

That's all I need—her asking her dead son to haunt me. Figures I end up talking to the craziest person in the room.

Faith followed the signs to the restroom. Her stomach was in full upheaval now, her hangover roaring back with a vengeance. She shoved the restroom door open, ran into the stall, and retched. Toilet water splashed her. She gagged and vomited again. After waiting a minute to make sure the worst had passed, she flushed, wiped the watery spew from her face, and sat on the toilet seat. Her skin felt warm to the touch.

Maybe I'm actually sick. She closed her eyes and leaned her head against the stall.

F aith smacked her pasty lips together and wiped her mouth with the back of her hand. The bitter, acidic film on her tongue . . . and she was drenched in sweat. Her eyes snapped open and her heart shot into her throat as she tried to process what was happening.

Did I fall asleep? I must have . . .

The memory of the meeting snapped into place. She remembered talking to Mrs. Henderson and escaping into the bathroom, throwing up, but then . . .

"Maybe it's my meds," she muttered, rubbing her eyes with her index finger and thumb. *Or maybe the six shots of whiskey?* her conscience fired back.

"Hello?" someone called out from the hallway and knocked on the restroom door. "Faith?"

Faith jumped up and shook her head. Big mistake. The little stall spun and she steadied herself by grabbing the metal toilet-paper holder. She felt like she'd only closed her eyes for a minute, but maybe it had been longer. *How long have I been in here?*

"Are you all right?"

She could place the voice now. It was the group leader, Robert. "One second." Faith hurried out of the stall and over to the sink. One look at her ashen face and she winced. The image of her father flashed like a strobe between her brain and the mirror. She pressed her eyes closed, washed her hands, and gave her mouth a quick rinse.

When she came out of the restroom, Robert was standing in the hallway with her water bottle and purse. He held them out to her. "I'm sorry. The group ended. I thought you'd left until I started putting the chairs away and found your stuff."

Faith took the purse and checked inside. Her wallet, a bag with her pills, the probation form, a pen, her phone. All still there.

Robert held up his keys and made a face that reminded her of an apologetic puppy—chin down, big brown eyes rounded and lifted up. "I don't want to rush you, but I have to lock the building."

"Sure. Sorry." Faith looked up and down the hallway, completely disoriented as to which way to go.

"Did you park out front or out back?" Robert asked.

"Out front."

"Follow me." Robert headed for the exit. Even though he was much taller than Faith, he seemed to hurry to keep pace with her. "Are you okay? Do you need a ride home?"

"No, thank you." Faith shoved the double doors open, walked down the granite steps, and stopped. She scanned the street. The locksmith's van with the magician statue on top was still there, but no Camry. "What the . . . ?"

"Are you sure you're all right?" Robert asked.

Faith spun around, and it was all she could do to not scream in his face. Fuming, she yanked her phone out of her purse and glared at the mischievously grinning magician, like he was responsible for making her car disappear. "Someone stole my car."

"Stole it? Are you sure?"

If it weren't for the concerned look on his face, Faith would have hit him with her purse. "I parked it right there." She thrust a finger toward the curb. "It's a legal parking space."

She spent five minutes talking to the police, who told her to wait until an officer came out. When she hung up, Robert was still standing there.

"You don't have to stay." Faith jammed her phone into her purse.

"I know." He grinned. "But sometimes a debacle is a little less of a debacle if there are two people."

Faith laughed. "Is debacle even a real word? And you managed to use it twice." The taste of genuine laughter was unnerving, especially under the circumstances, but welcome.

Robert blushed. "I think debacle was deemed dorky and banned years ago. It's fun to say, though, so I use it." He seemed unsure where to place his hands. They shifted in front of him, to his side, then to the back. Finally, he crossed his arms. "I'll just wait until the police come."

"Story of my life," Faith mumbled. "Wait, I really don't want to get a ride home from the cops."

"I can give you one if—"

"Great. I also forgot, I need you to sign this." She took out a folded piece of paper from her purse and a pen. "It's for my probation officer."

Robert stared down at the paper but didn't take it.

"I need you to sign it and say I attended tonight's meeting."

Robert's arms stayed crossed and his eyebrows pinched together.

Faith shook the paper. "I was there."

"Technically." Robert shifted uncomfortably. "But you came late and were only in the meeting for a little while . . ."

Faith's annoyance shifted into panic. Like a long snake of dominos tipping, she saw the consequences of not getting the paper signed—her probation officer, red pen in hand, marking a huge X on the form, the judge wagging a thick finger in Faith's face, the door to her cell rolling shut with a metal clack that echoed down the empty prison hall.

She scrambled for an excuse to convince him to sign the form, quickly dismissing several possibilities before feigning indignation and asking, "I'm going to get penalized for having menstrual miseries?"

Robert twitched and stammered like he'd swallowed a bug. "What? No . . . I—"

"Here I am, with the worst period of my life . . . "

"I'll sign it, I'll sign it. Um . . . I'm sorry you're not feeling well." Robert took the paper and signed.

"Thanks." Faith stuffed the form back into her purse. She stared at the empty curb, then at the magician, mocking her, his wand vibrating in the breeze. She let a string of profanities fly toward the little man, her missing car, and the world in general.

Robert rubbed the back of his neck with one hand. "I think if you were on TV, they'd need a little longer than a seven-second delay to cover that one."

Faith exhaled loudly. "That had to come out or I'd explode."

Robert nodded understandingly. "Sounds like it." He pointed back at the building. "Glad the elementary school was closed."

Faith smiled. "What's your deal? You a shrink?"

Robert shook his head. "I'm working on my counseling license, but I'm a survivor, too." He held up a hand. "Sorry, I guess you dislike the term."

"Survivor? I don't dislike it, I hate it. You sure apologize a lot."

"Bad habit." His smile was disarming. And charming. It brought out his square jaw and a slight dimple.

"How old are you?" Faith asked.

"Twenty-four."

"You're only a year older than me." Faith tried to remember him from school but drew a blank. "Are you from Marshfield?"

"No." His hands moved all around him again, looking for a place to land.

Faith waited for him to elaborate, but he didn't.

"Are you in the witness protection program?" Faith joked, trying to prod more information from him.

"Kinda." He clicked his tongue. "Actually, I'm working on putting the past behind me."

"I thought you weren't supposed to run away from the 'incident.'" Faith made air quotes.

"You shouldn't let it consume you, either. I've dealt with it, so now I'm starting fresh."

Faith looked down the street and tapped her foot. "Fresh? Good for you." Grinding her teeth, she crushed a sarcastic remark about no one ever breaking free.

"Here come the police," Robert said.

It took the cop forty-five minutes to take down Faith's information and fill out all the paperwork. Faith couldn't believe that Robert waited the whole time, sitting on the steps.

After the cruiser pulled away from the curb, Robert got up. "Would you still like that ride?"

Faith didn't have the heart to turn him down. The meeting had been over for an hour, and he could have been long gone. Instead, she gave a brief nod.

"My ride is around the corner." Robert started walking, and Faith followed. "The black Jeep."

The Jeep wasn't old, and it wasn't new either. Customized extra-wide, off-road tires, front-end winch, and flared fenders gave it a military feel.

"Do you know where Prescott and West Lane is?" Faith asked as he got her door.

"Sure do. It's only ten minutes from here."

They got in, and Faith picked up the scent of roses. She wasn't like most women; the smell made her stomach turn. They reminded her of funerals, of death. She couldn't stand them. Still, she was grateful for the ride, so she didn't say anything. She just powered down her window. As they drove, the night air refreshed her.

"I appreciate the ride."

"I'm heading that way. I'm right over on Whitlock. The white ranch. You must be in the apartment over the laundromat."

Faith cast a suspicious look at him from the corner of her eye. She sat up straight, pressing against the door, her fingers moving to the handle, cursing herself for getting into a car with someone she'd just met, no matter how nice he seemed. "How do you know where I live?"

"Lucky guess. They had a For Rent sign out in front for the last couple of months," Robert explained. "That's the only building with apartments nearby."

He smiled casually, unaware she had planned to bash his head into the steering wheel and jump out of the car if he turned out to be some crazed stalker. She'd dealt with that before because of the notoriety that came with the murders and the book. One time, a fan got herself committed to the same asylum Faith was in so she could "mother" Faith. Even after the woman was transferred and had a restraining order slapped against her, she showed up everywhere Faith did until she got arrested. Faith started twisting her ring. The woman died of a drug overdose two years ago. Her son wrote to tell Faith, thinking that might make her feel better. It didn't. Faith just wanted the woman to stop following her, not die.

The wind now felt too cold and the silence in the car too thick. "What do you do for work? Are you a cop?" Faith asked, wanting to get out of her own head.

"No. Right now, I make deliveries while I'm going to school. For a floral place."

That explains the smell. "It's right there," Faith said. She pointed to the two-story building on the corner.

When the Jeep pulled alongside the curb, she got another whiff of roses and practically dove out of the car. "Thanks," she muttered.

"Sure. If you need a ride, give me a call. I hope they find your car."

"In this town? The cops couldn't find their own asses."

Tuesday, April 10

Faith dashed across the street to the church. It was almost 10:15. If she was more than fifteen minutes late for the morning AA meeting, the moderator didn't have to sign her paperwork. Faith had her first check-in with her probation officer tomorrow and didn't want to start off on the wrong foot. Pushing away the frustration over her missing car, she broke into a sprint to race across the grass and up the gentle slope to the back of the church.

She rushed inside the door and skidded to a stop—the entire layout of the room had changed; the rows of chairs in front of the podium had been rearranged so that a dozen people sat in a circle facing each other. Apparently, the morning AA meeting was a discussion group.

Damn it.

The door banged behind her, cutting off all conversation and signaling everyone to turn and stare at Faith. She felt like a student standing in front of the class who'd forgotten the question, let alone the answer.

A middle-aged woman with long brunette hair motioned Faith toward an empty chair and smiled. Then she turned to a young man and asked, "How did that make you feel, Martin?"

Martin started talking as Faith slipped into her chair. Seated directly opposite her, Jane glanced up at Faith, smiled quickly, and put her head back down. It didn't take long to figure out what the topic of discussion was: Step 9. That's the step where you're supposed to make direct amends to anyone that your drinking has screwed over—as long as making amends doesn't mess up that person even more.

Faith had gone through the Twelve Steps several times and knew them all by heart. *Step 9: If you keep drinking, you keep adding to the list of people who get hurt. Drink, hurt people, make amends, repeat. A never-ending cycle of I'm sorry.* That's why Faith hated Step 9. It felt hollow. *How can you ever truly make amends?*

Back and forth the conversation went until they reached the mid-meeting break, and most of the people headed outside to smoke. The meeting leader walked over to Faith, who immediately broke into her apology. "I am so sorry I was late." Faith stood and pulled the form from her pocket. "My car—"

"No worries." The woman smiled as she reached out a slender hand and took the paper. "You weren't that late. Life happens, right? I'm just glad you made it. Welcome. I'm Rachel. Are you new?"

"To this meeting. I've been in recovery awhile. Can I get you to sign that?"

Rachel nodded and took out a pen. "Certainly. We have coffee on the table. Unfortunately, I think we're out of muffins. They go fast." The smile on her face came crashing down.

Faith followed Rachel's eyes. They were fixed on her name typed at the top of her probation form. For a moment, Rachel's mouth looked like a stuck garage door, clicking up and down. She finally settled on a tight-lipped smile and a nod, signed the form, and handed it back to Faith. "Well, nice to have you join us. Excuse me."

Faith watched her go. She was used to the darting glances, the whispers behind her back—but this was different. It wasn't just pity in Rachel's eyes. It was something more familiar, more personal.

Jane stepped over to Faith but not too close, like a squirrel, curious but ready to dart away at the first sign of a threat. "You came. I'm afraid there aren't any muffins left. You need to get here early to get the good ones." Jane reached into her jacket pocket, retrieved something wrapped in a napkin, and held it out toward Faith.

Faith shook her head. "I can't. You eat it."

"I already had mine. I got this for you. I was hoping you'd show up. It's chocolate chip."

"Really, you eat it. I heard you have to get here early to get the good ones."

Jane laughed, revealing more missing teeth. "I cheat. I live upstairs."

Faith cocked her head. "Upstairs? In the church?"

Jane nodded. "Pastor Hanson lets me stay in the missionary apartment. Rachel, that's his wife, she and him are really good people." She pressed the muffin into Faith's hands.

Rachel was in the back of the room talking to Martin. She glanced over toward Faith, and when their eyes connected, she gave that same tight-lipped smile. What was it about her? Did Faith know her from somewhere?

"Don't let her being the pastor's wife fool you," Jane said. "She understands where we're coming from."

Faith's stomach rumbled, and she absentmindedly took a bite of the muffin. "What do you mean?"

"She's a recovering addict, too. It's real sad; she started drinking after her sister and niece were murdered."

Anna . . . Faith started coughing. *Anna and Emily had an Aunt Rachel. That's why she looks familiar. Rachel Hanson is Mrs. Foster's sister.*

When she looked over at Rachel again, the tight-lipped smile was gone, replaced by naked fear.

Faith paced the apartment floor, trying to think of some way to fill up the hour she had to kill before her therapy appointment. She felt trapped without her car. She hadn't been able to work up the courage to tell her mother it had been stolen, dreading the conversation and the condemnation that were sure to follow the news. She finally decided to walk to the convenience store on the corner to pick up some milk. Just as she reached for her purse and patted it to be sure the phone was inside, it started ringing.

"Hello?"

"Faith Winters?" A man's voice.

"Who is this?"

"Sergeant McKenna of the Marshfield PD. We've located your vehicle."

"You did? Where? Is it stripped?" She was already pulling on her sneakers.

"We believe it's fine, but we'd like you to come and check it over. I have a patrol car in your area if you need assistance."

"I'll be right down." Faith couldn't believe they'd found her car at all, let alone intact and undamaged. She hurried downstairs and waited for the police to arrive. But as soon as the cruiser turned onto her street, she regretted accepting a ride. Her stomach flipped. *What was I thinking?* She hated police cars. To her they were like buzzards, signs that something bad had happened.

As the cruiser stopped at the curb, Faith rocked from side to side like someone about to jump into a freezing pool. The officer reached across the front seat and pushed open the passenger door. Faith held her breath and jumped in.

Ten minutes later, they pulled into a parking lot behind a closed furniture store, only a block away from the elementary school where the survivors' group met. Faith's car was in the middle of the lot; a police cruiser was parked off to the side. Two officers were talking to a short man in a dark-gray suit.

Faith scowled at the man in the rumpled suit and turned to the officer. "Do I have to sign anything?"

"We'd just like you to look the car over," he said. "And Detective Walker has some questions for you." He pointed to the man in the suit, who was now walking over.

Faith didn't need an introduction. She knew who Detective Lionel Walker was, and she also knew he was the last person she wanted to talk to. She hopped out of the cruiser and made a beeline for her Camry, hoping to reach it before he did.

Walker changed trajectory to intercept her. "Ms. Winters." He shifted his coffee cup to his left hand, stuck out his right, and stopped between Faith and her car. "Do you have a moment?"

Faith didn't shake his hand. She tried to keep a neutral expression on her face, but felt her eyes narrowing and a snarl forming. He hadn't changed since the first time she met him: overweight, receding curly red hair, ruddy cheeks, and eyes the size of peanuts. The knot of his ugly green tie was loose and crooked.

"You're working stolen cars now? This is about your speed. Big cases like that," Faith said.

He let the jab go. "Your car looks okay. Did you leave the keys in it?"

"No." She yanked her set out of her purse and dangled them. "I also made sure it was locked."

Like a portrait artist, the detective stood there, his eyes traveling around her face, studying her. Faith knew it was a thing with him. He'd ask a question and wait and wait, watching how you'd react. Maybe he saw some show on how to spot a liar and was waiting for Faith to blink or wiggle her ears. She didn't care. She was tired of the game. "I locked it. I'm sure." She stepped around him.

"I'd figure someone took it for a joy ride, but the lock seems fine, and they didn't pop the ignition. Did you lend *anyone* a key?"

"No, definitely not." She opened the door and got in. Her shoulders relaxed when the car started right up. "Do I have to sign anything?"

"Do you notice anything missing?"

Faith glanced around the car. She hadn't even put anything in it yet. "No. Everything's here." She pulled her door closed and rolled down the window. "Do I have to sign anything?"

Walker scanned the parking lot and then over his shoulder. Faith followed his gaze to the school where the support group met.

"Have you been drinking?" he asked.

"What does that have to do with my car being stolen?"

"Is it possible that you thought you parked in front of the school but you actually—"

"I could've been blind drunk and I wouldn't forget where I parked my car," Faith said, bristling.

"Don't get upset." He took a swig of coffee. "All I'm asking is if you may have gotten confused."

"I know where I parked my car."

Walker used the plastic lid of the coffee cup to scratch the stubble on his chin. "The reason I'm asking is, I heard that you allegedly saw the man you claimed was involved in your sister's murder."

Faith stiffened. "I didn't officially report anything."

"And I didn't officially hear anything. You know you can talk to me unofficially, Faith. A hundred percent off the record."

"I don't want to talk to you, period. You closed the case."

"I wasn't lead detective on the case, so closing it wasn't my call. I know your side, and if some new evidence has come up, I'll check it out. Look, Faith, I don't personally care if you've been drinking. I *do* care if something comes up about a case I worked, so I need to know if what you saw two nights ago was whiskey vision, or if you really think you saw the guy. I heard from a couple of people that you were three sheets to the wind."

"You've already made up your mind—again."

Walker grabbed the top of the door and got right in Faith's face. "Did you see the guy? Look, I already have all the details: brown four-door sedan with one rear whitewall, and you saw him outside of O'Lindey's heading toward Hingham. All I need from you is yes, I saw him, or no, I didn't. You know you can trust me, right?"

Faith stared out the windshield. If she knew anything about Detective Walker, it was that she *couldn't* trust him. "I know you didn't sign off on closing the case. I also know you never believed me about Rat Face."

"I—"

"Save it." Faith glared up at him. "I've read the police report. Someone gave it to my mom so she could use it as research for her book. You said I was 'too traumatized to be reliable.'" She pushed the button to raise the window.

He held up his hands defensively. "If you're going to quote me, at least be accurate. I wasn't talking about you seeing the guy in the parking lot. I was talking about whether the guy in the baseball hat that you saw coming out of the cabin was your father or not. Read the report again. This isn't just about you. Four people died that night. I'm thinking of the Foster family, too."

At the mention of the Fosters, Faith's shoulders slumped. *It is bigger than me.* She took a deep breath. "Yeah, I saw him. Now what're you going to do? Not believe me again?"

He held out a card to her. "Okay. If you see him again, or if you think of anything besides what you already told the police, call me."

"I can find your number." She didn't take the card.

He tossed the card through the window onto the passenger seat. "Then you need to use it. And you need to lay off the booze. If something happened to you, do you have any idea how it would affect your mother?"

Faith felt her lip curl. "You know she's remarried, right? Maybe you should put down that torch you're still carrying for her."

"What are you talking about? Your mother and I have been friends since we were kids. I've told you not to listen to gossip."

"Oh yeah, I remember. You gave me a big speech about not paying attention to what people said or what was in the papers. You just left out the fact that my father went out to the cabin to screw Mrs. Foster. I had to find that out in lunch period, and that he was paying to bang Sara Bradley, too. That made a hell of a headline: 'Madman Murderer Among Local Madam's Clients.' Remember that?"

Walker grimaced. "I'm sorry you had to hear about it that way. Is that what this is all about? This animosity?"

Faith scoffed. "No. My sister's killer is still out there because of you." She put the car into drive, and Walker stepped back. "*That's* the reason for my animosity."

"Don't listen to the gossip, Faith. Beverly and I are just friends. I know they've been running a bunch of crap stories because of the tenth anniversary, but . . . where did you get the idea that I liked your mother? Which paper?"

"I didn't read it in the paper." Faith took her foot off the brake. "My mother told me. Besides, it's written all over your face."

S oft beige carpet warmed Dr. Alex Melding's therapy meeting room. Two casual chairs faced each other, and the filtered natural light from skylights overhead created an atmosphere designed to set a person at ease. Large, framed degrees from a multitude of universities hung above rows of books, all carefully displayed to make you feel that you were under the care of a capable, highly educated professional. This was a place to unburden yourself of the complex emotions and baggage weighing you down. But this perfect therapy room with its perfect therapist was too perfect for Faith.

"How am I doing?" Faith repeated, leaning back in her chair. "Outstanding. Really, I'm living the dream."

Dr. Melding adjusted his glasses, but his face remained a neutral mask. He looked more like a young college professor than a therapist. His thinning hair was styled back, and while he wore polished shoes and pressed gray dress pants, his casual cotton shirt had a West Coast feel. "Sarcasm is your second-favorite defense mechanism."

"Second? I thought it was *numero uno*."

"No, that would be anger. Have you been drinking?"

"No. I just came from my AA meeting. I didn't have a beer on the walk over."

"I thought your drink of choice was whiskey. Odd choice, saying a beer."

"Sounds a little judgmental, Doc. And you just met me." Faith crossed her arms.

"I've read your records." Dr. Melding picked up a tablet. "They're extensive. And I've discussed your medical history, your trauma, and your treatment with your mother."

"You talked to my mother? Isn't that unethical? Kinda violates the whole doctor—patient privilege thing?" Faith's foot bounced up and down.

"That discussion occurred before I agreed to become your therapist." Dr. Melding folded his hands. "Are you taking your medication?"

"I take my meds."

"I'm not thrilled about the medication you're currently on. Given your history of alcohol abuse, it's not my first choice. Right now, my main concern is the Serofluxapine."

"Dr. Rodgers prescribed it. I'm fine with it. It's been working, and I'm not so doped up I sleep all day."

"If you were in an in-treatment situation where you could be closely monitored, I would prescribe it, too. But you're not. Considering your history of alcohol abuse, you're playing Russian roulette. Serofluxapine has several serious side effects if taken with alcohol, including insomnia, increased depression, hallucinations, suicidal thoughts—"

"Erectile dysfunction."

"Funny. But this is serious. I think we should rethink the Serofluxapine."

Faith shook her head. "No. I just got out. And I know how this works: if you change my meds, I have to go back in for at least a week's observation."

"I'd recommend thirty days."

It took an effort for Faith to keep her middle finger down. She glanced up at his collection of *Clinical Psychology* journals lining one of the bookshelves, then down at the unnaturally clean beige carpet. According to her official tally, this was psych visit 732, not including groups or family sessions, so she knew the game: talk as little as possible and say what they want to hear.

"What does my mother think?" Faith knew her mother had consulted with Dr. Rodgers on the medicine, and she didn't think Dr. Melding would be eager to tell his own partner that she had made the wrong choice.

Dr. Melding's fingers hesitated over the surface of his tablet as he observed Faith. "There's a new medication I was considering recommending, but unfortunately, you have a family history of Fabry disease, so that drug is inadvisable."

"I don't have Fabry. My sister did."

"You were tested?"

"It was negative. At least I didn't inherit that from my father, too."

"Your father couldn't be the carrier. I'm a little familiar with the disease—it's an inherited, albeit rare, genetic disorder. Fatigue and burning pain in the extremities are the primary symptoms. But Fabry is X-linked, so if your father had it, you'd have it, too. I'll have to ask your mother for her medical records."

"My mom doesn't have Fabry. It skipped over her."

"What did you mean when you said, *At least I didn't inherit that from my father, too?*"

"His eyes." Faith cast her own eyes downward. "I have the same eyes as his. I wish I didn't."

Dr. Melding perked up. "That's why you wore mirrored sunglasses in junior high?" He flipped the tablet around and typed a note, the keys snapping like someone walking on bubble wrap. "I found that detail particularly fascinating. It shows—"

"I take it you're a fan of *The Girl Who Lived*?" Faith scowled as she tugged on her hair. "That was in chapter 4. For the record, I find it kind of creepy that we're just skipping the whole 'getting to know you' phase." Dr. Melding started to speak, but Faith held up a hand. "No, no. This is my hour, right? I just met you, but you're spewing out all these facts about me. Personal stuff like I have anger issues and I drink whiskey. You even know I got expelled for refusing to take my sunglasses off, but I never told you any of that. I don't know you. I don't know anything about you, but you talk like you know me. Why? Because you've read about me in some book. You're supposed to be the psychiatrist, but that's not normal, Doc. In a normal relationship, we'd have some back-and-forth and those facts would have emerged slowly, like a budding flower. But you just reached into the dirt and ripped it out. Not cool. So not cool." Faith leaned even farther away from him. "And you believe everything you read?"

Dr. Melding's jaw flexed. Faith watched him mentally preparing what to say, like he was writing a bunch of words and then holding down the backspace key and starting again. "You're right," he said at last. "And that was a good analogy about ripping the plant out of the earth. I apologize."

The *mea culpa* caught Faith off-guard. No therapist had apologized before.

Dr. Melding crossed his legs, his brown eyes softening. "Why don't we hit the reset button? Shall we start with Marshfield? How does it feel, being back?"

Faith spent the remainder of the visit discussing her feelings. Or, more accurately, she talked about the feelings she guessed Dr. Melding *wanted* her to talk about. The fear, uncertainty, pain. *Yadda, yadda, yadda.* She knew better than to share her daydreams about vengeance and hate, and her obsessive desire to track down and eviscerate Rat Face. She'd opened up to a therapist once about how she really felt and ended up getting six months of triple therapy sessions and a double dose of meds that left her so zonked out she was practically drooling. Never again.

Finally, Dr. Melding ran down the list of expectations for the coming week. Work your program, take your meds, call if you have hallucinations or suicidal thoughts, *blah, blah, blah.*

"Our time is up for today." Dr. Melding clicked the stopwatch—the signal that the session was over. "Our next appointment is Thursday."

Faith forced a small smile. "Thank you, Dr. Melding. I'll be sure to follow your advice." She felt for her phone, grabbed her purse, and hurried out of the office.

14

With her group and her session finally out of the way, Faith's afternoon was open, and she knew exactly what she intended to do. No more driving around aimlessly, hoping to come across Rat Face's car. She had a plan. Henry needed to know more about Rat Face's car than "brown sedan." Henry had mentioned that Faith could leaf through some kind of police mug-shot book for cars, hoping something might jog her memory. But she hadn't heard from Henry, so Faith had to improvise.

She entered a coffee shop and, as she'd hoped, they had a rack at the back with the local *Auto Trader* magazine. She grabbed a couple issues and a latte, and took a seat in a leather chair in the corner.

Faith turned the pages, studying each photo, but she didn't really know what she was looking for, so she sipped her latte, imagined herself driving some of the hot-rods, and stopped to admire a Jeep and a cute little VW Bug. She flipped the next page and almost dropped her coffee. *That's the car.*

Well, not the *exact* car—the bumper on this one was half rusted away—but the same *kind* of car. A Crown Victoria. She closed her eyes and tried to remember the details of that night. Her memory had some whiskey fuzz on it, but she was pretty sure.

This could be helpful. She pulled out her phone and dialed Tommy. He and his friend could surely run some kind of search for Crown Victorias in the area.

Faith closed her eyes and pictured the brake lights coming on, the car stopping, Rat Face adjusting the side mirror to look back at her . . .

Wait. Faith's eyes opened. There had been something about the side-view mirror. Above it there had been . . . a second side mirror?

Why would there be two mirrors on the same side?

"Hello?" Tommy said on the other end of the phone.

Faith set her coffee down. Not two side mirrors. One mirror and one *spotlight.*

"Faith?"

And it didn't just look *like an old police car—it* was *an old police car.*

"Faith? Hello?" Tommy called into the phone.

"Tommy? Sorry. I, uh . . . I butt-dialed you."

"Are you okay? Did you get my text?"

"Yeah. Yeah, I'm fine. I mean, I did. Listen, I'll call you back." Faith hung up.

She focused on the picture. *Where does someone get an old police car?*

***

Aisle after aisle of alcohol stretched out before her at Murray's Wine and Spirits, a venerable Marshfield institution.

She felt a giggly urge to take a cart and race around the store, like one of those game-show contestants who gets five minutes to grab anything they want. Faith didn't care what she drank; she drank whiskey only because Rat Face did. She pictured him taking a swig from the bottle that night, the moon on the label. She may have been only twelve, but she never forgot the odor. Once she learned it was whiskey, she thought drinking it was some way of getting into Rat Face's head. But she'd just as soon drink mouthwash if it dulled the pain.

The guy behind the counter was about her age. He straightened up in his faded retro Galaxia T-shirt when Faith approached the counter. "Good evening."

"Hi," Faith said. "I'm looking for this guy."

She handed the clerk a sheet of paper—her own homemade "wanted" poster. After leaving the coffee shop, she'd taken a blank sheet of paper, sketched out a picture of Rat Face—the only thing she'd ever been able to draw from memory—and pasted the picture of the Crown Vic below it. She was particularly proud of the white correction fluid she'd used for the whitewall on the rear tire. She'd been showing the picture around town all afternoon. "He drinks whiskey."

"Are you a cop?" the clerk asked.

"No. The jerk hit my puppy."

The clerk's eyes widened and his expression hardened. "Lousy scumbag. Did he just take off?"

Faith did her best to make her lip tremble. It had taken a while to settle on this cover story. At first she said she was looking for a guy who was a killer, but the store owner freaked out and told her to go to the cops. At the next place she'd softened the story and said the guy backed into her car, but that hadn't evoked enough sympathy. Soon she figured out that everyone was eager to help a girl who'd lost her puppy.

"No, he stopped. That's when I smelled the whiskey." Faith made a sour face. "*Then* he took off. Have you ever seen him?"

"No. Around how old would you figure he is?"

"Close to thirty. He's got real bad teeth."

The clerk nodded. "Can I keep this? I'll pass it along to the other shifts."

"Would you? That's very thoughtful." She had made twenty copies of the sheet to begin with, and she was down to just a few now. It was going well. "Thank you." She forced herself to smile.

"Faith?" The voice behind her made her jump.

She turned to find Thad approaching with a shopping cart filled with bottles and boxes. He was tall, six foot three, with a bit of a paunch that he tried to hide behind an untucked, blue-and-white-striped golfing shirt. But with his sandy-blond hair and big, wide smile, he looked more like a surfer than a golfer.

"Hey." Faith's heart drummed in her chest. "I was just grabbing some smokes."

"Faith." Thad's face tightened.

It had been two years since he'd last visited her with her mother, but he looked like he'd aged much more than that. *Probably the booze*, Faith thought as she noticed his fully loaded shopping cart. The hypocrisy wasn't lost on her. He was upset that she was in a liquor store, when he himself apparently put away at least a pint a night.

"I wasn't drinking." Faith lifted her hands up like she was going through a security check. "Just getting cigarettes." She locked eyes with the clerk and nodded, praying he'd agree with her. His eyes had widened; she knew that look. At the mention of her name, he must have realized who she was. And as his expression changed, Faith recognized him, too. She had gone to school with him, possibly been in a couple of classes with him.

"Yeah," the clerk said. "You asked for cigarettes." He handed her a pack and a pack of matches.

Faith reached for her purse, but he shook his head.

"You already paid," he said quickly.

Faith remembered his name: Sam. And she remembered the last time she'd seen him. She was in line for a movie, and Sam and a bunch of his friends taunted her, asking if she was watching a slasher flick or starring in it. Faith had run out of the theater in tears.

"Well, that's a relief." Thad's shopping cart clinked as he pushed it up to the counter. "I don't want to be the bad guy, but I'd have to tell Beverly."

"Please don't. You're right, I shouldn't even come in here. I should go to the gas station for smokes."

"You know, that's a better plan. Hey, after this, I'm heading home—do you want to come over and—"

"No, no, I'm going to a meeting." Faith remembered that her mother knew her schedule. "I mean, I'm going to a meeting tomorrow, and I'm beat. I'll stop by soon."

"Beverly's been wanting to go out for dinner. We could go to The Wharf. You still love surf-and-turf, right?"

"That sounds great. I'm sorry. I should've stopped by already."

Thad smiled, and his demeanor changed. He seemed almost charismatic. "Not a problem. We totally understand. Get used to being back, and when you're ready, let us know, okay?"

"I will." Faith started for the door.

"Faith?" Sam said quietly. "I'll let you know if I hear anything."

Wednesday, April 11

Faith waited on the worn bench outside her probation officer's door in the basement of Jefferson Courthouse. The bench was shoehorned in between filing cabinets and boxes, but Faith found the confined, hidden space comforting. Hidden was good—though invisible would be better.

The door across from her shook and the doorknob rattled. Barbara Finney didn't even glance up as she pulled the door open with one hand and held onto an old landline, the cord stretched to its limit, with the other. She was in her early sixties, her gray hair cut short and one cowlick jutting away in a high arc. "All right, I'll call you later." She hung up and pivoted to face her desk.

Faith walked in and set down the coffee and muffin she'd picked up at the little store on the corner. "Faith Winters." She forced a smile that she hoped appeared friendly and not as awkward as it felt. "I hope you like cream." She deposited an assortment of sugar packets and sweeteners on the desk, forming a small mound.

"Barbara Finney." She gave her a firm handshake. "Take a seat." Barbara regarded the muffin and coffee. "That's a cheap bribe." Her thick bifocals swung back and forth from a cord around her neck as she reached over to grab the muffin.

The corner of Faith's mouth ticked up. "Next time I'll steal something more expensive."

"At least you made the drop before they caught you." Barbara flipped up the plastic lid of the coffee and took a long sip.

Do I detect a sense of humor here? Faith pulled out her signed forms and slid them across the desk.

"You got signatures? I'm impressed." Barbara inserted the pages into a desktop scanner. "Everything is digital now." She pointed out into the hallway. "Everything. Those cabinets hold the last papers to get scanned. Pretty soon they'll have an app for your phone and we can skip this step. I can't wait to see paper go. I feel like I'm sitting in the middle of a fire trap." She waved her hands in the air, and little muffin crumbs fell onto her desk. "So, your car is recovered and operational?"

"How do you know that?"

"You reported your car stolen, but I see that it was recovered." Barbara tapped her computer. "I see *all*." She deepened her voice and moved her hands around her monitor like it was a giant crystal ball. "Everything's connected." She chuckled. "And it's my job to keep tabs on you."

"Is your computer networked to the DMV?" Faith moved forward to the edge of her seat. "There's this guy. He drives an old Crown Vic and—"

"If you're even thinking of asking me to run an illegal search, think twice. It'll take a whole lot more than a muffin to get me to break the law." Barbara smiled, but the line had just been drawn.

"No. No. I wouldn't ask that." Faith scooted back in her seat.

"Good. Because I'm getting close to retirement, and I like my job." Barbara turned back to her computer and clicked a few buttons. The printer came to life and several sheets of paper slowly curled out. She picked up a manila folder, grabbed the papers, and slid them across her desk to Faith. "Now, why don't we start with the section outlining your responsibilities. Let's go over them, shall we?"

For the next twenty-five minutes, Barbara went over everything Faith had to do to stay on her good side—something Faith found herself surprisingly willing to do. Barbara grumbled, snarled, and threatened, but Faith could tell that underneath the gruff façade, Barbara really cared.

"Do you understand your obligations, Ms. Winters?"

"Clear as crystal."

Barbara took off her glasses, checked the clock, and sighed. "Time for my next appointment already? Gee, time flies."

Faith stood and reached for the door handle.

"Faith," Barbara said, "hang in there. But keep your nose clean. It doesn't matter how much I like you—if you violate probation, you're going back in for a long time."

16

Faith spent the remainder of the day handing out her makeshift wanted posters and searching for the man who haunted her nightmares, but as eight o'clock rolled around, she headed over to the survivors' group. A single raindrop landed smack in the middle of the windshield, the first salvo of a sudden torrent. Under cover of pelting rain, she drove slowly by the school, scanning for an open space, and gave the magician perched atop the locksmith's van the finger as she passed by.

So many cars! Some event was going on next door at the library, and she hoped this was simply spillover. The thought of a full house meeting made her want to circle around the school and head home. But leaving wasn't an option. Though she wasn't trapped in a locked room anymore, she was still a caged animal; the bars were just harder to see.

She pulled around to the lot in the back. Even there, three cars sat near the rear entrance. She parked between two of them—she felt safer that way—clicked off the engine, and sat watching the raindrops splatter against the windshield. Her breath started to fog the windows. She settled back in the seat and closed her eyes.

It wouldn't be so bad. She could pick up a hose at the hardware store and run it from the tailpipe to the back window. She would just fall asleep; she wouldn't feel a thing.

Her eyes fluttered open. *With my luck, someone will find me before I'm done, and I'll end up with brain damage and some big Russian nurse spoon-feeding me tapioca and changing my diaper.*

She shoved her door open, glared up at the sky, and stepped out into the rain. Despite not having an umbrella, she took the time to walk around the car and check all the door handles to be sure they were locked. She checked her options. The gutter had lost the fight to contain the curtain of water that separated her from the nearest entrance, but Faith dashed through the waterfall on the steps and heaved open the heavy door.

There was no sign back here pointing the way to the gymnasium. A darkened hallway stretched down the side of the building in both directions, and the red EXIT sign overhead cast a soft glow on the polished floor at her feet.

The rectangle of light cast by the open door slowly disappeared and the hallway became even darker. "Creepy," Faith muttered. She was tempted to go back outside and run around to the front entrance, but she didn't want to go out in the rain, so she headed right, which she knew was roughly where the gym ought to be.

Classrooms lined the hallway on one side, and on the other an occasional window looked out on the dark parking lot. The stillness of the hall made her glance back. She hated this jumpy feeling and could usually keep it in check, but not when she was overtired. Her footsteps echoed as she hurried through each shaft of light from classrooms where the lights had been left on. In the back of one room, an enormous fish tank illuminated a wall and two bright posters that read, *Keep trying!* and *You're already a success!* Usually, such empty messages would have turned Faith's stomach, but this time they produced a dull yearning. Faith had loved middle school—at first, anyway. It was the last place she'd felt good things. Hope, promise, love—

A click sounded in the hallway behind her. *The door?* Faith stared back into the darkness, but the shadows were too deep. She looked down at her hands. They had automatically balled up into tight fists—her body telling her what to do before her mind had a chance to disagree. There was a time when Faith felt the critical fight-or-flight instinct and she'd chosen wrong: flight. Over the years since, she suppressed that option until it no longer *was* an option. There would only be *fight.* If something came at her, she met it head-on, teeth bared.

The hallway door clicked shut. The red glow of the exit sign reflected off the wooden floor. A shadow passed through it.

Faith's breath caught in her throat.

Someone had just entered the building. Someone was following her.

Waiting at the end of the dark hallway.

Faith's chest rose and fell. She felt like a child quaking at the top of the cellar stairs, afraid of the darkness below. She was about to advance and demand that the person show himself, but she couldn't move. That flight instinct was buried, but it wasn't dead—and it chose this moment to find its voice.

Don't.

Fear trickled down her spine like a bead of sweat.

"Coward," she whispered. Shame and self-loathing ripped the word from her lungs and shoved it past her lips, compelling her to override her body's command to flee, and she stepped forward, toward whoever was back there, with the grit and determination of an advancing soldier.

Some people say you can feel darkness—that evil itself has a presence, a touch.

Faith felt it.

From the shadows down the hallway, as softly as a mother tucking in a child, a man began to hum.

Faith had heard that humming before.

This is not happening! Every cell of Faith's body told her to run, but she didn't. The image of her sister, the image that haunted her every waking moment and dominated her dreams at night, flashed into her mind. Kim's eyes wild with fear. Her mouth contorted in pain. Kim screaming at her to run, but her feet were rooted to the floor.

The sinister humming drew closer, reverberating off the walls like the buzz of angry hornets in a glass jar. The sound shot right through Faith, stripping her of courage, rattling her to her core.

Her body gave her no option at this point. She turned and ran, covering her ears to stop the hideous sound, but screams echoed in her head. She pulled her hands away, and the screams that had filled her head now filled the hallway.

Her screams.

Faith risked a glance over her shoulder, where shadows shifted in the darkness and footsteps in hot pursuit thundered down the hall.

She was being hunted. *Again.*

Up ahead, an adjoining corridor led off to the left that ought to take her toward the gym—and people. She flew around the corner, her cries broken only by gasps for air.

The hallway came to a dead end at a single door, but through its tiny glass window Faith could see the bright lights of the gymnasium. She smashed into the door going full tilt, but the door opened only a couple of inches before slamming into something. Faith kept shoving against it, but it wouldn't budge. Peering through the window, she saw some kind of equipment bin preventing the door from opening.

This is not happening. Faith's mind whirled in panic, but she realized the footsteps behind her had stopped. She pressed her back against the door, hoping to make herself less visible.

From out of the darkness, almost drowned out by her pounding heart, a faint sound echoed down the hall. The man was humming a tune.

Tears stung her eyes and her vision blurred. Her hands shook.

The footsteps started again. They were getting closer. The man was coming closer.

The humming grew louder, the tune was unmistakable: "Happy Birthday."

Not again! She tried to form words, but they wouldn't come, so her body took over again, letting out a bloodcurdling shriek.

"Hello?" someone called from behind the gymnasium door.

Faith lowered her shoulder and shoved at the door again. Through the three-inch gap she saw Nyah, in her hospital scrubs. Faith thrust her arm through the gap, desperately reaching for her. Pain shot up her forearm as the metal plate on the door scraped away skin.

"Please, please!" she begged. *"Let me in!"*

Nyah's face appeared in the gap. "Faith?"

"Open the door!" Faith cried.

"Okay, okay, just—" Nyah threw her weight against the equipment bin, but it didn't move.

Faith looked down the hallway behind her. She saw the silhouette of a man in the shadows, just beyond the pool of light coming from the gym—standing there, waiting. Watching.

Faith beat on the door. "Open it! Open it!"

"What's wrong?"

"Someone's coming. He's after me. Please. Please open the door."

Nyah turned away.

"Don't go!" Faith squeezed Nyah's hand tightly.

"I won't, I won't," Nyah assured her. "Robert! Help me move this thing!"

Faith looked back down the hallway. She couldn't see him now. Had he gone? Her eyes searched the shadows in vain. "Please don't leave me," she begged Nyah again.

"Faith, look at me." Nyah squeezed her hand. Faith looked into Nyah's dark-brown eyes. "I'm not going anywhere."

Faith could only nod. She needed to listen to make sure it had stopped. The humming. The footsteps, growing nearer.

Robert and Adam came running up behind Nyah. The two of them pushed the equipment bin clear of the door, and Faith, still holding Nyah's hand, stumbled into the gym. Nyah wrapped her arms around Faith, who began to shake uncontrollably.

Robert jogged down the hallway the way Faith had come, and Adam followed him.

Nyah rubbed Faith's back and spoke quietly and reassuringly. "Breathe. Okay? Just take deep breaths."

Faith's breath came back, and she didn't have to gulp in air anymore. Her heartbeat slowed a little. After a few minutes, Robert and Adam came back.

"Well?" Nyah said.

Robert shook his head. "We didn't find anybody."

"Did you see who chased you?" Nyah asked Faith.

Faith looked at the faces of the people around her. "No. But someone was following me."

"Are you sure?" Adam asked. "There wasn't anyone in the hallway or the parking lot."

"The floor was wet," Robert said. "The water could have been from two people."

"But it could have just been from her, too." Adam pointed at Faith. "It's not like you're Tonto and can tell by the puddles if two people were there."

From outside the school, the faint sound of sirens grew louder.

"Who called the police?" Nyah asked.

"Mrs. Henderson," Robert said. "She went for her phone the second she heard the scream."

***

In the sanctuary of the gym, Nyah was bandaging Faith's arm using a little emergency kit that Gus, the older gentleman, had located. Mrs. Henderson held Faith's other hand. Robert stood behind her right shoulder, Adam on the other side. In front of Faith stood a policeman with his hands on his hips and a skeptical look on his face.

"So, no one here actually saw a person?"

"Someone came in the door after me. I heard it closing," Faith said.

"But you didn't actually *see* anyone, right? The door is weighted, so it takes its time closing."

"Maybe you pressed the handicapped button?" Brian called out from over at the coffee table. "The door takes forever to close after that."

"No. I heard it close after me, then it opened again," Faith said. "And I heard him too. He was humming."

The policeman raised a disbelieving eyebrow. "While he was running after you, he was humming?"

"You don't have to be an ass about it," Faith snapped.

Mrs. Henderson gave Faith's hand a squeeze.

"He started humming when I got stuck at the gym door," Faith said, glaring at the cop. "He was trying to mess with my head. The guy who killed my sister did exactly the same thing."

"Your father killed your sister," the policeman said, but from the look on his face, Faith guessed he hadn't meant to say that out loud.

"You're the girl who lived?" Brian said, cookie crumbs tumbling from his mouth.

Gus shot Brian a look. Brian closed his mouth and stared.

"Someone was chasing me," Faith said. "When I got stuck at the door, he started humming 'Happy Birthday.' It was my birthday the day after the killings. I—I'm positive someone followed me into the school!"

The policeman hooked his thumbs into his gun belt. "My partner circled the building inside and out. He didn't see anyone. Neither did I. Neither did anyone else here." He looked around the group. "Did anyone else hear anything? Any humming?"

No one said anything.

"Well, I'll write it up." He obviously viewed the whole incident as a waste of time. "Do you need an escort home?"

Faith shook her head.

Everyone waited as the policeman walked away, his shoes tapping against the gym floor. When he had gone, Robert knelt down in front of her. "Do you want someone to give you a ride home now, or would you rather stay at the meeting and—"

"Stay." Just the thought of being alone made her feel like she was being dangled off a skyscraper, her knuckles turning white as she clung to her chair.

Robert nodded. "Okay. Why don't we all take our seats and . . . Brian, why don't you start? How was your day?"

Faith didn't participate—didn't even listen to what was said—but she was grateful to have other people around her.

Nyah sat close on one side and Mrs. Henderson on the other, and eventually Faith was calmed by their presence. When it came time for a break, Gus and Adam bolted outside for a smoke, but Nyah didn't move.

"You smoke, don't you?" Faith asked.

Nyah nodded. "Tried to quit a million times. Maybe next time it'll stick."

"You can go have one. I'm fine."

"No. I'm good."

"Go."

"Are you sure?"

"I'm fine. Thanks."

Nyah hurried to the door but hesitated, glancing back with a look of concern on her face, like Faith was one of her patients she was worried about, only stepping outside when Faith motioned for her to go. Faith hoped for a nurse like Nyah if she ever ended up in the hospital again.

Mrs. Henderson gave Faith's arm a squeeze and a gentle pat.

"Thanks, Mrs. Henderson," Faith said.

"You poor dear. You've had quite a fright tonight."

Faith gave a one-shouldered shrug. "I'll get over it."

"I'm sure you will." Mrs. Henderson folded her knitting in her lap. "But don't you worry. You're not alone." She lowered her voice and leaned close. "I spoke with my son. I'm sure he'll help."

Oh, no, not this again! She didn't feel like dealing with crazy on top of everything else, but the old woman had been very kind.

"Thanks," Faith said. "I need all the help I can get."

Mrs. Henderson smiled and picked up her knitting. Faith followed the rhythm of the needles and the steady movement of red yarn. Mrs. Henderson paused mid-stitch and looked up. "I wonder if the man in the hallway was the driver you saw? I was worried about that."

"Worried about what?" Faith's heartbeat sounded to her like a kitchen mixer banging off the side of the bowl.

"When I heard that you saw the driver outside of O'Lindey's, it made me go all pins and needles. I just knew . . ." Her hand trembled as she touched her chest. "I knew that if you saw him, then most likely he saw you, too."

Faith's stomach tightened at the thought. "Rat Face stopped when I screamed, but . . ." Faith leaned away from Mrs. Henderson. "How did you know I saw him?"

Mrs. Henderson's needles began moving again. "My son told me."

Each click of the needle now sent Faith's heart beating faster. Faith squinted to study Mrs. Henderson more closely. She couldn't quite tell if the woman had that off-balance look that she'd seen in some people's eyes at Brookdale. For Faith, there were two kinds of crazy. There was the life-has-beat-me-down-and-I-need-some-help type of mental illness, and then there was the Joker type of crazy. That kind would kill you. Faith made a mental note to avoid extended conversations with Mrs. Henderson from now on. The woman officially creeped her out.

Fortunately, Mrs. Henderson seemed happy to knit in silence, unaware or not caring that Faith sat there twisting her ring, watching her.

Faith put her head in her hands and tried to push the man's eerie song out of her mind by silently reciting a nursery rhyme from childhood:

Hush, little girl, rest your head.
Hush, little girl, stay in bed.
The sun and your friends are fast asleep.
Now's not a time to cry and weep.

For in your dreams, there we'll be.
Hurry now, and follow me.

After a few minutes, someone touched her back.

"Are you all right?" Nyah asked.

Faith looked up. Everyone had come back from break and returned to their seats. All eyes were on her, all worried.

"Yeah." Faith sat up and squared her shoulders. "I'm okay. I'll be fine."

Faith could tell they didn't believe her false bravado. They didn't believe her because they knew what it was like to lie to themselves. Every morning they strapped on that mask of bravery and prayed that a stiff breeze wouldn't blow it off and reveal to the world how terrified they felt.

R obert parked behind her at the laundromat after insisting on following her home. "For safety," he said, and she didn't argue. Now, as she got out of her car and looked up at her darkened building, she didn't want him to leave.

Faith walked back to the Jeep and gestured for him to put down his window. "I'm probably setting the cause of women back twenty years, but... would you mind coming up to my apartment?" Looking at Robert's shirt and not his eyes, she felt the color rising in her cheeks. "Just to check that it's safe. Then you can go."

"Sure. I—I didn't think you meant . . ." Robert stammered, climbing out of the Jeep. "Lead the way."

Faith led him to the staircase at the side of the building, and said, "After you."

Robert started up, glancing back every few steps. At her door, he stepped to the side so she could unlock it, but she handed him the key instead, and he unlocked it for her.

She followed him inside. Besides the main room, there wasn't much to check out, but he dutifully slid back the closet's pocket door and checked the small space anyway. He went into the bathroom. She heard him pull aside the shower curtain, and winced, not from nerves but because she remembered the pile of underwear tossed in the corner.

He came back into the main room, where Faith was standing by the kitchen table, and nodded. "All clear."

"Thanks," Faith said softly. "It's just . . . the, um, the anniversary of my incident is tomorrow. Ten years. I think it's making me crazy."

"No need to apologize. That's what the group is here for. Besides, it's nice to be needed." Robert stood there, his eyes darting around the apartment, his hands in full fidget mode. After an awkward pause, he started for the door.

Faith shifted in front of him. "Can I offer you something to eat?"

"I'm fine."

"It's no problem. I just . . . I bet you're hungry." Internally, she groaned at her desperation not to be alone.

Robert glanced at her face and his eyes softened. "Sure."

Faith pulled open the door to her little refrigerator, then quickly closed it, doubting he wanted a package of creamer or soy sauce, the only items her refrigerator contained. She tried the nearest cabinet, where she kept the ramen and oatmeal, and pulled out one of each.

"You can't resist, right?"

Robert laughed.

Faith lifted the instant ramen cup a little higher, and he nodded. "Ramen it is." She put the oatmeal back, got herself a cup of noodles, and peeled back the lids. "Do you want to sit down?"

"Sure." He lowered himself onto a stool and sat ramrod-straight, rubbing his hands on his jeans. "Do you need any help?"

"Making ramen? Nope." She popped the *p*. "How about some tea?"

"That'd be great."

Faith grabbed an unopened box of tea and struggled with the clear wrap. "I guess they vacuum-seal these things." She lifted a steak knife from the butcher's block, cut the plastic, and took out a bag. "It's Earl Grey." She filled the little teakettle at the sink.

"Have you made an anniversary plan?" Robert asked.

Apparently, he wasn't going to bother with small talk. Faith didn't have an anniversary plan, but she wasn't going to let him know that. "My mom's my support contact." She set the kettle on the stove and the ramen cups in the microwave, punched five minutes into the microwave, and pressed start.

Robert sat up even straighter. "I don't mean to pry, but— she wasn't affected by your incident, too?"

Faith crossed her arms and leaned against the sink. "No one told you who I am?"

Robert looked honestly puzzled. "No one in the group would share that information even if they knew your background. It's not right."

"You sound like a Boy Scout."

"You say that like it's a bad thing."

"Good point. It's just . . . I'm used to the whispers and looks. I kind of assume people say, 'That's the girl from Reed Lake,' as soon as I walk out of the room." She huffed. "If they wait that long. Sometimes they say it when I walk in."

"I know the feeling. But no, I don't know your story. Do you want to share?"

Faith sniffed. Something was burning. "Damn it."

Faith shut the burner off. She had turned on the wrong burner, and the plastic handle of the steak knife was smoldering on the stove. Robert grabbed the handle at the top and flicked the knife into the sink, waving away the foul-smelling smoke cloud that shrouded him when the water hit the hot knife.

"I'm an idiot." Faith jerked opened a window. "At least the smoke alarm didn't go off."

"Have you checked the batteries? You should, because it should have gone off."

"Up until a minute ago, a fire was pretty low on my list of things to be paranoid about."

Robert inspected the knife. There was only a divot where it had rested on the burner. "It's still good. And now you have a finger grip." He grinned and flashed a dimple.

The microwave dinged.

Faith reached to open it but Robert held up a hand. "You should leave it in there for a minute before you take it out."

Faith smirked. "Wow, you really are a Boy Scout. Do you obey all the rules?"

Robert blushed. "Five minutes was a little too long. It'll be too hot."

Faith slumped against the sink and looked down at the knife. "That was stupid."

"Don't beat yourself up. Look, anniversaries are the biggest trigger. I can ask Nyah if it's okay to give you her number. I'll leave you mine, too."

"I'm good. If you need me, I'll be at O'Lindey's."

Robert frowned. "Not funny."

Faith held up her hands in mock surrender. "It was a joke. Gallows humor." She cringed at her choice of words.

Robert sat back down. "Seriously, Faith, you need a plan. A support network. It's an anniversary."

"I'll hide under the bed. There, it's a plan." Faith took the ramen cups out of the microwave and handed one to Robert.

"Fork or spoon?"

"Um, both, I guess. Fork for the noodles, spoon for the soup."

"Good answer." Faith took a seat and blew the steam from the top of her cup. "So. What's your story?"

Robert looked down at the ramen. "I'm working on my counseling license."

"I thought you're a survivor. Why would you want to be a therapist? Aren't you sick of hearing all the stories?" Faith asked.

"I think that's why I want to be a therapist. Maybe being a survivor makes a difference, you know?"

"Could be." Faith shrugged. "I know it's better in group if people know where you're coming from. That's why I hate starting a new group. You don't know everyone's *incident* yet."

"Is that what you think about at group?"

"Yeah," Faith admitted. "I mean, like I said, I assume everyone knows mine, but you wonder about everyone else. I'm looking at Nyah, and I'm curious what happened to her. And why is Gus there? He's an old guy. How long ago did it happen? Is he still freaked out by it? Does this ever end? That kind of stuff."

"Well, being curious is part of human nature. I try to just see the people, though. What happened to us doesn't define us," Robert said.

"Yes, it does. My incident made me."

"No, no." Robert waved his spoon for emphasis. "What happened to you is external. It's not who you are."

Faith blew on her noodles again, then slurped some down. "I don't agree. Are you kind of okay with everything that happened to you?"

Robert made a face. "Okay with it?"

"I don't know the right word. Grounded? Sane? Are you on the edge of Crazy Town, and if I share my screwed-up thoughts with you, will that push you over into some full-blown psychotic meltdown?"

"I like to think I'm . . . grounded, as you said. I know my limitations. To be honest, it's a little uncomfortable being here and talking with you like this."

Faith pulled her legs up under her. "Why?"

He poked at the ramen. "I'm used to listening, but you seem to be making the conversation two-way."

"That's what a conversation is," Faith said. "Besides, I want to know what you think." She took another bite of noodles. "Once I totally information-dumped on my roommate. Well, technically, she was a cellmate. Anyway, she went sort of nuts afterward, and when they carted her away, she was screaming some of the stuff I told her about. I really don't want a three-peat."

"A repeat?"

"No, three-peat. See, I figured the first time was just a fluke. I didn't think what was in my head was so off-the-wall crazy that it would make someone else nuts too, you know? So I tried telling the story to my new cellmate and . . . same thing happened."

"Okay. Now you've got me a little nervous, but I want you to be honest with me."

Faith dropped her spoon in her cup and set it on the table. "I'm a monster. Like Frankenstein's. Seriously. I died that night. Everything inside me did." She tapped the side of her head. "This is a dead shell. I look the same on the outside, but when everything happened, it killed that little girl everyone called Faith. All that she was is gone. So what happened, that really *is* me. My incident killed me, and I came back as this freak."

Robert was etching the side of the ramen cup with his thumbnail. "No."

"You don't agree?"

"Not with all of it. I understand what you feel about dying. I even understand about feeling like a monster. But something happening to you doesn't make you. It can feel like it kills you, but it still isn't you. It happened. It changed you, but it's not Faith."

Faith leaned forward. "What's Faith? I hope you can tell me, because I don't know. I woke up in this world of suck, where everything I had is dead and gone. I breathe. I move. But I can't feel anything good anymore. I remember what feeling good felt like—some. Bits and pieces. But it's like looking in a broken mirror. I can't even stand my own face."

"But you're beautiful." Judging by Robert's expression, the words had escaped his mouth without his brain's permission. He quickly looked down.

Faith snorted. "I look like my father. That's all I see when I look in a mirror. It's a good thing I'm not a guy, or I'd grow a beard down to my knees."

Robert coughed and put down his cup.

"It's okay to laugh," Faith said, getting up to get him a glass of water.

"I didn't want to be rude."

"Choking on noodles isn't a good alternative."

Robert coughed again.

"So, what's your incident?" Faith asked, setting the water in front of him.

Robert froze. The muscles in his forearms tightened till they showed through his long-sleeved shirt. "It's in the past."

"Ah." Faith narrowed her eyes. "I was kind of rocking this whole transparency thing." She pointed back and forth between them. "But I get it. You want *me* to share, but not you. Right?"

"No, it's just . . . you said yourself, people judge. I understand how you feel when you walk into a place and everyone knows what happened to you. That's why I moved here. I wanted a fresh start, a new name, a new life. No more looks from everyone in town. And now no one knows me or my story."

Faith glared at the table. "So it's okay for everyone else to spill their guts and hang out their dirty secrets, but not you? You were just in group asking people to share, but that doesn't work for you?"

"I've done it before. I shared my story before I moved, plenty of times, and that experience helped me deal with my incident, but sharing is voluntary. Now I choose not to."

"Great. Me, too. Go ahead and ask me if I want to share. I'm dying to tell you my answer."

"Look, I'm sorry if I upset you. It's just, my incident . . . it's different."

Faith waited for him to continue, but Robert remained silent.

"Whatever." Faith grabbed her cup and shoveled ramen into her mouth.

Robert stood up. "Well. Thank you for the noodles."

Faith didn't look up.

After his footsteps faded away, she set down her cup, reached over, and ran her finger over the letter *K* he'd absentmindedly etched into the Styrofoam—and felt even more alone.

For a brief moment, when she started her own search for Rat Face, Faith had felt empowered. Whoever had chased her down the school hallways and reduced her to a blubbering, queasy mess on the floor of the gymnasium had chosen exactly the right way to strip away every bit of that newfound confidence. Now she was afraid again—but this time was different.

This time she hated her fear even more than she hated the man who kept it alive in her. This time she'd fight. This time she'd defend herself. All she needed was a gun. And she knew exactly where to get one.

She pulled into the driveway of her grandmother's sprawling English Tudor, hoping no one was home. Faith and her mother had moved in here after the murders, but Faith had never thought of the place as home. Even after her grandmother died, less than a year after they moved in with her, it was still "Grandma's house" in her mind.

Faith punched in the code for the garage—the same as it had always been, her grandmother's birthday—and the door rose.

laxed as she scanned the huge garage with three
ertible and her mother's BMW weren't there—
eater MG, under a tarp where it had always

ning was different, and it took Faith a moment to
ze what it was. They'd taken away her grandfather's
workbench. The lathe and the racks that had held his saws and
chisels and planes were gone. Although her grandfather had
made his money in real estate, Faith always remembered him in
overalls covered in sawdust. She pictured him sanding away with
the radio on, listening to a baseball game, remembered his smile
when she took him a glass of iced tea from her grandmother. He
had made everything from birdhouses to clocks, but now there
was no trace of him. Just the faintest whiff of woodiness.

She turned away and went inside, paying no attention to any
details in the interior. She had no desire to stir up demons from
the past; she wanted only one thing from this house. She strode
straight to the second floor and paused outside a guest bedroom.
It was now an office but once—in another life, it felt—she and
Kim slept there whenever their parents went out of town.

A memory of Kim braiding Faith's long hair twisted her
heart in knots.

Pushing the memory aside, she leapt up and snagged the rope
that pulled down the attic stairs. A curtain of dust fell and the
stairs opened, creaking loudly in protest.

It looked like her mother hadn't been up here in years—
maybe not since they'd moved in.

This place is a tomb. After the murders, Faith's mother had
been close to catatonic, so her grandmother hired some movers,
and they simply packed everything into boxes and deposited
them up here. Apart from clothes, most of the boxes had never
been opened. *Here lie the ruins of the Winters family.*

In reality, they all died that night. Even her mother. Faith lost her father and sister, but her mother . . . Not only had her daughter been murdered but the police insisted her husband had killed her along with Anna and Mrs. Foster, and then shot himself in the head.

Her mother didn't believe the police at first. Faith remembered her screaming at Detective Walker that he was stupid to even suggest such a thing, even hitting him on the chest, until he had to take her in a hug and restrain her. But when the Sara-Jane story broke, her mother crumbled, and when she put herself together again, she had rearranged her molecules somehow to believe that her husband, the father of her children, had been a deranged murderer and serial adulterer.

Attic dust caught in Faith's nose and tears struggled to break free. She caught sight of one of her old teddy bears, gritted her teeth, and willed the tears back. She needed strength.

In some ways, Faith envied her mother's strength. She had managed to fight her way back to life. She not only held onto her therapy business but expanded it. Went on to write a bestseller. And privately, Faith didn't believe her mother had needed to marry Thad. He just showed up after seeing her mother on TV and wormed his way back into her life.

Running her hand over a stack of boxes, Faith realized one had been opened, the packing tape unsealed. Curious, she looked inside, and immediately wished she hadn't. *Photographs from the old house*. On top was one that used to sit on the mantelpiece in the living room. The four of them at the lake. Everyone was smiling. Faith's father had his left arm around his wife and his right arm squished Faith and Kimberly together at his side.

Faith's tears made a faint ticking sound as they fell onto the glass. Her sister looked so happy, so beautiful. On an impulse, Faith removed the picture from the box before closing it up. She didn't have much time. She made a conscious decision not to look at any more boxes and squeezed through the junk toward the back wall.

Something popped and she jumped, while her stomach seemed to plummet through the floor. *What was that? Old houses make lots of sounds, right?* Or was Rat Face in the house, trying to step quietly, trying not to touch anything? Had he followed her, waiting in the brown sedan while she went through a bunch of stupid pictures? He was making his way through the living room now, toward the attic steps. Oh, why hadn't she pulled up the steps? Another pop, a board groaning with someone's weight?

She quietly scooted over to the opening in the floor and positioned her feet so that as soon as his loathsome face appeared, she could kick him right down the stairs again. When, after a full five minutes, the pops and creaks never organized themselves into the nightmare she had so clearly seen, she cursed her stupidity again. *That's why you're here, idiot. So you never have to feel this way again.* At the very back of the attic, behind yet more boxes, was a tiny half-size door leading to a crawlspace. As far as Faith knew, no one ever opened that door. No one but her. Faith worked her fingers into the crack beside the door and pulled it open.

The mahogany box was still there.

Faith pulled it out, flipped back the brass latch, and opened the lid. Her father's pearl-handled six-shooter cowboy pistol lay inside. It had originally been locked in her grandfather's gun safe, but years ago, after the incident at school, Faith had found the key, removed the gun, and brought it up here. She had intended to kill herself, but she chickened out and hid the gun instead. Her mother soon realized it was missing, but Faith never admitted to stealing it and never revealed where it was.

As she ran her hand over the weapon, she was glad she kept this secret.

Let him come at me now.

It was almost 11:00 p.m., but Faith's mind wasn't interested in sleeping. After ten more minutes lying awake on the bed in her apartment, she rolled onto her stomach, reached down for the air vent, pulled the metal grille aside, and felt around blindly until her fingers closed around the cold metal of the old cowboy gun. She held it in front of her face, curious as to whether the pearl handle was real. She laid her hand flat against the side and spun the chamber.

Do bullets go bad?

It was over ten years since it had been fired. Her father had taught her to shoot, and she knew how to fire a rifle and a small pistol—but he had said the cowboy gun had too much of a kick for little Faith. He let Kim do it, though.

Faith pictured her sister's sassy grin of victory as she shot down the targets at the gun range. *Why couldn't she protect herself that night?* Faith picked up the photo beside her of her family as it once was. *Kim, I'm sorry. I should have done something.*

She rolled onto her back again and felt tears streak out the corners of her eyes and soak into the pillow.

Four hours. That's how long the police think I hid under that log. Was Kim alive while I was hiding?

Faith put the barrel of the gun in her mouth and sucked in a breath when the cold metal touched her tongue.

What about Anna and her mother? If I'd gotten help, would they have lived?

Her finger curled around the trigger.

Would the police have caught those men if I'd gone for help? Have they killed even more people because I let them get away?

The gun rattled against her teeth as her hand shook.

Sole survivor. The old nurse's words from ten years ago were still as clear as day. It was in the hospital, right after everything happened. She hadn't made her first suicide attempt, but she wanted to die even then. The nurse must have known. It was probably written all over her face—oh, how she had wanted to die—because she had made a special point of telling Faith that she *had* to live. That the police needed her. She was the *sole survivor*, and if she died, who would ID the killers?

Why me? Why not Kim? Why not Anna?

Faith yanked the gun from her mouth and sat up in disgust. She wasn't even sure which disgusted her more: her desire to pull the trigger or her failure to go through with it. Both solutions were cowardly. And that's what she was: a coward.

She wanted a drink. No, she needed one.

The gun felt heavy in her hand. If she was caught outside with it, she'd violate her probation. And the bar was just down the street. Besides, her, drunk and with a gun? That was a recipe for someone to die.

She got up, hid the gun back inside the floor vent, laid the picture face down on the bed, and got dressed.

***

She thundered down the stairs and zipped her sweatshirt against the cool night as she went. She glanced at her phone. Quarter past eleven—still plenty of time to get blind drunk. The phone buzzed in her hand. Tommy. She ignored it.

A light gust of wind sent a discarded wrapper past her and down the sidewalk. As she followed it with her eyes, she saw a man across the street, leaning against a red Camaro. Under different circumstances, the man might have turned her head. He was tall, broad-shouldered, and narrow-waisted. Strong. But on the street at night, across from her apartment . . .

Is he watching me?

Then she saw the glow from his cigarette, and he blew out a big puff of smoke.

He's just having a smoke. I'm getting paranoid. She shoved her phone deep into her purse and continued walking toward the bar. She considered going back for the gun, but she'd already lost too much drinking time to turn back now. The bar was only a block away.

The same bartender with the yellowish eyes looked up as she walked in. A few patrons were scattered about. Three looked to be construction workers, with dust-covered jeans, matching green work shirts, and heavy boots. Two men in their fifties nursed beers at the end of the bar. Two others guys, roughly her age, shot pool.

Faith headed for the bar, took out two twenties, and held up four fingers.

"I toldja before. Two at a time," the bartender said.

"Fine. Tell me when the twenties are done. Two shots of Pale Night."

She pounded the first shot before he'd finished filling the second. She gulped that and held up two fingers.

The bartender cast a sideways glance behind her at the door before pouring two more glasses and walking away.

As Faith knocked back a third shot, the bell above the door rang. Glancing at the mirror behind the bartender, she watched Camaro Guy enter the bar. She tapped her ring on the counter, rapid little clicks like a telegraph operator sending out a distress signal, as she watched him scan the room. *Is he following me?*

One of the construction workers in the corner waved, and Camaro Guy headed over to them.

Faith started breathing again. She downed the other shot and held up two more fingers.

The little bell above the door rang again. She checked the mirror to see Robert walk in. He spotted Faith immediately, like he'd known she was there. He approached her with an odd look on his face. In his eyes, she saw the swirl of emotions: concern, disappointment, hesitation . . .

"You shouldn't have come," Faith muttered.

Robert thrust his hands into his pockets. "I was going to say the same thing to you."

"How'd you find me?"

"You said you'd be here."

"When I said that, I was talking about tomorrow, and I was kidding."

"I'll go if—"

"If I want?" Faith stared into his eyes.

Robert's mouth tightened. He looked like he was struggling to breathe. *Maybe he's an alcoholic, too? A lot of survivors are.*

She hated herself even more, but she couldn't deal with her own pain let alone be responsible for his. "Just leave," she said.

"Will you call your sponsor?"

"No. Go. *Now.*" She hadn't meant to raise her voice. The pool players stared, eager for an excuse to flex their beer muscles.

"Please," she whispered. "Go."

Without another word, Robert turned and left the bar. He didn't look back.

For a minute Faith wanted to leave, too, to go anywhere else. Instead, she waved at the bartender and held up two fingers.

After he poured, one of the construction workers strutted over. The A&R Construction logo on his shirt was stretched tight across his massive chest, like he benched Mack trucks. "You okay?" he asked.

If she had needed his help with Robert, his arrival was two minutes too late. "You kinda missed the boat." She chuckled sarcastically and shook her head.

"Can I buy you a drink?"

"No. Get lost."

His buddies burst out laughing. The guy swore under his breath and faked a casual saunter back to the far side of the bar.

Faith watched him go and then immediately forgot him. She felt herself drifting to another place, another time. By merely shutting her eyes, she was right back where she always went—in front of the cabin. As always, the cabin was in flames, fierce red streaks reaching for the sky, darkened by black clouds of soot rising into the night.

She took another shot. She wished her vision were real. She'd run forward and throw herself into the fire, and she could be with Kim again.

A commotion in the corner got her attention. The construction workers were leaving, exchanging loud farewells with the Camaro driver. As they walked out the door, Camaro Guy strode to the bar and took a stool two seats down from Faith. He leaned against the counter, one foot on the rung of the stool. How she wished she could be like that: large and in charge.

Just looking at him relaxed her a little. He set his beer bottle on the bar—some kind of fancy import with a red-and-black label.

Surprised this dump serves anything decent. She squared her shoulders and downed another shot.

When her glass banged off the bar, the stranger's face cracked into a crooked smile. "I'd offer to buy you a drink, but it looks like you got your own system going."

Faith huffed. If she had to guess, she'd say he was close to thirty, but with his good-ol'-boy grin and tousled hair, it was hard to tell.

"Why don't I try something different, then?" he said. "How about I ask real nice? Can I have one of your drinks?"

Faith rolled her eyes.

"Pretty please?" He moved over and took the stool next to her.

Faith held her hand up for the bartender. "Get him another beer."

Camaro Guy nodded to the bartender. "Another Fashingbauer." He took a sip and smiled at Faith. "Thank you. I'm Hunter."

"Faith."

"Interesting system you got there." He pointed at the shot glasses.

Faith clicked her tongue. "It's patented."

"Really?" Hunter grabbed a pretzel. He looked amused, but Faith was sure he was flirting now. "I think I should sue you for infringement. I invented two-fisted drinking. But I recommend beer. That whiskey?"

"Yeah. I need something strong."

Hunter rested an elbow on the bar. "Now, there's a story behind that."

"That's a closed book."

"Fair enough. What would you like to talk about?" He gave the distinct impression that he didn't really care what they talked about—least of all the crap going on inside her head—and right now she really liked that.

"You." Faith knocked back the shot and held up two fingers to the bartender, then locked on Hunter's brown eyes. "Talk about you."

And Hunter talked. Just as he seemed to control the environment when he walked in, he controlled the conversation now. He talked about a trip he just took to New York City, hiking the Appalachian Trail, and his car, but he didn't ask any more questions. It was as if he understood that Faith just felt like listening—that she needed to get outside her own thoughts for a little while.

Eventually, Faith felt gravity pulling her head forward and her eyelids down. She looked at the clock—twelve fifteen. *Uh-oh. Death Day.* She didn't know how many shots she'd had, but she'd left drunk in the dust a long time ago and had almost reached oblivion.

"Do you have someplace to be?" He put a twenty down on the bar for another round. "I can give you a ride home later."

Faith shook her head. She was wasted, but there was no way she was going to get in a car with some guy she'd just met at a bar. "No thanks." She stumbled off the bar stool. His strong arms caught her around the waist and easily kept her upright.

"Well, thanks for listening." Hunter smiled.

Faith weaved as she headed for the door. She tugged it twice before pushing it open.

A yellow VW Bug was parked at the curb with Robert's Jeep behind it. As Faith stepped onto the sidewalk, the Bug's doors opened and Robert and Nyah stepped out. "Hey, Faith," Nyah said.

"You called Nyah?" Faith slurred. She closed one eye but still couldn't focus.

"We watch out for each other, and it looks like you need it," Nyah said.

"I'm going home," Faith mumbled. "I don't need babysitters." Faith turned to walk away and would have fallen if Nyah hadn't caught her. "And you suck," she snapped at Robert. "Mister My-Life's-Great-and-I-Don't-Have-to-Share. That's crap. You know that?"

"I didn't mean it that way," Robert said.

"Well, that's how it is, right? But I don't care. I'm fine. I get a do-over fresh start for my stuff, too."

"Now you're just a babbling drunk," Nyah said. "You're coming with me."

"No, I'm not." Faith wrapped her arms around herself.

Nyah looked at Faith like she had three heads. "Right now I bet you can't even spell your own name. You really think stumbling down the sidewalk alone is a good idea?"

Faith shook her head and the world spun.

"I think you should let your friends help you," Nyah said.

"Just you. He's not my friend. You are." Faith pointed at Nyah. "You bandaged my arm, but Mister Wait-a-Minute Ramen doesn't share, so he can go suck mud. I'm not going home with him."

"You're not going home," Nyah said. "You're crashing at my place. Let's go." She put her arm around Faith's waist and led her over to the Bug.

Faith groaned. She looked at her feet and saw four of them until she closed one eye again. "Fine. Fine. My survival buddies are here to rescue me," she slurred, swaying. "What can go wrong?"

Nyah guided her carefully into the passenger seat. "Keep your head out the window until we get there," she said. "I just cleaned the floor mats."

Thursday, April 12
Death Day

J effrey shut off the TV and stomped to the front door for the fifth time in the last hour. Each time his hand touched the chill of the metal doorknob, he stopped—thinking of his friend's black eyes and the warning not to leave the house.

Don't piss him off. Don't do it, Jeffrey cautioned himself. He glanced at the clock: 12:35 a.m. If he rushed, he could still make last call. He yanked the door open and jumped sideways as if shocked when his phone vibrated in his pocket.

He fumbled to answer it. "What? I'm here."

"Are you home, Jeffie?" The man's voice was a singsong.

"Yeah." Jeffrey's hands shook as he took out a cigarette and peered into the darkness. "Where else would I be? But listen, I need a drink and I'm out of booze. I figure I could make last call at—"

"What kind of moron are you?" The words snapped like wet wood in a fire. "I told you I'd take care of it, didn't I?"

Jeffrey's heart sped up and a hopeful smile spread across his face. "Did you do something? Did you run her over?"

"Stop talking. I swear just listening to you has the potential to make someone stupid. One minute on the phone with you and my IQ has dropped ten points. No, I didn't run her over. See, you don't think. That's your problem, Jeffie. First off, you can't rush these things. There's no fun in a quickie. You need to make it last."

Jeffrey pounded the doorframe. "This one's not a game. She can ruin me." Anger-tinged panic roared through him like a brush fire. "If they catch me, it's over for *both* of us."

Jeffrey waited for a reply, and in the growing silence, his confidence also grew. *He doesn't want to get caught either.* Jeffrey took a long drag on his cigarette, but his sense of relief was short-lived—the silence on the other end of the phone was broken by laughter.

"Well, look out, everyone, Jeffie here has grown a pair and now he's a big boy." The man laughed again, but when he spoke, his voice was hard. "Did you just threaten *me?*"

"No. No, I would never do that. You know that. I was just . . . I just meant if I got caught, they might put it together. You and me. You know? I would never, never tell anyone. Remember the cats? Did I say anything? Nothing. I took the fall. I said nothing."

"Calm down, buddy. Relax. I know you'd never, never, ever say anything. Right?"

"I wouldn't. I swear it on my mother's grave."

"Damn, I can't ask for better than that. That's why I'm taking care of this problem. But we've got to do it my way. Understand?"

"Your way." Jeffrey switched hands with the phone and wiped his sweaty palm on his pants.

"And wouldn't you know, I'm doing something about it right now. Guess where I am at this very moment?" The man started humming a game show countdown.

Jeffrey sucked on the cigarette so hard flames flicked at the end. "I—I—I—"

The man made a loud buzzer sound. "Time's up! Wrong! The correct answer is: *Lying in her bed.*"

Jeffrey exhaled and started coughing. "No way. No friggin' way. She's dead?"

"What the hell are you talking about, Jeffie? You think just because I said I'm lying in her bed that means she's, like, dead and naked next to me? That is *seriously* messed up. You're one of those kinky psychos who likes to hang out with dead people. You should get some help, you twisted freak." The man started laughing again.

Jeffrey pressed the heel of his hand against an eye. He felt like his head was going to explode, but he didn't know if he was going to burst into tears or throw a fit and start smashing everything in sight.

"I'm in her apartment!" the man boasted. "And you would not believe the stuff she has. I found something priceless. Tell you what, I'll bring it over."

Jeffrey straightened up and his throat tightened. "Over here?" His breath was now coming in short gulps.

"Roll out the welcome mat, my friend, because I've just got to show you this stuff. It's most impressive. I also have a case of red and white, and a bottle of Pale Night whiskey with your name on it."

In spite of the promise of booze, he was the last person Jeffrey wanted to see right now. Just the thought of him coming made Jeffrey quietly close the front door. "Are you sure? You don't have to. It's late, man."

"Too late? Get out. It's not like we're going to wake up your mom—she's dead!" The man laughed. "You're not laughing, Jeffie. See, I knew you were still sore, but don't worry, I'll swing by with my presents, and you know what? You and I have a party to plan. That's right, so give me fifteen minutes, and I swear on your mother's grave that I'm going to put a big smile on your face."

Faith groaned into her pillow and slid her tongue across sticky teeth. Her stomach churned as she smelled stale smoke, whiskey, and . . . roses.

Faith sat up, and quickly regretted the sudden motion. Her clothes were gone, and she was dressed only in an unfamiliar oversize T-shirt. She rolled off the floral couch and stumbled around in a panic, blinking to make sense of the photos of strangers on the walls, the long coffee table, and a tan kitchen countertop wiped clean. The neat, small apartment she found herself in was deserted. On the kitchen table, she found a bottle of water, a bottle of aspirin, and a note with her name on it.

If your pity party's over, there's a meeting tonight that we hope you're at. I washed your clothes and they're in the bathroom. I'm not an AA sponsor, so you should call yours. Sober up before you call me or Robert. You owe him an apology.
— Nyah

Faith put the note in her pocket and chugged the water. As it went down, bits and pieces of the previous night came back to her. *Apologize to Robert? What did I do?* It was as if she were looking through a kaleidoscope at first, then shards popped into place, one after another, and formed an embarrassing picture.

She remembered getting out of the Bug and falling. That must have been outside Nyah's apartment. Robert ran to help her up; she was crying—bawling. Fragments of the words she spewed in hate as he carried her up the stairs floated to the surface of her memory like garbage on water. She had ripped into him, slurring how sorry she was for him. Told him he'd never get a fresh start. Called him a coward for not facing what happened.

Her stomach clenched and her mouth flooded with heat. She was going to vomit—now. She banged open two doors before finding the bathroom, lifting the lid just in time.

I'm a monster.

The memory of the pained look on Robert's face made her vomit again. She cleaned up the bathroom, changed into her clothes, grabbed her purse, and slunk out the door. Keeping her head down, she walked until she recognized where she was, then headed home. The only thing she wanted to do was take a shower.

Her temples throbbed as she trudged up the rickety steps to her apartment. She stuck her key in the lock, but as she turned it, she felt no resistance, and it made no sound.

I'm sure I locked it.

She pushed the door open. Sitting in the middle of her kitchen table was the photo of her family. Someone had taken it off the bed and propped it up, facing the door.

Her heart hammering along with the pounding in her head, Faith yanked out her phone and punched in her mother's number.

"Faith? Are you all right? I've called you several times and—"

"Did you come over here?" Faith turned the photo facedown. "Did you come *into* my apartment?"

"Of course not. Is everything all right?"

Faith's eyes scanned the room. Everything else seemed to be in its place. *Maybe I just . . .* Faith looked down. The air vent where she had hidden the gun was open, the metal cover sitting beside the hole in the floor.

"Are you still there? Faith? Is everything okay?"

Faith raced over to the vent and felt around inside. The vent was empty. The gun was gone.

"No, no, no . . ." she muttered.

"Faith? What's going on?"

"Someone's broken into my apartment."

"Get out and go to a neighbor's—now." Her mother hung up.

"Mom? Mom?"

Faith hit redial and got voicemail. "Damn it." Her mother was no doubt on the phone with the police—which meant both the police *and* her mother would be here any minute.

Faith peeled off her clothes as she ran into the bathroom. She grabbed her toothbrush and toothpaste, got in the shower, and frantically scrubbed her mouth and tongue while the hot water ran over her. She gargled a few times and jumped out. She was drying her hair with a towel when she heard the first sirens.

"Crap." Faith grabbed a T-shirt and pair of sweats, not even taking the time to put on underwear.

The sirens stopped outside her apartment, and footsteps came thundering up the stairs. They stopped on the landing. "Marshfield Police, coming in!" yelled a familiar voice.

Faith tugged open the door. "Tommy, wait!"

Tommy stood outside the door with his gun drawn, down by his hip. He swore. "Your mother said you went to a neighbor's. Get out of here!" He grabbed her arm and dragged her out of the apartment. "Is anyone inside?"

"No. Not now."

"Wait here." Tommy went into the apartment. It took less than thirty seconds for him to make sure the place was empty.

Another siren was echoing down the street now, people on the sidewalk stopping to stare at the dark-green sedan that raced down the street with its police light flashing.

Tommy holstered his gun as he came to the doorway. His nose wrinkled. "Are you drunk?"

"No. I . . . "

He shot her a look that was equal parts sympathy and disappointment. "You were drinking last night."

"No, I wasn't."

"You called me."

A sharp pain ran between Faith's temples. "I did?"

"I guess you really lit it up last night. You sounded wasted. I called you back, but you said you were with your sponsor so I let it go."

Faith rubbed her eyes with her index finger and thumb. "What did I say?"

Tommy looked away. "Nothing. Drunk-speak. Forget about it."

The hurt expression on his face didn't match his words. Faith must have said something hateful and now she felt even lower. "Tommy, I'm sorry. I . . . "

The sedan screeched to a stop behind Tommy's cruiser, and Detective Walker jumped out.

"Get inside," Tommy said, handing her a package of mints. "Don't tell anyone you were drinking."

Faith walked over to the table and slumped into the chair.

When the chubby detective came through the door, he was sweating and breathing hard. His frown deepened as he looked around. He gestured for Tommy to join him outside on the balcony, where the two men spoke in hushed tones. Tommy seemed to be doing most of the talking. Finally, they both came back inside.

"Are you okay?" Walker asked Faith.

Faith nodded.

"What happened?" The detective stood behind the stool while Tommy waited in the doorway.

"I came home this morning—"

Walker flipped open his notebook. "Where were you last night?"

Faith glanced over his shoulder at Tommy, who gave just the slightest shake of his head.

"My sponsor's. I was having a . . . She's helping me transition, so I slept over. When I came home, the front door was unlocked."

"Did you lock it before you left?"

"Of course I locked it. But it wasn't locked when I came home. And this"—Faith picked the picture up so he could see it—"was propped up in the middle of the table."

"It's a picture of your family." Walker looked at her, confused, then glanced back at Tommy.

"But you didn't leave it there, right, Faith?" Tommy said hesitantly.

"No. I'd left it on the bed. When I came back, someone had put it there so I'd see it when I opened the door." Faith reached out and laid the picture facedown.

Walker tapped his notebook with his pen as he looked around the apartment. "Okay, I need you to provide me with a list of what's missing."

Faith looked at the air vent and swallowed. The only thing that seemed to be missing was the gun—and she could hardly mention that.

When she didn't say anything, Walker raised his eyebrows. "Something of value was taken, wasn't it?"

Faith's eyes shifted away from the vent. "Unless they like ramen, I have nothing to take."

"Nothing was taken?"

"That's right."

Walker closed his notebook. "So your complaint is that someone broke into your apartment, took a picture off the bed, and put it on the table."

Faith nodded and Tommy hung his head.

"What about your medicine?" Walker asked.

Faith went over to the cabinet where she kept her pills and opened it up. "They're all here."

"Can you tell if any are missing?"

Faith picked up a bottle and pretended to count. "Wait a minute . . . the bastard took two aspirin! Way to go, Sherlock, you cracked another case."

Walker scowled. He pointed at Tommy and then the door. Tommy looked like he was about to protest, but the glare from his superior was too much. Tommy went and stood outside, closing the door behind him.

Walker spun around, stomped across the floor, and glared at Faith. "Save the 'poor me' act and get off the hate wagon," he snapped. "You're the one who called in a burglary. Answer my questions."

Faith opened three different bottles and took a pill from each. She popped them in her mouth and swallowed. "I didn't call you. My mother did."

Right on cue, her mother burst through the door. Her eyes were red, and she looked like she hadn't slept. She rushed over to Faith and grabbed her shoulders. "Are you okay? Are you okay?"

Faith nodded and pulled free. "I'm fine."

"Beverly?" Walker said. "May I speak with you outside?"

Faith's stomach dropped. She knew she was going to sound crazy. "Mom, someone broke in. They did."

Faith's mother stepped between the detective and her daughter and held up a hand. "I'm sure Lionel's not saying they didn't. You just need to calm down, okay?"

Oh, Lionel, is it? Faith felt guilty as she looked at her mother's trembling hand and red-rimmed eyes. She sat back down in the chair.

They spoke outside for several minutes. When they came back in, Faith's mother looked even more upset than before. She hurried over and took Faith's hand. "Faith, what happened to you last night? I called several times. Did you go drinking?"

Faith shook her head. "I had a rough night, but I wasn't drinking."

"Then where did you go? Lionel says you didn't sleep here last night."

"I . . . I was having a hard time, so I called my sponsor."

"Amanda?"

"No. I didn't drink. It wasn't about that. It was my survivors' group sponsor. I spent the night at her house. My phone died."

Don't make up too many details.

Faith's mother smiled at Faith like she'd come home with an A on a test, and let out a relieved sigh. "You should have called me. I don't think I slept." She looked up at Lionel. "She was at her sponsor's," she repeated, like it explained everything.

Lionel took his notebook out again. "Can you please take another look at your medicine and let me know if any is missing?"

Faith took a deep breath. "Do I look like the type who keeps track of how many little pills are in there? No. It could all be there. It might not be. It's not OxyContin."

"I can figure it out." Faith's mother hurried over to the cabinet and began counting pills. After a minute, her eyebrows knitted together. "Actually, there are too many here."

"I forgot to take them last night," Faith admitted.

Her mother looked disappointed.

"Beverly, would you mind waiting outside while I speak to Faith?"

"All her pills are here," Faith's mother repeated.

Lionel nodded. "Thank you for figuring that out. I have a couple more questions that would be best handled without her mother in the room."

Faith's mother cast a nervous glance at Faith. "Is that okay, honey?"

"I'm fine, Mom."

Her mother squeezed her hand and then walked out onto the landing.

The door clicked closed and Lionel scratched his chin. "Who have you had in the apartment recently?" Lionel asked.

Faith thought for a moment. Besides her mother and Henry, there was only one other person: Robert. "Just this guy Robert. He's the moderator of my survivors' group."

"No one else?"

Faith rolled her eyes. "No one that would do this."

"Maybe it was one of your friends. Have you been using?"

"First off, I don't *have* friends. And I haven't been using."

"Does this Robert have a last name?" Lionel asked.

"I'm sure he does, but I don't know it. It's an anonymous group, like AA."

"Why was he over? Is he a boyfriend?"

"No. He came back to the apartment with me after a meeting," Faith said.

"So Robert's not a boyfriend, but he brought you home? Do you have a boyfriend?"

"I'm beating guys off with a bat." Faith got up, took an old glass out of the sink, gave it a quick rinse, and filled it up with water. "You'd figure with my being famous and all, the guys would come running—but, shocker, no boyfriend."

"I know you had to come back to Marshfield as part of your probation deal, but you could put in for a transfer. Just be honest with the judge. Tell them that there are too many ghosts here." His voice made Faith look up; it didn't have its usual edge. "You could go someplace else. Someplace where no one knows you."

Faith wanted to smash the glass, but resisted the temptation. Lionel actually looked sincere. "Where am I going to go? Everyone knows me as 'the girl who lived.' Thanks, Mom." She raised her glass in mock salute.

"Faith . . . I'll be honest . . ." Lionel set his notebook down on the table.

"You know, whenever someone says that, I immediately think of all the times they were *not* honest with me."

Lionel ignored the remark. "I'm worried about you." He tapped the side of his head. "First you think you see the guy from the parking lot. Then your car gets stolen, but it's right around the corner from where you said you left it. Yesterday you thought someone was following you, but no one, out of all the other people in the building, saw or heard anything. And now this?"

Faith rubbed her face. She did sound crazy. If only she could tell him about the gun.

"And you're lying. To your mother at least. You didn't take her calls because your phone died? Really? If you're gonna lie, can't you do better than that?"

She didn't know what to say, so she didn't say anything.

"I know today is hard for you," Lionel said.

Faith groaned. She didn't need to be reminded. Death Day. Worse than that: the tenth anniversary. She raised her water glass. "Happy anniversary."

Lionel grabbed hold of her wrist. "Don't you dare drink to that." His eyes flashed and his anger seemed genuine.

Faith pulled her hand free. "Don't lecture me." She poured the water into the sink, where there were a few dirty dishes. She had a sudden thought to hide the knife she'd burned last night from Lionel's prying eyes, but she didn't see it. *Did I put it away already?* Hiding her concern, she said coldly, "If you're not going to do anything, I'm late for a meeting."

Her mother stuck her head inside. Obviously, she'd been listening. "Can I come in now?" she asked.

"I was just leaving." As he brushed past Faith's mother, she mouthed "Thank you." Lionel nodded, glanced back at Faith, and stomped out the door.

Faith's mother closed the door and hurried inside. Faith felt like she'd been punched in the gut. Her mother was crying. "I'm sorry. I'm so sorry I ever wrote that stupid book. I never thought . . . I . . . " Tears ran down her cheeks.

Faith felt guilty for her mother's tears, but also . . . pleased. She hated that book. It was basically a raw biography of her life in the twisted aftermath of the incident, revealing to the whole world how Faith's life unraveled—as told by the poor mother who tried to help her daughter but failed. Even the title mocked Faith: *The Girl Who Lived.* As if what she did now counted as "living."

"That's the problem." Faith glared at her mother. "You didn't think about *me* when you wrote that stupid book."

"You're *all* I thought about!"

Faith took a step back. She couldn't remember the last time her unflappable mother had raised her voice, let alone yelled.

"I lost my husband! I lost Kim! And I lost you, too. I was going out of my mind, and Dr. Melding said I should write down what I felt." Her mother's right hand stroked her own left arm like she was cradling a cat and petting it.

"Writing about personal stuff that I was going through is one thing, but letting other people read I went crazy made me even more of a circus freak. I shared what was going on inside me." Faith jammed her fingers against her chest. "I trusted you, Mom. You didn't talk to me for three months after. *You had me put away for three months.*"

"You know why." A tear ran down the bridge of her nose.

"Yeah, but so did everybody at school, and at that horrible psych hospital you put me into. Everyone knew you just wanted to throw me away, forget about me. What did you write? *I look at my daughter and feel the same as if I were gazing at a book or a table that belongs to someone else. If she were a book, I imagine the story inside might mean something to another person but I, on the other hand, have no desire to read it.*"

"That's why I wrote *The Girl Who Lived*. I felt cut off from you, so I tried to get closer."

"You might as well have put hidden cameras in my friggin' bathroom. You wrote down everything."

"I asked you, you know." Faith's mother picked up some spilled napkins off the floor and blew her nose. "You gave me permission to write it and you read it first. You said I could publish it. I didn't think anyone would read it, but I . . . I can't change the past. All I can say is, I'm sorry."

Faith didn't remember her mother asking. Maybe she did, but Faith was so drugged up at the time, her mother could have asked her if it was okay to paint her butt purple and leave her on a busy highway and she would have said yes.

"So I should blame Dr. Melding for you writing the book?"

Her mother's shoulders trembled, and she shook her head. "No. It's my fault. I wrote it."

Faith wanted to hold her and be held, but the pain was still raw. She crossed her arms and stared at her mother. She tried to come off as uncaring, looking at her mother like she meant nothing more to her than the table, wanting to impose the same pain on her mother as was inflicted on her. But the truth was, distance was the last thing Faith wanted. She needed a mom now more than ever, but . . .

Her mother stepped closer. "I'm so worried about you," she whispered. "Have you been drinking again? Did you black out?" Her eyes scanned Faith's face.

"No." Faith eyed the door. Oh, how she wanted to run, to get away from Marshfield and just keeping going. She repeated her prize-winning test answer yet again. "I slept at my sponsor's place."

"Lionel's concerned, too. He asked if you should go back to Brookdale."

"*What?* Why? Because someone broke into my apartment?"

"He said it wasn't just because of that. He said there've been other incidents of you . . . thinking something happened."

"They *did* happen, Mom! Someone stole my car and—"

"Honey, you need to calm down."

"Oh, do I?" Faith's voice rose. "Your ex-boyfriend wants to put me back in Brookdale, and I should calm down?"

"I never dated Lionel."

"Really, were you too busy banging Thad?"

Faith's mother stood as stiff as a judge and stared her down. "Whether you want to hear it or not, Thad loves you. You've made it perfectly clear that you don't want to consider him your stepfather—"

"He's not."

"Technically, he is."

"Considering the guy you picked to be my real father was such a loser, you'll forgive me if I don't want to celebrate Father's Day, the sequel."

Faith's mother closed her eyes and took three deep breaths. "I can understand that. But Faith, I got a second chance to do things differently, so I did. And I'm glad I did. I hope that one day you realize that's the most important gift that you can be given. You deserve another chance, too."

Faith scoffed.

"You do. And a lot of people want to see you succeed, including Lionel."

"He just wants to succeed with *you*."

Her mother waved her hand dismissively. "Don't be silly. Lionel and I have been friends since we were kids—nothing more. And he does have your best interests at heart." Her mother picked up her purse. "At least let me take you to breakfast. Today is going to be rough for both of us."

Faith glanced up at her mother, holding her purse in front of her with both hands, a hopeful look on her face like a kid who just asked for a cookie.

She's trying.

"Sure." Faith grabbed her keys off the table. *Rough day? I'll bet it's worse than that.* Faith followed her mom to the door, turned to look around the apartment—stopping at the picture frame flat against the table, where she'd left it after talking with Lionel—and locked the door behind her.

22

Faith's mother parked the car in front of the church.

"Are you sure I can't give you a ride to Dr. Melding's after your meeting?"

"I'm positive. I'll be fine."

"And you promise you won't be alone tonight? I know you don't want to be with me, but you can't be alone."

"I'll be with my sponsor," Faith lied. "Totally safe."

"Okay. That's good. Call me. And make sure your phone is charged."

"Thanks for breakfast," Faith managed to say as she got out of the car.

Beverly was smiling but not with her eyes; they were watching Faith like she was about to step off the curb and into the path of an oncoming truck. Then her mother waved and pulled out into the street. Even after the car had disappeared from sight, Faith stood staring at the spot, like a little kid standing in front of school, wishing her mother would come back. When she was a child, she felt as close to her mother as a baby kangaroo in the pouch, but that bond had already started to come undone before the killings—after Kim was diagnosed with Fabry disease.

That call from the doctor's landed like a nuclear warhead in the middle of her happy family, blowing the dynamic apart and scattering everyone. Faith's father became withdrawn and distant, spending more and more time alone at the cabin. Faith felt invisible to her mother. The therapist said this kind of detachment could occur under certain circumstances. Kim was sick. Her mother was focusing her attention on the more vulnerable child. Unfortunately for Faith, Kim took *all* of her mother's love and attention.

Why won't she protect me now that I'm the one who needs her?

Faith's shoulders slumped as she walked up the concrete path to the church. Her mother was going through the motions of acting like a mom, but that's how it felt—forced and distant.

She's trying, Faith reminded herself. Dr. Rodgers told her to focus on that fact. *I have to try, too.*

As Faith slipped inside the meeting room at the church, all heads turned. She didn't see Jane. Slipping into the closest seat, she crossed her arms and legs, tucked her chin to her chest, and picked a spot on the floor to stare at.

She could white-knuckle it through this meeting.

Through this day.

Through this life.

She did her best to listen, but she couldn't concentrate. It was Death Day. That was the only thing on her mind. The one day of the year that all the others rotated around. *Death Day.* Now that it was here, the familiar feeling—that the earth would split open at any second and swallow her whole—electrified each nerve.

Time felt like it was moving backward. She had no idea how long she'd been sitting there when someone asked, "Faith, did you want to contribute?"

Faith glanced up to find Rachel looking at her expectantly. She realized she must have muttered something aloud. "No. I'm sorry. No." Faith stared off and began counting the flower petals in the wallpaper border below the ceiling.

Faith was up to 247 petals when her phone vibrated in her pocket. She peeked at the caller ID—Murray's Wine and Spirits. She jumped up and hurried for the doors. "Hello?"

"Faith, it's Sam. Sam Green from Murray's. We spoke the other night. I think I may have a lead on the guy who hit your dog."

"My dog? Yes . . . My puppy. Snoopy." She winced as she said the first dog name that popped into her head. "You know who he is?"

"Not yet. But Steve, he works weekends, he remembered a guy like that. Steve couldn't remember if he bought whiskey, but he did drive an old Crown Vic. Steve said they talked, and the guy said he'd just moved back to town."

"Did Steve know anything else? Did he get a name?"

"No, but at least you know the guy's local. I told everyone to keep an eye out for him. I'll call you when I hear something else."

"Thanks, Sam."

Faith hung up. She didn't know how to get in touch with Henry; she just seemed to show up, so she tried Tommy.

Tommy answered in a whisper. "I have to call you back," he said.

"Tommy, I've got some information. Well, I think. Rat Face lives in Marshfield now."

"I can't talk. I'm getting called into the chief's office right now. It's about you."

"About me? What about me?"

"The owner of Murray's Wine and Spirits just came into the station. He said you really freaked him out. He has some poster that you made. He said you threatened to kill the guy on the poster when you found him."

"What? No. I just asked the owner if he'd seen Rat Face! That's it. I didn't threaten anybody."

"You didn't say anything about killing anyone?"

Faith exhaled. "He asked me what I was going to do to Rat Face when I found him. I said put a bullet in his head. What was I supposed to say?"

There was a long silence on the other end of the phone. "Do me a favor? Go home. I'll swing by when I'm done with my shift."

"When's that?"

"Eight."

"Fine. Whatever."

Tommy hung up.

The church doors opened, and people started for their cars. Apparently, the meeting was over. *That was a lot of petals, I guess. But I made it through. Thank you, Dr. Rodgers.* She hurried back inside and found Rachel talking to Martin, who was stacking chairs. Faith waited until Martin left, then she took the paper out of her pocket.

"I'm sorry I had to take that call," Faith said. "And I know I was a little late. And I guess maybe you could tell I wasn't really paying very good attention. It's just, today's the day that . . . " She trailed off as she realized that there was no need for her to explain. It was Death Day for Rachel, too.

"Faith, I want to apologize," Rachel said softly.

"For what?" Faith's voice was low, almost hostile. The more Rachel spoke, the more Faith thought about Anna's mother and her best friend, and that stirred up pain. Faith knew Rachel wasn't responsible for her pain, but her rage was heating up all the same.

"You've done nothing wrong," Rachel said. "But I've never reached out to you. I should have. My sister liked you and your family very much."

The paper in Faith's hand crumpled as her fingers tightened into fists. "You did nothing. I'm the one who should be doing the apologizing. My father... my father was responsible for your sister's . . . for Anna. It was his fault they died."

"Oh, Faith." Rachel took a step forward, and Faith took a step back.

"I don't think he killed them," Faith said. Her words were halting and selected with effort. "But he *got* them killed. If your sister hadn't come to meet my father in the cabin, she wouldn't have died."

"My sister and your father were *not* having an affair," Rachel said. "Your father was a good man. He wasn't unfaithful to your mother."

Grief squeezed Faith's chest and curled her lip into a snarl. "Look, I get you not wanting to think ill of your sister, but you don't know that."

"My sister did not have an affair with your father," Rachel repeated emphatically. "Jessica and I were like best friends. We told each other everything. She would have told me if there had been anything going on between her and your father."

Faith made a face. She couldn't help it. She'd seen enough denial. Battered women who denied that their husbands beat them. Children who insisted their parents hadn't molested them. *They can't face the pain. Rachel can't either.*

"You don't know that," Faith repeated. "Only my father and Jessica knew the truth."

"Jessica would have told me." Her lips were twitching.

"Really?" Faith's voice dipped into sarcasm now. She was responding like a wounded dog, biting back at anyone getting close to her, but she was helpless to stop. "Maybe she was embarrassed to admit to her holier-than-thou pastor's wife sister she was committing adultery?"

Rachel's eyes filled with tears. "No." She took a deep breath. "Jessica knew I wasn't holy. She knew about my *own* affair."

That closed Faith's mouth.

"I wasn't the same person then. I married young. I wasn't prepared to be a minister's wife." Rachel exhaled and looked at the ceiling. "I'm making excuses. Forgive me. I was wrong. It's that simple. I broke my marriage vows, and I was having an affair with an old boyfriend. Jessica was trying to get me to salvage my marriage. That's the kind of woman she was. So, yes. I can say that she wasn't having an affair with your father, and I believe that with every fiber of my being."

Anger swept through Faith like a flame. She wanted to say something about her father paying for sex with Sara-Jane Bradley, but she bit her lip—literally. Not knowing what else to say, she unclenched her hand and thrust the paper forward. "Can you please sign this?"

"Of course." Rachel's hand trembled as she walked over to the coffee table, smoothed out the paper, and signed it.

Faith held her hand out for the paper. "I don't know if I believe you yet. Not that I think you're lying. Well, you might be lying to yourself."

Rachel gave her back the form. "I understand that you have reason to doubt, but I know the truth—in here." She touched her chest. "I also want to say thank you for being such an example of forgiveness, with Jane."

Jane? Faith was about to correct Rachel that there was nothing that she needed to forgive Jane for—but at that instant the sick woman's name clicked into place. Faith started trembling, not from fear, but rage. "Jane is Sara-Jane Bradley?"

Rachel's eyes widened. "You didn't know?"

"Didn't *know*?" Faith forced the words through clenched teeth. "If I knew that toothless *ghoul* was the woman who managed to turn my life into more of a living hell than it already was, I would have helped her into her grave. Where is she?"

"Faith, no. You're wrong."

"Wrong? I'm *wrong*? No, I'm not. Listen, you might be Anna's aunt, but don't talk to me about not *getting it.* You're the one who doesn't *get it.* You're lying to yourself with all this forgiveness crap. Tell Jane, or Sara, or whatever that whore is calling herself now that if I see her on the street, she'd better run."

"Faith!"

Faith smashed the doors open and ran outside.

"Faith! Wait!" Rachel chased after her. "Jane admitted she lied about your father. She followed the Twelve Steps. I was her sponsor. She made the whole affair up to try to get a lighter sentence for herself."

Faith spun around again. She felt like her head was about to explode. "That's a lie, too."

"Didn't the police tell you?" Rachel said.

"The cops? Jane didn't tell the cops. I don't believe it."

"Yes, she did. I went with her. I helped her get a lawyer first, just in case there was an issue with her plea deal."

"Why aren't the police looking for the real killers then?"

"They didn't believe her. They said because of her drinking and the car accident, she wasn't reliable now."

Faith's stomach heaved. *No, please, not again!* She ran over to the edge of the parking lot and doubled over, and the stomach cramps passed.

Rachel came up behind her, but Faith held up her hand. "Stop. Just stop."

"Faith, I'm sorry. I'm making it worse. I just—"

She was strong enough to run, so that's what she did. She didn't know where she was going, just that she had to get away.

Faith ran all the way across downtown. When she stepped inside Dr. Melding's office, soaked in sweat, she headed for the water cooler. Thankfully, Leesa, Dr. Melding's assistant, didn't comment on her appearance. Faith gulped down five little cups of water before crumpling the paper cup and dropping it in the trash.

Leesa glanced down at the phone and back up at Faith. "He's still on the phone. I'll let you know as soon as he's off."

Faith grabbed a handful of mints out of the bright-yellow bowl. She crunched down on the mints and dragged the pieces around her mouth with her tongue, trying to mask her breath.

Despite her tired legs, Faith paced while she waited. For once she was on time for something, and Dr. Melding was running late. That made her nervous. *Shrinks are never late. What's he doing?* And, more importantly, who was he talking to? She could make a pretty good guess.

When at last the door to his office opened, Faith went inside and flopped onto the soft tan chair as Dr. Melding walked over to his desk.

"Hello, Faith," Dr. Melding said, his back to her. He leaned over his desk and picked up his tablet. "I'm sorry to keep you waiting."

Sitting beneath the skylight, she felt like a bug under a microscope, her every motion about to be analyzed and assessed. She picked a bookshelf behind Dr. Melding and started counting books.

When Dr. Melding turned around, his expression seemed tense, tight, and his posture unnaturally straight and serious.

"So, you've been talking to my mom?"

"She's concerned."

Ha! I was right!

"We had a great talk. We went to breakfast and everything's fine."

Dr. Melding walked over to the other chair and sat. "Why don't you tell me what happened." He had that look Faith's doctors would get right before they tried to lock her up.

She didn't know where to begin. Her mother must have told Dr. Melding about the car and the break-in. Probably about her suspicions that Faith was drinking, too. Trying to hide anything would look bad, so she decided to put a positive spin on it instead. She tried to emphasize the good and downplay the bad of recent events. She took her time explaining her AA and survivors' group meetings, hoping to eat up as much of the session as possible.

Finally, Dr. Melding adjusted his glasses and said, "Faith, I'm recommending that we switch your medicine."

Faith groaned inwardly. She did *not* want to change meds. And it wasn't so much because she cared what drugs she put in her body, but because when changing meds, most doctors insisted on hospitalization so the patient could be "monitored in a controlled environment" and receive "specialized care." Faith knew that all Dr. Melding had to do was say the word and she was on the fast track to the mental hospital for a guaranteed thirty-day incarceration.

"My meds are working."

Dr. Melding shook his stylus. "Not effectively, it would seem. My only hesitation is the family history of Fabry disease, and I can't find any record of you being tested for it. Do you know who performed the test and when?"

"We were all tested for it right after Kim was diagnosed. It was with the family doctor. A little over ten years ago."

"Perfect. I'll have them send the results over." Dr. Melding smiled for the first time that morning. "And once we decide on the right meds, I'm going to recommend intensive in-patient therapy until we get you regulated. Besides, I think you could benefit from the daily structure."

Faith's reaction was swift and hostile—her middle finger shot out and she ripped off a couple choice swear words.

Dr. Melding took his glasses off. "Obviously, you're having coping issues. But with a change in your medication—"

"You can't change my medicine. I won't let you."

"I'm sure your mother—"

"Isn't me. And as far as coping issues, today's *the* day. You know that, right?"

"I'm aware that it's the anniversary of—"

"Were you aware that I came home this morning to find my apartment robbed?" Faith's hands gestured wildly as she spoke. "Seriously, Doc, give me a break. That happens today, *the* day, and I still manage to have breakfast with my mother, hit up an AA meeting, and make it on time to my appointment with you. But you say I have *coping issues*. Under the circumstances, I think I'm coping just fine. And you don't know the half of it." Faith leapt to her feet.

"If you'll sit down, we can discuss this."

"If I sit down and we talk, at the end of that conversation are you still sending me to the funny farm no matter what I say?"

Dr. Melding thought for a moment before nodding. "I hold to my earlier assessment. Yes."

Faith slammed the heels of her hands into the padded chair and shoved it over. The top of the chair missed the carpet and landed on the hard wood with a loud bang. She stuck her middle finger up again. "I hold to my earlier assessment of you, too. You're an—"

The door to Dr. Melding's office opened and his assistant peered in nervously.

"Everything's under control, Leesa," Dr. Melding reassured her.

"Sorry to bother you." Leesa started to close the door.

"No bother." Faith marched across the room and grabbed the door before it could shut.

"You know, your actions leave me no choice now, Faith," Dr. Melding said.

"Yeah, yeah, yeah. Oh, I almost forgot." She held up both middle fingers. "Thanks for telling my mother it would be a good idea to write a book about my life turning to crap, you friggin' genius. You made my life even worse."

She slammed the door behind her as she stormed out, sending the framed certificates and degrees clinking and tapping on the other side of the wall.

Faith stopped in front of a white, one-story ranch house with a lawn that looked like a golf course and saw Robert's customized Jeep parked in the driveway. A brick walkway was bordered by crocuses. The front door was deep red and flower boxes filled with bright gold, white, and purple flowers adorned each window. Robert's house made Faith wonder if his therapist had suggested working with flowers the way Dr. Rodgers had recommended counting for her. Either way, he certainly took pride in the lawn. She rang the doorbell and waited.

Robert answered the door in bare feet, wearing a T-shirt and jeans.

After she stormed out of Dr. Melding's office, she'd headed right here. Yet now that she was standing in front of Robert, she didn't really know why.

He looked up and down the empty street. "Oh, no. Did your car get stolen again?"

"No." Faith gave a slight chuckle. "The way my morning's going, though, I'd expect it to burst into flames. No . . . I just went out for a walk."

"I didn't expect you'd stop by. How do you know where I live?"

"You told me when you gave me a ride home. You said you lived on Whitlock and I saw your Jeep."

Robert stepped to the side. "Do you want to come in?"

"You're inviting me in, even after my epic tirade?"

"You were drunk."

"I still said things . . . " Faith twisted her ring. "I can remember some of what I said, and I know it was bad. So I'm pretty sure it was all bad. I'm sorry. That's it." She turned to go.

"You're just leaving?"

"Yeah. I'm going away for a while. I figured I should apologize before I bounce. Tell Nyah that I said thanks."

"Wait a second. Are you leaving right now? Like, leaving town? How?"

Faith turned back around to face him. "What do you mean, how?"

"Well," Robert rubbed the back of his neck, "that paper you had me sign, it's for a probation officer. I didn't think you could just take off if you were on probation."

Faith stared at him.

"Are you sure you want to make that decision today? It's the anniversary, right?"

"It *is*?" Sarcasm dripped off Faith's tongue, but she immediately regretted it. "Sorry. It's just. . . . I'm having a rough day."

"I'm sorry. I just meant that you really shouldn't make any big decisions today. Can leaving wait?"

"I kinda don't have a choice."

Robert's eyebrows rose. "I don't understand. Do you want to come in?"

Faith looked back at the road. She knew skipping town was stupid, but she wasn't going to go back to Brookdale—especially today.

"I have two different kinds of ramen," Robert boasted. "Chicken or shrimp. I also make a mean grilled cheese."

Faith sighed. "How can I refuse?"

Robert's house felt even smaller on the inside than it looked on the outside, but it was clean and bright. Tall windows in the front room let in lots of light and the walls were a cheerful yellow. He led Faith to the kitchen. "I put some tea on. Do you want some?"

Faith stopped in the kitchen doorway. "You drink tea?"

"I'm just trying it. I'm addicted to caffeine, so I'm trying to cut back on coffee."

He handed her a mug. Faith took one look at his and burst out laughing. Tags attached to four teabags hung over the edge of his cup. "Robert, you do know that some teas have a whole lot of caffeine, right? You must be wired."

"No way. No wonder I didn't sleep last night!" Robert laughed too. "I thought the tea was really weak, so I kinda upped the dose. Maybe I can offer you some water or . . . " His voice trailed off.

"Or what?" Faith asked.

"I was going to ask if you wanted some iced tea that I just made, but I won't tell you how many bags I put in."

Faith laughed again. "Water's fine." She sat down at the kitchen table and rubbed the side of her head. She still didn't have enough hair to twirl around her finger like she used to.

"Do you need some aspirin?"

"No, thanks. I think I'm well over my limit."

Robert took cheese and butter from the refrigerator and grabbed a loaf of bread from a cabinet.

"You were serious?" Faith said. "You don't really have to make me a grilled cheese sandwich."

"I was about to make myself one anyway. Sit back and relax."

"Should I have it tested for poison after what I said to you last night?"

Robert's smile vanished. "Seriously, forget about that. You were drunk, and . . . " He cleared his throat.

"And?"

"I was going to say in pain, but I don't want to tell you how you're feeling. But I did think about what you said."

Faith cringed. "I thought you said forget about that."

Robert pulled out a knife and started spreading butter on each slice of bread. "I meant the part about sharing. You said it was wrong for me to ask you to share and for me not to. You were right."

Faith rested her elbow on the table and her head in her hand. "I don't hear that very often."

"Well, you were. Are." He turned on the stove and put a pan on. "My incident happened five years ago."

Faith jumped in quickly. "Look, I'd be the world's biggest hypocrite if I didn't say that you don't have to tell me. I agree with you. I don't think you have to share. I think it's fine to keep it bottled up inside. I mean, come on, it's working wonders for me." She rolled her eyes.

"That's why I want to tell you." Faith didn't stop him this time. "I had just bought my girlfriend a ring."

"Like an engagement ring?"

Robert nodded. "You're sort of not supposed to interrupt when someone shares."

"Sorry. I just . . . " Faith closed her mouth.

"I was nervous about it, and I told the guy at the jewelry store what my plans were." Robert slid the sandwiches into the pan.

"Right down to the place and time that I was going to propose."

Faith started twisting her own ring. *This isn't going to end well.*

He picked up the spatula and his hand shook. "So, I drove out to this private spot with my girl. It was sunset and warm and just perfect. I was so nervous about asking her, I didn't hear them coming until it was too late. They wore masks. It turned out, the guy from the jewelry store told his brother, and they figured they'd get an easy score and steal the ring. One of them had a gun. I thought they just wanted the ring, but . . . after they tied me up . . . "

He lifted up the corner of one of the sandwiches and set it back in the pan. "I was begging them. I had never begged before. Not like that. They were laughing as they hurt her. I started screaming, and one of them broke my jaw."

Robert didn't say anything more until he took the sandwiches out of the pan. "Sorry. I think they're a little overdone."

Faith shook her head but didn't speak. She waited a second to make sure her voice didn't crack. "Did she live?"

Robert pulled up a chair and sat down. "Yeah. She, um . . . I don't blame her, but she couldn't really . . . It wasn't healthy for her to be around me. I reminded her of everything."

"So you left?"

"I would have waited for her, but she asked me to go. It's complicated. There's more. A lot more, but . . . "

Faith held up a hand. "I get it. You don't have to say anything else. Believe me, I get it."

They ate in silence. Faith racked her brain for something to say, and Robert seemed lost in his own thoughts.

"Do you want another sandwich?" he asked when she finished.

"No, I couldn't eat another bite. Thank you." She tried to put more into her voice than just an acknowledgment of the homemade sandwich.

When Robert took the plates to the sink, Faith stood up.

"I should go."

"Do you have to?" Robert stepped forward suddenly, then stopped. "I mean . . . are you okay?"

"I've got a lot going on. My therapist wants to change my meds and send me back to Brookdale." He didn't seem to recognize the name. "It's a mental hospital."

"I'm sorry," Robert said, and he looked like he meant it. "Do you want me to reach out to him? I don't know if it will do any good, but—you've been through a lot these last couple of days."

"No. But thanks for the offer. It won't do any good."

"Will you at least call Nyah?"

"I will," Faith lied.

"Do you need a ride somewhere?"

"No. I'm just going to walk home. Enjoy my freedom while I have it."

Robert followed her to the front door. "Listen. You can say no, but I'm just concerned about you. And if I need to call you . . . can I have your phone number?"

Faith looked down at her feet. There was something about Robert that seemed unpolluted by this world and everything that happened to him. Robert was *good*. Just the thought of being close to someone like that and fouling it up left a bitter taste in her mouth. And Faith would foul it up. No question about that. She was toxic.

She shook her head. "Thanks for the sandwich." She turned and strode down the walkway.

A s Faith pulled her duffel bag out of the closet, she couldn't believe how quickly she'd fallen apart. She hadn't made it on the outside for even a week. In only four days, she'd gone on two benders—the first within twenty-four hours—and had managed to squeeze in multiple run-ins with the law. Like one of those prisoners who gets paroled, can't handle it, and intentionally screws up to get thrown back in.

There was a knock at the door. Faith quickly shoved the duffel bag back in the closet and went to answer it.

Henry walked in without saying hello. She looked like she wanted to take Faith's head off her shoulders. She stomped around the table, put both hands down on it, and leaned forward.

"You're a human wrecking ball." The ligaments in her neck protruded. "I can't believe you got drunk *again*. And what's this?" Henry pulled one of Faith's "wanted" posters out of her pocket and tossed it on the table.

"I remembered what kind of car the guy was driving. You disappeared, so I went looking for him myself."

"Don't go there." Henry pushed off the table and started pacing around the small apartment. "You don't get to play the 'I'm all alone, no one's helping me' card. Do you have the slightest idea of the danger you're in, or how badly you've mangled prosecuting this case?" She stopped at the window and looked down at the street.

"You can't prosecute the guy unless you catch him," Faith snapped. "I think you're getting a little ahead of yourself worrying about a conviction. Unless—is he out in the car?" she added sarcastically.

"This isn't a joke, Faith. Your little 'wanted, dead or alive' poster put a bull's-eye on your back. Let me level with you, and I want you to really listen for once. I think you *did* see the rat-faced man. Yes, I do. And you know what that makes me? It makes me the only law enforcement agent in town who believes you."

Faith didn't know what to say, so she remained silent. But her heart rose at Henry's words. Never, not once, had she even had the glimmer that a cop really heard what she was saying— let alone believed her.

"But you know what else I think? I think Rat Face saw you, too. And now they're coming after you."

"They?"

"Rat Face and the man you saw at the cabin. They're a team." Henry shook her head. "You don't have a clue." She picked up a screw that was lying on the windowsill and rolled it between her thumb and forefinger. "A year ago, you saw Rat Face in Greenville Notch. Do you remember why you went there then?"

"Yeah. I went looking for Rat Face. A family that was camping in the state park out there was murdered. I thought the killings were similar to my family's."

"They were. And there've been more killings. At least six, and those are just the ones I can link."

Faith couldn't believe her ears. "What makes you think they're linked?"

"A number of factors. Remote location, one victim killed by self-inflicted gunshot wound, others by multiple stab wounds, trophy-taking—"

"Trophy-taking?"

"A lot of serial killers take trophies. An article of clothing, sometimes a tooth or even a finger. All of the victims in these cases were missing some item of jewelry."

Faith was confused. "My dad didn't wear jewelry."

"He wore a watch, yes?"

Faith nodded. Her father had worn a gold watch with an old leather band. Always, even when he went fishing. In fact, it had even had an inscription on the back, *Time for Fishin'*, or something like that.

"There was no watch found on his body. Perhaps it fell off or perhaps. . . " Henry shrugged. "Serial killers don't stop, Faith. They keep going until they're caught—or dead."

Faith looked into Henry's steely eyes, trying to read them. "You don't believe my father was the killer."

"I think your father was a victim."

Faith put her hands on the table and tried to control the tremors running up and down her legs. It had taken ten years to hear those words from someone in law enforcement, and now that she had, it felt like all the hate and frustration propping her up and fueling her rage had suddenly vanished.

Henry continued, "The local police's case was weak from the start. The strongest evidence was that the gun used belonged to your father. A man killing his mistress and then himself? Sure, happens more often than you'd think. But a man *also* killing his mistress's daughter—*and* his own daughter—simply for being in the wrong place at the wrong time? No. Never happens. Sara-Jane Bradley's testimony added to the suspected motive, but the police should have reopened the case after she confessed that she lied."

"But they didn't reopen the case. That's why I have to do something."

"What you *have* to do is stay out of it, Faith!" Henry stormed back over to the table. She took a deep breath and her voice softened. "Look. Let me do my job. I've been making progress, but your antics have put everything, including yourself, at risk. Do you know what perps do, nine times out of ten, when they feel the heat, when they think they're being looked at?" She waited for her words to sink in. "They skip town and disappear. And that's when they *think* they're being looked for. Thanks to your little wanted poster, these guys *know*."

"I just want to find them. I never thought they'd run from me."

"They might, they might not. Sometimes a cornered rat turns and fights. And right now, there are two things keeping them in Marshfield. The anniversary . . . and you. Freaks like this can't pass up a chance to relive their crimes. Like an athlete watching an old highlight reel of the game of his life, play by play, they want to feel those emotions again. That thrill is a powerful motivation for them to stay put—and so is tormenting you, Faith. Since you spotted Rat Face, they're after you. And enjoying it a great deal, I'd wager."

"Good," Faith said, trying to sound confident. "I'll play their game."

Henry slammed her hand down onto the table, making Faith jump. "This is not a *game*, Faith. They're playing with you, but once they get tired or we get too close, you're dead."

I'm already dead, Faith wanted to say. Instead she said, "Fine. What do you want me to do?"

Henry spoke in the calmest voice yet. "Let's go over a few things. First, the local PD think you're insane. Your car is stolen, but the police locate it around the corner from where you parked it. Then there's the incident in the elementary school hallway where no one else saw or heard anything, even though there were half a dozen people present. And now you claim your apartment was broken into but nothing was taken. Think that through. They broke in only to take a picture off your bed and set it up on this table?"

"I'm missing a knife, too."

"You think they took a knife? What kind of knife?"

"A steak knife. I accidentally left it on the stove and the handle melted. I looked everywhere but it's gone. I haven't told the cops about it yet."

"Maybe you threw it out?"

"I didn't. I know it sounds crazy," Faith admitted.

"Yes, it does."

Faith shifted uncomfortably under Henry's steely gaze. She felt like Henry was seeing right through her story and her, revealing her lie. Like she was in one of those airport scanners that see through your clothes.

"Do you think I'm crazy?"

Henry didn't answer that question. "When did you get a picture of your family? There were none here when I came before." She tapped the screw against the table.

"I got it from my grandmother's house. My mother's house now."

"Where did you put it?"

"In the closet."

Henry slowly rolled the screw between her thumb and forefinger. "Get it," she said. "And get whatever else you took from your mother's house, too."

Faith chewed her bottom lip. What had given her away? Henry was able to read her like a book. She went into the closet and came back with the photo.

Henry handed Faith the screw and took the photo. As Henry studied the picture, Faith looked down at the screw in her hand. Puzzled, she glanced at the air vent—and saw that it was missing a screw.

Henry smiled. "What did you hide in the air vent?"

"What?"

Henry crossed her arms. "Remember, one lie and I'm gone. What were you hiding?"

Faith exhaled. "I hid my father's gun there. It's gone now."

"So, they *did* steal something! I knew it. And that's why you couldn't tell Walker—it would violate your probation. Like I said, you're a human wrecking ball. Why did *you* want a gun?"

"I wanted to protect myself," Faith said quickly. "Someone's coming after me, and I wanted more options than hiding under a log. What was I supposed to do?"

"I'm not buying that," Henry said. "If you were scared, why didn't you ask for protective custody?"

"You just said the police think I'm crazy! No way would they give me protective custody when my only complaints were the car and a break-in where somebody moved my photograph. Besides, I'd rather fend for myself."

"You sure you didn't have another purpose in mind when you got that gun?"

"What are you asking?" Faith asked, although she knew the answer.

"I'm asking if I'm going to lose my only witness because she's going to take her own life."

Faith tried to stop herself, but she was slowly rocking back and forth. The pressure in her head was building and she felt like the dam was about to break.

"You're drinking again," Henry said. "Are you suicidal now, too? If you are, I have to report it."

"Go ahead!" Faith roared. "Dr. Melding is changing my medicine. That means I'm getting locked up again anyway."

Henry's gray eyes hardened. "You haven't answered the question."

Faith glared. "You don't have to worry about losing your crazy, unreliable witness. But just so we're clear, I've been wanting to eat a bullet since Kim died. There's not a day that goes by that I don't wish for that, pray for it. But I'm not going to off myself until I kill the bastards who killed Kim. Is that what you want to hear? Fine. I'm the girl who lived, and I'm gonna live until they *pay*. Now get out."

Henry stood her ground.

"I'm serious. My sponsor is coming to pick me up, and I need to get ready. Get out."

"You can't stay in Marshfield, Faith. You need to go back to Brookdale."

"But you just said I'm part of the reason they don't run. If you take me out of the equation, they could skip town. I'm not going to kill myself."

"I believe you." Henry's voice was actually soft now. "But I need time to sort everything out. I got an extension on the case. One more week. I'm running down a lead from Greenville Notch, but until I see if that pans out I need you to be somewhere safe. When will Dr. Melding send you back?"

Faith shrugged. "I would guess tomorrow."

"I think you should go."

"I think I don't have a choice."

"Do you have someone to be with tonight?" Henry asked.

"I'll be with my sponsor." *Such a useful lie.* "You can stop worrying."

"Okay then, one last thing. You can't involve the local PD anymore. Don't talk to any of them, including Officer Carson."

"Tommy? Why?"

"Because I think someone on the force could be involved."

"What?"

"That's all I can say for now. I'll be in touch."

Yeah, sure. When it's convenient for you.

Faith closed the door after her thoughtfully. So, she had an ally in law enforcement . . . and an enemy.

Faith was almost there. She knew exactly where she was going when she got in the car, but the truth didn't sink in until now—she was going to the cabin. And she'd known for a long time now that she'd make this trip. She just hadn't admitted it to herself.

Is this how animals feel? Like the swallows of Capistrano? She'd done a report on them in middle school. Like paper clips to a magnet, they were drawn back to the same spot, helpless in the grip of instinct, unable to go in any other direction.

Memories of many light-hearted car rides with Kim up to the cabin—especially the last one—flickered like the sun and trees outside her window. In the ten years since she'd been here, trees and foliage had grown up and died, but the forest looked the same. Lost in thought, she came to the turnoff to Reed Lake before she knew it. The car skidded as she cut the wheel, but she made the turn and the Camry jostled and bumped its way down the unpaved road.

At last the north parking lot came into view, and she was glad to see it was empty. She was afraid the tenth anniversary might attract vultures from the news, or some stupid kids. Faith drove as far away as possible from the spot where Kim had parked that night, and backed into a space. From under the passenger seat she pulled out a bottle of Pale Night whiskey. A liter. It was a split-second choice in the liquor store and that little voice in her head had freaked out the whole ride here, but it was too late to stop now.

She kept it in the bag as she opened it and drank straight from the bottle like an athlete chugging water after a run. It burned her throat, but knowing she was about to step into oblivion felt wonderful. As she took another long gulp, she knew that just as surely as she had been drawn to this place, she was going to finish off the bottle.

Faith glanced at the spot near the trailhead where Kim had parked that night. For the millionth time, she wished she could turn back time—prayed that she could go back and do something, anything, and prevent Kim's death. She could have thrown a tantrum when she saw Rat Face—insisted they turn around and go home. She could have suggested they call someone, convinced Kim to stay home in the first place . . .

Coulda, woulda, shoulda. Didn't.

She tipped the bottle back, ignored the burn, and let the whiskey flow. The spot of sunlight she was staring at slowly faded and turned to shadow. Faith looked around. The trees had grown much darker; the sun was setting.

It was time.

After another deep swig from the bottle, Faith opened the car door, stumbling sideways so hard her hand touched the gravel. The ground listed like a ship at sea as she straightened up, slammed the door closed, and crossed the parking lot like a condemned woman trudging to the gallows. The closer she got to the start of the path, the heavier her legs felt.

Kim had walked down this path. So had her father. So had Anna and her mother.

So had their killers.

Faith stopped. Unseen insects buzzed away in the woods. The air was warm. She shut her eyes and tried to remember what it was like to enjoy this place, but the memories collided and canceled each other out. It was like trying to imagine a car you loved that was later destroyed in a car crash: one second you're thinking of the wind on your face, and then suddenly you're at the part where your face smashes through the windshield. Faith's mind refused to hold onto the happy thoughts. This had been her favorite place on earth, her childhood sanctuary. Now it was a graveyard.

She fumbled with the cap on the bottle, took a long sip, wiped her mouth with her forearm, and started walking again, fueled by whiskey courage. The sky darkened as she took the last turn. The path dipped down and then back up again—and there it was.

The cabin was still standing. Faith hadn't known if it would be. Why her mother kept it was a mystery. She should have sold it. Faith had often hoped someone had burned it to the ground. But it looked . . . the same. She almost expected to see Anna's bike there.

A memory surfaced of Faith and her mother sitting on the steps, watching fireflies dance in the summer night. Faith closed her eyes and inhaled deeply, letting the peaceful vision embrace her. She swayed from the whiskey, took a step forward to balance herself, and another memory superimposed itself over the first—Kim, stumbling down the stairs, bleeding from her wounds, her cries ever weaker.

Faith looked down at her feet in the grass to confirm what her mind and heart already knew. She was now standing in the exact spot where she had stood that night. Consciously or unconsciously, this very spot had been her destination. It had always been her destination.

I should have died that night, right here. If I hadn't run . . .

Tears streamed down her face. If she still had the gun, she would do it now. Here. At this spot. She wouldn't back out, not here.

She closed her eyes and played out the scene in her head. Lifting the gun. The cold metal against her temple. The thin trigger against her finger. Half an inch of effort, and all her pain would end, and she could die and be with Kim.

Faith's hand went to her belt. It was leather. It would do.

She unbuckled it, but as she started to slide it out she noticed, through the cabin window, something move. It was just a brief flicker of motion, but she saw it.

Is someone inside the cabin?

This is not happening. Not today.

Her legs shook and her hands trembled as she fumbled to refasten her belt, not taking her eyes off the darkened window. Something moved again. Whatever it was caught the fading light, gleamed briefly, flickered. A mirror?

No, it moved.

She crept toward the door, staying low and looping around to avoid being seen from the window. When she reached the door, she leaned close to the rough wood and listened. All she heard was her heartbeat pounding in her ears and trees creaking in the breeze.

If someone's inside, wouldn't I hear them walking?

She tried to picture the inside of the cabin. She hadn't been inside that night, but she had seen pictures of the horrific aftermath. Those pictures had unleashed demons that tormented her to this day. She clutched her stomach. The grief was raw and real, but it paled in comparison to the anger that suddenly erupted inside her. There were probably some dumb kids in there playing Haunted House, making a game out of her family's tragedy, the brutal slaughter of four people.

That thought was the spark that set her off.

Faith grabbed the door handle and shoved her shoulder against the wood with all her might. To her surprise, the door was unlocked. It burst open, and she barreled inside.

The cabin was dark, but between the open door and window, there was enough light to see. The single room was empty and trash littered the floor.

She scanned the room, blinking sweat from her eyes. *I know I saw something. I'm not that crazy.*

Empty beer bottles sat on a table, and more trash. *Someone has been here. That could have been ages ago. There's clearly no one here now.*

A faint bump came from above. Faith looked up at the rafters. She found the source of the noise—and the movement. A single shiny, red-and-silver balloon with a short streamer gently bumped against a beam.

What the hell?

Faith walked closer to the table. What had looked like trash was actually an empty cupcake wrapper, a half-melted candle, and a kid's party horn—the kind with a paper tube that shoots out and makes noise.

Someone had a party here?

Faith had put up with the questions. Tolerated, albeit barely, the film crews that had descended on the fifth anniversary. But this was too much. Her right hand balled into a fist. Rage filled her mouth, blazed from her eyes, ran like liquid flames through her core.

Who would have a party in this cabin? What kind of monster . . .

She glared at herself in the old mirror that still hung on the wall. Her breath came in short puffs between clenched teeth. Her familiar face stared back at her, but all she saw was her father's eyes.

White-hot fury shot up her spine and through her head and she bellowed as she punched the image in the face.

Glass shattered, and half the mirror fell to the floor. Pain raced up her arm, but she struck again. Blood splattered the wall as more glass flew. The third strike knocked out the rest of the glass except a small sliver that twisted back and forth.

Even in that bloodstained shard, her father's eyes stared back at her.

She grabbed a chair and catapulted it into the mirror, knocking all the remaining pieces to the floor.

Panting, she looked down. Hundreds of reflections of her blood-spattered face stared back, eyes ablaze like blue stars. She staggered into the table. The beer bottles tipped over and rolled across the table and off the edge, popping glass and droplets of amber liquid into the air.

Who would celebrate this day? What sick bastard would have a party where four people were butchered?

Faith grabbed the last bottle, the only one standing, and prepared to smash it.

Her arm froze. Her fingers loosened, and she dropped the bottle at her feet, her whole body shaking. This bottle wasn't empty; it hadn't even been opened. And it was ice cold.

She rushed to the door and looked out frantically—though terrified of what she might see. There, down at the pond and walking her way, was someone with a flashlight. But as soon as Faith spotted him, his flashlight went out.

Like the Devil himself was behind her, Faith bolted out the door and raced back up the path toward the parking lot. The path dipped down and back up again, and just as the last light of the day slipped through the trees, she thought she saw, on the path ahead of her, the silhouette of a man, just one shade darker than the dusk.

This is not happening!

Her scream of horror caught in her throat and came out as a sick moan. Willing her whiskey legs to be strong, she darted into the dark woods and ran till her lungs burned and her vision blurred with stinging sweat. The branches scraped her face and tore at her clothes, but she didn't slow down.

A rocky outcrop rose up on her left and she raced toward it, scrambled over the rocks, and dropped down out of sight. One enormous rock had a split running straight up the middle, and Faith wedged herself into that cleft and kept her breath quiet. Her heart pounded and her chest heaved, but she forced herself to remain still.

A branch snapped nearby, echoing off the rocks like thunder. The booze had made her light-headed, and she'd give her right arm for water right now, but her thinking wasn't cloudy. Maybe she wasn't completely certain she'd seen a flicker in the window or a man on the path, but someone was definitely chasing her now. The sounds of twigs and leaves crunching beneath unseen feet were coming closer.

Are they looking for me? Is it Rat Face and the other man? Did they see me?

The beam of a flashlight danced across the branches and shone on the rocks where she hid.

Faith squeezed her eyes shut and clutched the rock. Seconds ticked by. She felt her lips moving and realized she was silently saying *Please, God*, over and over again. The twigs and leaves stopped crackling and rustling.

She risked opening one eye. The light was gone. A man called out, but too far away for her to understand the words. Her ears strained to hear, as the voice became fainter and faded away.

She stood up and fought back a sob. The woods were silent now. It was exactly like that night. Hiding. Afraid. Listening for them to come back and find her.

Are you hiding? Where are you? Woods? She remembered the man calling out to her that night. And singing. She felt cold fingers squeezing her heart as the melody ran through her head.

The terror of hiding in the same dark woods, chased by unknown men, running like a scared rabbit . . . All of it rushed back. She'd never been able to recall that night clearly. But now she wasn't remembering—she was *reliving it*. Even right after it happened, she hadn't remembered it this well. The old detective had been kind, but he'd insisted she walk him through every detail. Rat Face. Kim. Running through the woods. What the man said.

She'd tried to answer the detective's questions through her quivering sobs, while her blood- and mud-caked face swelled and throbbed. But now she knew something that the terrified little girl hadn't remembered right. Faith realized she'd heard the man's words, but she hadn't understood them.

He'd said, *Where are you, Woods?*

"He wasn't asking where I was," Faith whispered. "He was calling to Rat Face. Woods. Rat Face's name is Woods."

F aith stumbled out of the woods and onto the road just as a car approached and had to swerve around her. The horn blared and the driver shouted something, but she didn't hear the words and figured she wouldn't want to. She took her phone out and winced, noticing a deep slice in her knuckle and lots of blood. She kept her thumb pressed down on the phone's fingerprint sensor, but because of the blood, it didn't register. She licked her thumb and was about to try again when blue lights flashed behind her.

Faith stepped to the side of the road as a police cruiser skidded to a stop. She thought about running, but quickly dismissed the idea. The way she was still swaying, she wouldn't make it ten yards.

Tommy leapt out. "Hell, no," he muttered as he rushed over to her.

"I remembered something." Faith reached out for him, and Tommy grabbed her wrist.

"Do I need to call an ambulance? Did you slice your wrists?" Tommy turned her hands over and scanned her arms.

"No. I'm okay."

"You look like a damn horror movie." Panic made his voice even louder. "Is this blood from your hand?" Tommy's grip tightened. "Is this all *your* blood?"

Faith yanked her hand free. "I cut my hand. It's not that bad."

Tommy marched her over to the cruiser and showed Faith her reflection.

"Okay, that's . . . kinda scary." Faith wiped at her face but only succeeded in smearing the blood around.

"That was you coming out of the cabin?" Tommy asked.

"What? Did you follow me?" Faith took a step back, remembering Henry's warning about talking to police, even Tommy.

Tommy held onto her arm. "Was it you?" he demanded. "Look, I haven't called it in yet, but I'm going to have to. Did you trash the cabin and get blood all over it?"

"It was open." Faith shook her head. "Wait—that was you by the lake? Why did you turn off your flashlight? Why were you following me?"

"I turned off my light when I saw someone coming out of the cabin. And I wasn't following you." Tommy opened the back door of the cruiser. "Just get in. You're drunk."

Faith froze. "You're taking me in?"

"I should, but no. You just violated your probation twice over, so shut up and get in the car." He reached into the front seat and pulled out a box of tissues and a packet of wipes. "Try not to bleed all over the place."

Faith climbed into the back, and Tommy ran around to the driver seat. He shut the lights off, hit the gas, and grabbed his radio. "This is Car 23. Over."

"Car 23, go."

"I'm ten-seven for the next hour."

"Ten-four." The radio clicked off.

"What's a ten-seven?" Faith asked.

"I told them I'm going offline for an hour. Put pressure on your hand."

Faith pressed some tissues against the largest cut.

Tommy pulled out his phone. "Jay? I need a favor. Are you home? Great. Be there in five." He hung up.

"Who was that?"

"I can't take you to the hospital." Tommy pulled down the rearview mirror and frowned at her. "Use the wipes on your face before we get there, please." He angled the mirror so Faith could see herself.

Blood was smeared across her face the way soldiers apply camouflage. She tried her best to clean up her face.

"How did you get out here? Tell me you weren't driving," Tommy said.

"I didn't drink and drive. I drank in the parking lot. My car's still there." Faith wrinkled her nose. "You were at the lake? How come I didn't see your car?"

"I parked in the south lot."

"But it takes twice as long to get to the cabin from there," Faith said. "Why would you park there?"

Tommy took a right onto a side street. He looked back once and then stared straight ahead. "Because I didn't want to walk the same way Kim did."

They drove in silence the rest of the way. Tommy pulled into the driveway of a duplex and parked next to a pickup truck. As he was letting Faith out of the car, a man about Tommy's age opened the front door of the house and rushed out.

"Is she okay? What's her status?" he asked.

"She sliced a knuckle open. I think she needs stitches, Jay."

When Jay got close to Faith, he made a face. "She's drunk."

"I know," Tommy replied.

Jay turned Faith's hand over. She pulled the tissues away so he could inspect the wound on her knuckle. "She needs stitches for that one, for sure," he said. "So the question is, why aren't you taking her to the hospital?"

"*She* is right here," Faith said, pointing at herself. "You don't have to talk about me in third person."

"Shut up, Faith," Tommy said.

Jay's eyes widened. The two men stared at each other for almost a full minute before Jay spoke. "Bring her in." He turned and marched toward the front door.

Faith stood her ground, pressing the soaked tissues harder against her hand. She needed help, but Henry's warning made her think twice about going into an unknown house with two men.

A woman carrying a toddler on her hip came to the doorway. She took one look at Faith and Tommy, then glared at Jay. "Why not the hospital, Jay?" she asked.

Jay whispered something in her ear.

"At least tell me why it has to be my kitchen?"

"The light is best in there. Look, I knew her sister. I owe Kim this."

The little boy laid his head against his mother's chest and gave Faith a small wave. Faith smiled but didn't wave back. She didn't want the boy to see her bloody hands.

Jay's wife and son disappeared into the house without another word.

Faith followed Tommy and Jay down a narrow hallway and into the kitchen. Jay gestured to them to sit at the round table in the corner, which had two chairs, a booster seat, and two high chairs, and Faith and Tommy watched while he put clean dish towels on the table and started setting out medical supplies.

"Are you a doctor?" Faith asked.

"EMT."

"I have to go clean up my cruiser," Tommy said. "Just in case."

Jay nodded, and Tommy hurried out of the kitchen.

"He hates blood," Jay said. "How much have you had to drink?"

"A little over a pint, so I should be good."

Jay shook his head. "That just means you're going to bleed a lot."

"At least I won't feel it."

Jay shook his head again. "You will." He started to clean her hand. "What did you punch? Was it someone's mouth?"

"No."

"Don't lie. You can get bacteria that can kill you from broken teeth."

"It was a mirror."

Jay frowned. "You really should be going to the hospital."

"I can't."

Faith gritted her teeth as Jay cleaned out the wound. He was right. It hurt like hell.

Jay held her hand up to the light, and a shard of mirror flashed. He grabbed a pair of tweezers and deftly removed it.

"Look. As far as I know, you fell in your kitchen. I'm giving you temporary stitches and telling you to go to the hospital."

"I'll still need to go to the hospital?" Faith asked, confused.

Jay rolled his eyes. "That's the story we're going with to cover my ass. I shouldn't be doing this, but Kim was my friend. I have a family to watch out for, so stick to the story, okay?"

Faith nodded. "I will. Thank you."

Jay exhaled and picked up a needle. "You won't be using this hand for at least a week. If you do, you'll pull the stitches right out. I'd give it two weeks to be sure."

"I appreciate it. If I could do something for you . . . "

"Make a fist with your left hand," Jay instructed.

She did, and Jay began stitching her right hand up. The needle hurt worse than the mirror. Each time he punctured the skin she winced.

"And yes, you can do me a favor." Jay kept his focus on her hand as he talked. "Tommy's never gotten over your sister. Do you know that he wears her engagement ring on a chain around his neck? I know it eats him up seeing you screwed up."

Faith grimaced but didn't know how to respond.

"Every time you ask Tommy to do something, I keep worrying you're going to jack him up at work. He's a rookie cop, and he keeps butting heads with the chief for you. Since you've been back, he's been skating on thin ice. First, he asks all his friends and cops to look for a car that can't be found. Then he gets everyone looking for your car, and it turns out you just forgot where you parked it."

"It was stolen," Faith snarled.

Jay pulled the cut tight. "Even the other cops are turning on Tommy. Not just the chief. I don't know what you did tonight, and I don't want to know, but if you really want to do me a favor, leave Tommy out of it. He became a cop because of what happened to Kim. You're going to ruin the one thing he's got left. If you do that, you'll be killing him. Understand?" He locked eyes with her and didn't drop his gaze until she acknowledged with a nod.

His touch was firm but gentle as he gave her hand a final inspection. "Okay. I just need to wrap it up." Five minutes later, her hand was encased in a bulky ball of gauze covered with an

Ace bandage. Jay threw his gloves in the trash and washed his hands. "You're going to need to keep it dry for forty-eight hours. Then you change that bandage." He came back to the table with tape, a roll of gauze, and an Ace bandage in a bag, and handed it to her.

"Thanks." Faith sat back in the chair. "Wait a second. Are you the friend Tommy said he was going out with that night?"

Jay nodded. She obviously didn't need to tell him what she meant by *that night*.

"Kim didn't believe Tommy went out with you," Faith said. "He'd been lying to her. He said he went with his father the weekend before, but his father was out of town."

"Tommy never told you?"

"Told me what?"

"Tommy wasn't with me that night. He was working. He got a job as an on-call operator on third shift."

"Why wouldn't he tell Kim that?"

"Because he was saving up to buy her that engagement ring."

***

Faith sat silently in the back of the cruiser as Tommy drove her back to her apartment. She watched him in the rearview mirror, saw the lines around his eyes. He looked older than his years. Not tired or sleepy, but actually ground up by life.

I was wrong about him.

Tommy glanced back at her. "We can get your car tomorrow. I still can't let you drive."

"Thanks . . . for watching out for me."

"You have to knock it off, Faith. Drinking's going to kill you. I'm just glad I found you and not another cop."

"If you weren't following me, then why were you at the cabin?"

Tommy stared straight ahead. "I leave flowers there every year."

"Every year?"

Tommy nodded. "I miss her."

Faith looked down at her hands. Fresh tears fell on her bandage.

"What was it that you remembered?" Tommy asked.

"What?"

"When I found you, you said you remembered something."

Woods.

Faith sat forward on the edge of the seat and looked at Tommy. She suddenly remembered a day, a long time ago, when he and Kim took her to the town fair. All they did that day was laugh. She'd loved Tommy like a big brother back then.

Jay's words echoed. *Leave Tommy out of it. He's skating on thin ice.* She shook her head and pushed back in the seat.

"Nothing. I just got confused. Sorry."

"I'm sorry I scared you. I saw you at the cabin and then you ran. As a cop, when someone sees me and runs, I figure it means they're doing something wrong."

"You scared the absolute crap outta me! Why didn't you identify yourself?"

"I did. But not at first, I guess. Look, seeing you there freaked me out, okay? When you came out of the cabin, I thought . . . " Tommy cleared his throat. "I thought you were Kim. You looked just like her."

Faith didn't know what to say. *I guess I'm not the only one who's gone crazy.*

"Did you go out to the cabin with that guy from your survivors' group?" Tommy asked.

"Robert? No."

"Okay, good. Something about the guy bothers me. So, shouldn't we go find your friends and give them a ride home? Were they drinking, too?"

"Huh?" Faith said, confused. "I went out there alone."

"Don't lie to me, Faith. After you bolted into the woods, I saw your two friends waiting for you up ahead on the path. They made a run for it toward the parking lot. After I lost you, I backtracked toward the lot, but they were gone by the time I got there. Did they have a separate car?"

Faith's skin grew cold. *Two* men?

It was them.

It was *them* on that same gravel path with her, in the same woods. On the same night of the year. It was *them*. She was certain of it.

"Tommy, pull over. I think I'm going to be sick."

A s he walked through the front doors of Murray's Wine and Spirits, Jeffrey checked how much cash he had in his pocket. Not enough for whiskey. He headed for the cheap beer in the back, grabbed a six-pack, and took it to the front counter.

"You just made it." Behind the counter, the clerk smiled cheerfully. "You get everything you need, buddy?"

"Yeah," Jeffrey mumbled.

The clerk rang up his purchase but didn't press enter. "I forgot to check your ID."

Jeffrey scowled. There was something about the way the clerk was looking at him that bothered him. "I forgot it. I've been in here a hundred times. You've never asked for it before."

The clerk cleared his throat. "Maybe you left it out in your car. You drive an old Crown Vic, right? I was thinking about getting one at auction. How much did yours cost?"

The question brought Jeffrey up short. He looked down at the floor and shook his head. "You're thinking of the wrong guy.

I drive a pickup. I'll come back with my license." He headed for the door.

"We're closing in, like, two minutes," the clerk shouted after him.

As Jeffrey drove his truck out of the lot, he pulled out his phone and punched in a number. His hands were shaking. "You gotta do something," he said as soon as the call went through.

"Jeff." The voice on the other end was calm. "I told you I'm taking care of things. Some things take time."

"It's taking too long." Jeffrey powered down his window. When the wind whistled in, he recognized his mistake, but it was too late.

"You didn't leave your house, did you, Jeff?"

"I . . . uh, I had to. I needed something to drink."

There was a long sigh. "Jeff, Jeff, Jeff. I *just* had drinks with you."

Jeffrey ran his hand over his sweaty forehead. "I wanted some whiskey."

"Now I'm hurt. I go to all the trouble of setting up an anniversary party, and you tell me beer isn't good enough for you?"

"No, no, it was fine. The party was good, until it got interrupted." Jeffrey rolled to a stop at a red light.

"Is it my fault you ditched the rest of the beer in the woods?"

"That cop was chasing us. I had to lighten the load."

"No, he wasn't. See, there you go again, reading too much into the situation. He was chasing the girl. And you know, Jeff, I would have gone and gotten you some whiskey. All you had to do was call."

"I'm sorry. I'm sorry, okay? I'm going out of my mind stuck in that house all the time."

The man laughed. "Calm down. I'm just busting on you, man."

"Can't we stop playing around with this chick? She's gonna get us arrested."

"I'm not ready to stop playing yet. She's just fighting back a little, that's all. She's kicking and scratching. And I like it."

"But the guy at the liquor store was asking if I drove a Crown Vic. I think she talked to him. She ain't playin'—she's *looking* for me."

"Like I said, it's all part of the game. Which she's gonna lose. She doesn't even know it's not just us. How can she beat us if she doesn't even know who all the players are?"

"Let's just kill her and move on."

"What fun would just killing her be? Don't ask me again." The man's voice was sharp now. "Did the guy asking questions at the store follow you or see your truck?"

"No," Jeffrey lied. He had parked at the side of the building, but he had no way of knowing if the clerk had seen his truck or not.

"Then go home and let me handle this."

"Okay. I'm pulling into my driveway now."

"One more thing. What was the name of the shrink they made you see—you know, after you killed those cats?"

Jeffrey huffed loudly into the phone.

"Don't go crying over spilled milk just because you got blamed." The man laughed. "Get it?"

"Whatever." Jeffrey pulled into his driveway and shut off the car. That was the day all this started—with the cats.

"What was his name?" the man repeated.

"Meldern? Melding? Something like that. His office was over on Heritage Street. Why?"

"No reason."

"Seriously. Why are you asking about my old shrink?"

"Do you know what killed those cats, Jeff?" The man started humming the *Jeopardy!* theme song.

The tune made Jeffrey break out in a sweat. "You did. With a knife."

The man made a loud noise like a game show buzzer. "WRONG! The correct answer is . . . 'What is curiosity?'" The man laughed. "Don't feel bad. You would have been wrong anyway because you didn't phrase your answer in the form of a question."

Jeffrey was breathing heavily now.

"Oh, there you go getting all worked up again, Jeff. You *have* to lighten up. If you really want to know the truth, I'm looking for a new therapist. The lady I'm seeing now is just not working out for me. I hate to say it, but I think I'm a complete psychopath, and she doesn't even have a clue."

Friday, April 13

The front door of Tommy's apartment closed with a click, and Faith sat straight up on the couch, blinking herself awake. Her hand throbbed, her head pounded, and her stomach felt like she'd been in a sit-up contest and lost. Rubbing her eyes with her left hand, she glanced around the little apartment. It was almost as small as her own, though at least Tommy's apartment had a bedroom. Besides the comfortable couch, the biggest thing in it was the TV. The place was a mess, too—a real bachelor pad. The coffee table in front of her was covered in papers, magazines, and several soda cans. Her purse and keys had been placed on top of a pizza box, along with a note:

Your car is out front. Leave it here if you want. There's a breakfast sandwich and an iced coffee in the fridge for you. I'll call you after my shift.
Tommy

Faith closed her eyes. Tommy must have gotten a friend to go with him and bring back her car. Another favor she owed him for. As she set down the note, she saw something was written on the other side. She flipped it over.

P.S. Happy Birthday.

"Happy birthday?" Faith muttered. *Ha.*

She hadn't had a happy birthday since she was twelve, and hadn't even considered having a birthday party since then. What was there to celebrate? Another day of being alive? *Woo-hoo.*

Her stomach churning, she walked to the kitchen area, grabbed a glass from the cabinet with her left hand, then had to set it down to open the refrigerator. *Using one hand is going to take some getting used to.*

Tommy should have written that there was *only* a breakfast sandwich and iced coffee in the fridge. Well, that plus a half-gallon of milk and a bottle of ketchup. Tommy clearly wasn't dating anyone—that made Faith feel even worse. She knew that Tommy's parents had moved away a while back, which meant Tommy was very much alone.

Her stomach wasn't ready for coffee or a sandwich yet, so she poured a glass of milk to quiet her rumbling belly. The booze was wreaking havoc on her insides. She chugged three gulps of the milk before realizing it had gone bad. Clamping a hand on her mouth, she raced for the bathroom, but the first door she opened led to a closet. She gagged again, ran into Tommy's bedroom, and saw another open door and a bathroom. As she dashed through Tommy's messy bedroom, she knew she wouldn't make it to the toilet. She practically dove into the little bathroom and threw up in the sink. Repeatedly.

When she was convinced she was done, she cleaned up the basin and looked in the mirror.

Much worse than she had feared. *I need to take a shower and change. If they come to take me to Brookdale and find me looking like this, they'll put me under suicide watch for sure.* Dried blood matted her hair and was clumped along her jaw. Dark circles rimmed both eyes. Even the bright blue of the irises seemed to have darkened, as if storm clouds had passed over them. She didn't look anything like her father now—or herself, for that matter. *How do ya like my makeover?*

She washed her face the best she could with one hand, and dried off with a towel. She considered showering here, but without new clothes, what was the point? She'd have to go back to her apartment.

Faith stepped out of the bathroom and stopped dead in her tracks. She'd never seen anything like this except in the movies, either when the police or FBI were working a case, or in the darkened home of some obsessed psycho killer. In her haste to run to Tommy's bathroom, she hadn't seen the complex mosaic of pictures, papers, and notes that he had spread across one whole wall, with red strings connecting the various pieces.

There were photos of the cabin at Reed Lake, of the parking lot, the beach, and Faith's old house. One of the flyers Faith had made was there, too—pinned right next to the actual police sketch of the rat-faced man.

Her stomach threatened another insurrection. Tommy had been searching for Kim's killer, too, all this time. Faith squeezed her eyes shut. He must have been in so much pain. He had loved Kim—intended to marry her—but she'd been ripped away from him, just like she had been ripped away from Faith. That must have destroyed him.

And he was still pursuing her killer.

Faith hurried out to the living room and grabbed her purse. She'd been wrong not to trust Tommy. If Henry was too busy to help her, Tommy would. Tommy could search through the police database for Woods.

As she took out her phone, a piece of paper poking out from underneath the pizza box caught her attention. The red lettering at the top read *NOTICE OF REPRIMAND.*

Faith picked up the paper and sat down on the couch to read it. Tommy was being investigated by Internal Affairs. He was accused of looking up vehicle registrations belonging to early-model Crown Victoria sedans, and he had refused to provide a reason for his search without speaking with a representative first. A disciplinary hearing was scheduled for next week.

Jay's words haunted her: *Leave Tommy out of it. You're going to ruin the one thing he's got left. If you do that, you'll be killing him.*

30

etective Lionel Walker pulled up to find two patrol cars, a fire truck, an ambulance, and an unmarked detective's car already parked haphazardly in front of the large white colonial that had been converted into office space years ago.

As Lionel got out of his car, a man about his age, in a dark-brown suit, walked over from the ambulance—Frank Higgins, the night detective. Marshfield only had two detectives, so Lionel and Frank had to decide who would take which shift. Luckily for Lionel, Frank had actually chosen the evening shift.

Frank was a short man with a fondness for sweets, which was evident in his growing stomach. His dark skin made the streaks of gray in his hair even brighter, but that gray was his only sign of age. He was energetic, a fast walker, and an even faster talker. Maybe it was all the sweets.

"It's a mess inside." Frank stroked his throat and grimaced. "The doctor's assistant found him when she opened the office this morning. The victim's office is on the bottom floor. A doctor, Alex Melding. Shrink. He's got a partner."

"Beverly Winters."

Frank nodded and took out a small bag of candy and offered one to Lionel, which Lionel declined. Frank popped a couple into his mouth. "Yep. And with her name attached to this, you know Chief Dennis is going to be all over it."

"What did you get out of the assistant?"

"Nothing. Her name's Leesa Boyd, but I only know that much because I was told by a guy at the dentist's office. The poor girl is absolutely hysterical. The EMTs have her on oxygen, and she's still hyperventilated twice since I've been here."

"Have you talked to anyone else?"

"There was no one else to talk to. I've got a call in to Beverly Winters to have her come out here."

Lionel scratched his jaw. "I wish you'd called me about that first, Frank."

Frank shrugged. "Standard procedure, Lionel. I can't do her any favors."

"I'm not asking for any. But if Beverly Winters is linked to this—now, of all times—and the press gets ahold of it, this whole place is going to go crazy. Reporters are already running around spouting decade-old gossip and theories. You add murder to the mix, it's only gonna fuel the flames. Let's lock it down before that has a chance to happen."

They stopped outside the doctor's waiting room so Lionel could slip a pair of surgical shoe covers over his well-worn shoes. "How long has the crime scene unit been here?" he asked.

"A little over an hour. They already processed the waiting room. I tried to call you several times."

"My phone was off." They passed through the waiting area, and Lionel looked into the office, where a photographer was taking pictures. Lionel gave a low whistle.

"The crime seems to have been confined to the office," Frank said. "It doesn't look like the good doc put up much of a fight. No defensive wounds on his hands."

The doctor may not have fought back, but that didn't make the attack any less violent. Blood was everywhere. The doctor's legs were under his desk, and his body was twisted at an odd angle.

"Looks like whoever did this really didn't like the doctor," Frank said. "This is total overkill. I counted at least two dozen knife wounds."

"Where's the ME?" Lionel asked.

"En route from Weymouth. He should be here shortly. But I want to show you something."

Frank stepped into the room while Lionel remained in the doorway. The last thing he wanted to do was step on something before it was documented. He'd worked hundreds of crime scenes in his almost twenty years on the force, but this was only his second murder scene. The first was Reed Lake. He had a feeling this one was going to be a bigger circus than the first.

Frank squatted and pointed. "We've got a partial bloody footprint just off the carpet on the hardwood. Hank already sent it to the 3-D boys. It's smudged, but I think we can use it."

"What size is it?" Lionel asked, peering at the delicate print.

"It's small. I'm just guessing, but I'd say a woman's running shoe. It's a real narrow print. We've already ruled out the assistant. She wears heels every day."

Lionel exhaled and looked over at the victim. "The timing of this is going to be a huge issue."

Frank shrugged and popped another candy into his mouth. "We won't know anything definitively until the ME does her thing. Right now, we can only estimate sometime after eight last night."

Lionel stared at the body. "I meant the date, Frank. Yesterday was the tenth anniversary of the Reed Lake killings. I can see the copycat headlines now."

"Do you think it's connected? You worked that scene—you see similarities?"

Lionel shuddered. He wished he could forget those killings. Especially the poor girl. "The excessive knife wounds. The amount of blood splatter . . . What was he doing here so late?" He scanned the blood-smeared desk.

Frank cocked an eyebrow. "That's one of the questions I have for Beverly. The dentist in the next office said that Dr. Melding worked late a lot."

"Maybe he was doing paperwork," Lionel said, half to himself. He put his hands on his belt, pulling back his jacket and revealing his gun and a new holster.

"You're really carrying that around with you?" Frank pointed at Lionel's Taser.

"You better start carrying yours. The chief wants everyone carrying nonlethal and—" A flash from the photographer's camera cut off his thoughts. When the light flashed, something on the doctor's neck sparkled. Lionel turned to the photographer. "Hank, take the same picture you just did. I saw something because of your flash. Use the same angle."

The camera flashed again and Lionel moved closer to the body on the floor. "Did you see something in his throat?" He pointed. "Watch when the flash goes off. Take it again, Hank."

The photographer clicked again.

"I saw something, too." Frank knelt down and peered at the doctor's neck. "Well, isn't that the damnedest thing . . ."

"What is it?" Lionel asked.

"There's only the end of it sticking out, but I think it's one of those things you tap on the screen of those tablet thingies."

Frank snapped his fingers. "A stylus. Someone stuck a stylus in this guy's throat."

31

Faith's only hope of staying out of Brookdale now was to beg her mother. She'd sworn she'd never do that, but she had no choice. She needed to find Rat Face before he found her—and to do that, she had to be on the outside. So, right now, she had to get out of her bloody clothes, clean up, and get to her appointment with her probation officer. If she was to have any chance of convincing her mother that she didn't need to change her meds or go back to Brookdale, she had to prove she was doing everything right.

She parked in front of her apartment and turned the engine off, but didn't get out. She was shaking. Was it safe to go upstairs? She wanted to tell Henry she had found out about Woods and the Crown Vic, but she couldn't find Henry's number on her phone. There wasn't time anyway. Henry had said she would get in touch with her, and she believed her.

Her reflection appeared as the phone screen blackened. She still looked rough, but . . . there was something different. Was it something in her eyes, or the way she held her head up? Faith got out of the car. "I can do this," she muttered as she marched for the stairway. She took the steps two at a time, but when she turned the corner to the balcony that led to her apartment, she stopped cold.

Cowering in front of her apartment door was Sara-Jane Bradley. She held out a small basket covered in napkins. "Ninth step, ninth step," she said, like some kind of mantra. Her whole body trembled.

As Faith stalked forward, matted blood in her hair, murder in her eyes, and fully intending to toss this woman off the balcony, Sara-Jane recoiled. Her lips moved again, but no sound came out. She slid down the door and held the basket above her head, like a lowly peasant making an offering to her queen.

Faith's anger waned at the pitiful sight. Besides, she needed to hear the truth from her. She reached over Sara-Jane, unlocked the door, and opened it. "In," she said.

Sara-Jane's eyes widened. And then the last person Faith thought she would ever let into her apartment walked inside.

"I'm so sorry," Sara-Jane said softly.

"Sit down. Talk." Faith grabbed the stool and pointed to the chair.

Sara-Jane set the napkin-covered basket down on the table and sat down, then took a folded piece of paper from her pocket and handed it to her.

Faith tossed it onto the table. "No. Say it to my face."

Sara-Jane looked like she was about to burst into tears. "I should have brought my sponsor. Please don't hurt me." She lifted a thin arm. It shook. Faith could see a bandage where she'd recently had blood taken. Beneath it was a dark bruise.

Faith rose from the table, filled a glass of water, and handed it to her. "I talked to Rachel. She was my friend's aunt. She's the only reason I'm doing this. Talk."

Sara-Jane nodded. "Sorry, this is probably a really bad time with your hand like that and all."

"Talk. Just talk already."

"I lied. Your father—"

Faith shook her head. "Start at the beginning."

Sara-Jane looked down at the paper. "I wrote it down."

"I said I want to hear it from your own mouth."

The truth was, Faith already knew the story of the "Marshfield Madam." Everyone did. If it weren't for Faith herself surviving Reed Lake, Sara-Jane Bradley would have been Marshfield's most infamous resident. And someone had written a book about her, too. A book Faith had read.

It detailed how Sara-Jane had gone from being a prim and proper housewife to the founder of a call girl service. What made that service even more salacious was its name: Soccer Moms. On paper, Soccer Moms was a nonprofit booster club, providing local teams with equipment. They even started a preschool soccer program in town. Sara-Jane herself was a fixture on the soccer fields and at other public events, working the crowds and fund-raising. But that was all a front.

Behind the scenes, Sara-Jane was networking with the other moms—the pretty ones whom she'd known for years, the ones she trusted. She hired them as call girls, enticing them with flexible "mothers' hours" and the opportunity to earn big cash under the table. All they had to do was show up looking great, entertain, and have some fun—all while their kids were at school and their husbands were at work. It was an ingenious system: the moms' hours matched perfectly with the nine-to-five hours of the johns, and the pretty suburban housewives could show up at lunchtime in the city in broad daylight. Business boomed . . . until one of the girls found a conscience and dropped a dime on Sara-Jane.

"Talk," Faith repeated.

"Did you read that book about me?" She twisted a napkin in her fingers as she spoke.

Faith nodded.

"Well, it's all true, pretty much. I sold myself so I could have nice things." She held up her thin arms. "I was drinking a lot and incredibly selfish back then. I didn't think about who got hurt, not even when I got arrested. After that, I was just thinking about how I could stay out of jail. Me, me, me. It wasn't until the accident and I met Rachel that I changed."

"There's no accident in your book."

Sara-Jane took a jagged breath. "The book stops at the trial. I spent two years in prison. My husband left me and I had no money, so I moved in with my mom. I should've picked someplace much farther away to live, but . . . with no money, I didn't have much choice. It was live with my mom, or nothing."

Faith knew how that felt. But what Sara-Jane told her next was a surprise. "Anyway, a couple weeks after I moved back there, someone ran me over—on purpose."

"They hit you with a car?"

"Twice. Well, three times actually. They ran me over, then kinda backed up and pulled forward again. Rachel came to visit me in the hospital and rehab center. She's really nice. I started working my program in rehab. After that my mom passed, but the Hansons let me stay at the church. I try to help out there and it makes it easy for me to keep working my program."

Faith stared hard at her. "Why did you put my father on your list?"

"I'm sorry I hurt you."

"You have no idea."

"I read your mother's book, too."

Faith forced herself to look away. She was afraid she'd do something she'd regret. "That book doesn't begin to describe anything about me."

"I'm truly sorry, Faith."

Faith had expected Sara-Jane to say something about her own book, or her own pain. This simple apology caught her off-guard. It stripped away her anger—but that only made the wounds beneath it smolder.

"Why did you put my father on your list?" she repeated.

Sara-Jane put her hands in her lap. "You know they offered me a reduced sentence in exchange for my client list. So, I gave it to them. But then they said they were rethinking the deal. I'd be looking at fifteen years. I couldn't do that. I had two kids. So when these two detectives came in, Griffin and Walker, and started asking me about your father . . . I saw a way out. They kept asking and asking, and I knew it was valuable to them. So I lied. I'm sorry. I am so very sorry." She started to sob. Her shoulders trembled. "I'm a vile human being."

Faith's phone beeped a reminder signal. She had to leave for the probation office in fifteen minutes, and she still needed to take a shower.

"When did you tell the cops you lied?" she asked.

Sara-Jane's chin now rested on her hand, which was serving as a kickstand for her wobbly head. She looked exhausted. "Two, two and a half years ago."

"Who specifically did you tell?"

"Walker. He's the chubby one with the curly hair, right?"

Faith nodded. "And what did he do with the information?"

Sara-Jane sat back and her eyebrows knitted together. "Nothing, I guess."

Faith stood up. "You gotta go."

To her surprise, Sara-Jane didn't bolt. She remained sitting. "I'm sorry." She pushed the basket closer to Faith and pulled back the napkins. It was filled with cookies and muffins. "Do you forgive me?"

"Why didn't you apologize to my mother?"

Sara-Jane's hands shook. "I did. I wrote her a note. I tried to give it to her, but she wouldn't take it. She wouldn't talk to me."

"Can you blame her?"

"No," Sara-Jane said quietly.

A thought popped into Faith's head, and she asked the question before thinking it through. "Did they ever catch who ran you over?"

Sara-Jane looked down. "No. I figured it was someone whose marriage I destroyed. You wouldn't believe how many people would have motive. And I . . . I kinda deserved it." Sara-Jane got up and went to the door. "But I like to think that your mother did read my letter."

"I thought she didn't take it."

"She didn't." Sara-Jane smiled. "But your stepfather did. He's a nice man. He said he'd give it to her."

On the way to the courthouse, Faith frantically looked through her call logs, trying to find Henry's number. She knew Henry was following up a lead in Greenville Notch, but her silence caused Faith's anger to boil—along with her fear.

She hurried through the marble corridors of the courthouse toward the basement, nervously eyeing every policeman she passed. Henry thought the police might be involved, but was Henry the one who was now in danger? She needed to tell Henry that Woods had moved back to town.

"Sorry I'm late." Faith flopped down in the chair in Barbara's office, then gasped.

A woman she'd never seen before sat at Barbara's desk. Her blond hair was teased and sprayed into a neat hair helmet. It looked a bit like cotton candy, but there was nothing sweet about this woman. She cast an annoyed glare over her glasses at Faith and frowned, the corners of her mouth pulling her entire face into a grumpy scowl.

"Where's Barbara?" Faith asked.

"Mrs. Finney is out of state on a personal matter. I'll be handling your appointment today. I'm Mrs. Torres."

Faith winced. She didn't have her paperwork. She had been hoping to sweet-talk Barbara, but this woman looked as approachable as a viper.

"Let me pull up your file. You are . . . ?" Mrs. Torres spun around in her chair to face the computer.

"Faith Winters."

Mrs. Torres didn't react to the name, which told Faith she wasn't from Marshfield.

Mrs. Torres typed in Faith's name, and her file filled the screen, including her mug shot.

"Does that system have everyone in town?" Faith asked.

"Only if you have a criminal record," Mrs. Torres said smugly. "Do you have your paperwork?"

Faith stared at the computer screen. She didn't need Henry to call her back. She didn't need Tommy to risk his career. The answer to the question that had haunted her for ten years was on that machine. All she had to do was search for a man named Woods and look through the pictures and she would find him. She just needed a way to get Mrs. Torres out of the room.

"Do you have your paperwork?" Mrs. Torres repeated.

"I . . . I must have left it in the car," Faith lied. "I'll run and get it."

"I don't have all day, young lady."

"Five minutes." Faith held up her hand. "My car is right out back. Thank you."

Faith hurried out of the office and down the hall. But as soon as she had turned the corner, she stopped to think.

I could call the building and have her paged. No, they'd just call her office. Maybe I could sneak in at night? Who am I kidding? It's a courthouse. It's got guards and alarms and—the fire alarm.

It was right across the hall from where she stood. She ran over to it and reached for the handle.

If I pull the fire alarm, Mrs. Torres might lock her office. She could also lock down the computer . . .

A plan formed in Faith's mind. She strode quickly out of the courthouse, went to her car, and grabbed her probation folder. She hadn't done any of the work that Barbara had wanted her to do, but that didn't matter now. She yanked open the glove compartment and snatched the cigarettes and matches Sam had given her in the liquor store.

Faith went back inside, past Barbara's office, to the restrooms. The women's restroom was occupied, but the family restroom was all hers. Faith searched the ceiling. The smoke detector was mounted directly over the sink. *Perfect.*

Faith grabbed a long trail of toilet paper, scrunched it up, and put it in the sink. Her fingers trembled as she lit the cigarette, fumbling to light the match with her left hand. She finally managed to get it going, taking four rapid puffs until it glowed brightly. Then she set the cigarette inside the pack of matches, careful not to touch the burning embers to the match heads, and folded the lid over the cigarette to keep it in place. She looked at her improvised timer and pulled the burning end of the cigarette closer to the match heads. She had to guess how long it would take for the cigarette to burn down, hit the match heads, and light all the matches. Once the cigarette hit the matches, the matches would light the toilet paper and the whole thing would set off the smoke detector.

That was the plan, anyway.

Faith slipped out the door and went to Barbara's office. She cast a glance at the computer screen. Mrs. Torres had already locked it; a little password entry box was right in the middle of the screen.

Faith held out her folder. "I got my paperwork. Can you check off my things?"

Mrs. Torres looked pointedly at the clock; Faith had been gone almost fifteen minutes. Her annoyed face curled even more when she wrinkled her nose. "You smell of cigarettes. Did you stop and have a smoke on your way back?"

"No, of course not. I don't smoke. I, uh . . . had to go right through the smoking section. It was packed. Like Beijing on a bad day."

"Isn't that the most disgusting habit. They should just ban it."

Faith nodded. Right now, she'd agree if Mrs. Torres said the moon was made of marshmallows. "I'm so sorry I took so long. I've just—I've been having a really bad week. But you have no idea how important this is."

Mrs. Torres frowned. "If it's so important to you, I would suggest that next time you come on time and prepared."

"I will. I promise."

Mrs. Torres unlocked her computer and opened up Faith's folder. As Mrs. Torres fanned through the pages and no alarm went off, Faith became concerned that the cigarette had just gone out.

"I don't see your job search report or your group signatures."

"What?" Faith feigned shock. "Can I please see that?" She took the folder back. "I applied to three stores in person and a number of them online." She pretended to search through the papers—slowly. "Webber's Market. I saw them on Monday. Best Burger. The manager there really liked me."

"I'm glad to hear it. But I need the papers."

Faith pretended to go through the folder a second time.

Mrs. Torres drummed her fingernails loudly on the desk. "Miss Winters, I really—"

The fire alarm blared to life and red lights flashed on.

Faith tried not to smile.

Mrs. Torres popped out of her chair. She started to turn toward the computer, but Faith leapt up and grabbed her arm. "We have to go! Barbara always said this office was a death trap in a fire."

Mrs. Torres grabbed her purse and turned once again toward the computer.

"Right now!" Faith actually pulled her around the desk toward the door. "All those boxes of paper in the hall are like kindling. We've got to go!"

Mrs. Torres's eyes widened, and she allowed Faith to pull her into the hallway.

The hall was now crowded with people covering their ears and hurrying for the exit. The alarm shrieked overhead as red lights flashed. Faith let Mrs. Torres get ahead of her, and as soon as the woman turned the corner toward the stairs, Faith spun around and headed back to Barbara's office.

Faith slipped inside, closed the door, sat down at the computer, and grimaced as she worked the mouse with her left hand. She clicked the magnifying glass in the corner. A search screen appeared.

Yes.

Faith typed "Woods" in the field for last name, pecking at each key with her left index finger. She checked the drop-down option for "male." There was also a date range field. She selected twenty years ago until now. She pressed enter and an hourglass appeared.

Faith tapped her foot and bit her lip.

The hourglass slowly spun.

Faith heard voices in the hallway. They were coming closer. The alarm still blared and the lights still flashed but the voices were becoming louder. *Why aren't they leaving, too?*

Faith leapt out of the chair and flicked off the office light. The voices were definitely moving her way. The sound of a door opening down the hallway, then a voice again.

"Hello?" a man called out. "All clear."

Faith glanced at the doorknob—she'd need a key to lock it and there wasn't enough space to hide behind the door. She wedged herself between the desk and a bookshelf, tucking her head between her knees just in time.

The door to Barbara's office opened, the light flicked on, and Faith held her breath. But it was only a second before the light went off again, the man shouted, "All clear!" and the door closed.

Faith peeked up at the screen. The search had finished. She stayed on her knees as she grabbed the mouse and clicked "print all." The printer behind the desk came to life.

The computer screen counted down the pages. Ten, nine, eight, seven . . .

Faith chewed on her lip until it bled. Like a chipmunk darting out of its hole for a nut, each time a page came out of the printer, she reached up, snatched it, and hid back under the desk. Only when the last page printed did Faith come out for good. Listening for sounds outside the office, she closed all the search windows on the computer, stuffed her treasure into her probation folder, and crept out into the hallway. She was halfway to the stairs when a man shouted behind her.

"Hey, you! What are you still doing in here?"

Faith turned around to find a security guard striding toward her. He wore a navy-blue shirt with a gold badge. She turned on the waterworks. "I can't find the way out!" She grabbed the man's arm. "I was using the bathroom, and the alarm went off, and then someone shut off the lights. I . . . Please, where's the exit?" She covered her face with her bandaged hand and sobbed.

The security guard's face softened. He took her by her good hand and jogged with her to the exit.

"Thank you, sir. Thank you," Faith said. He held the door open and fresh air hit her face. She put her head down, hurried down the stairs, and slipped into the crowd that had formed in the parking lot.

Two fire trucks had already pulled up. Faith prayed that she hadn't started a real fire. She ran to her car, tossed the folder onto the passenger seat, got in, and slammed the door shut. In the bubble of her car a warm glow of relief washed over her. She began to shake. It wasn't fear she felt, but something else.

Something good.

She had done it.

The answer she had waited ten years for sat a foot away from her. She held her breath as she picked up the folder from the seat. She paged through the printout slowly. On the fourth page, her heart stopped.

Jeffrey Woods.

Rat Face.

She had finally found him.

Jeffrey had a number of arrests, starting when he was a teen. His first conviction was for animal cruelty. Her eyes widened when she saw the name of the arresting officer: Lionel Walker.

A sharp rap on the window made Faith scream.

Detective Lionel Walker stood outside. He stepped back, looking startled himself now, and motioned for Faith to get out.

Faith quickly closed the folder and placed it back on the passenger seat. *Did he follow me? Does he know I made the fire? No, that's crazy. The police station is next door. Maybe he just happened to see me and wants to talk to me about my apartment?*

Lionel's expression was somber. Faith was used to the look. She'd seen it so many times in people's faces as she was dragged off to be incarcerated: a mix of pity and inevitability.

Faith swallowed.

Lionel motioned again for her to get out of the car.

Faith powered down the window. "Is this about my apartment? Or the car?"

"No. I need you to come to the station with me."

Faith could feel her heart thumping like an unbalanced washing machine. "I can't. I have a group."

"It'll have to wait."

"I can't." Faith tried to put the transmission into drive, but with just her left hand, she couldn't before Lionel stepped closer to the car and put his hand on the door.

"Faith. Please."

"Can't you just tell me here?"

"No. Right now, I'm asking nicely. If I have to ask again, I'm taking you in cuffs."

Faith fought back tears as she got out of the car.

Faith stared at the empty chair across from her. *When is Detective Walker coming back?* He'd barely said two words to her since he walked her over to the police station from the courthouse. He spent the whole time making calls and ordering people around. Then he led her to this interrogation room, sat her down, and left. That was over twenty minutes ago.

She couldn't tell Lionel about Jeffrey Woods. Right now, Lionel was the last person she'd trust. Faith glanced at the camera in the corner of the room and stared down at the table. She needed to reach Henry—she trusted Henry. But where was she? Had something bad happened to her?

It was at least another ten minutes before the door finally opened and the detective came in. He rested his hand on the back of the chair opposite Faith. His funeral face was still in place. "I'm sorry, Faith, but I had to bring you in to talk to you." He pointed to the camera. "Everything we say is being recorded."

Faith rubbed her bandaged hand and didn't look up. Her stomach was doing flips. The fire didn't just violate her probation, it brought on a string of new charges, and from the look on Lionel's face, she was certain he thought she started it. She tried to brace herself for what was coming.

"I want to hear your side of the story. Can you please tell me what happened?"

Faith closed her eyes. She didn't even know where to start. "I don't know what to say."

"Just start at the beginning. What happened when you got to the office?"

"I was late. I ran in, but Barbara wasn't there. If she was, I would have asked, but—"

"Who?" Lionel finally sat down.

"Barbara Finney. My probation officer."

Lionel looked confused. He pulled his chair closer to the table and leaned in. "Are you all right, Faith? When's the last time you spoke to your mother?"

"I haven't talked to her since yesterday. She left me a bunch of messages, but I haven't had time to listen to them. Why?"

Lionel put his hand on his forehead and ran it over his hair until it rested on the back of his neck, then let out a long sigh and looked up at her. "I'm sorry to have to tell you this, but Dr. Melding is dead."

"What? How? When?" Faith's chest tightened like she had jumped in a freezing pool.

"His assistant found him this morning. She's pretty shaken up."

There was a knock on the door and a black man in a brown suit stuck his head in. "Lionel, Chief wants to see us both."

"I'm in the middle of something."

"He said now. It's about . . . " The man tipped his head toward Faith.

Lionel stood up with a grumble. "I'll be right back."

When Lionel left, the room seemed to get smaller. Faith struggled to process her doctor's death, but one question stood out from all the others: *Why bring me to the police station to tell me?*

A few minutes later, the door opened again. This time Lionel was accompanied by Faith's mother.

Faith had no explanation for her rapid and intense reaction, but as soon as she saw her mother, she burst into tears.

"Shh. It's okay. Shh . . . " Beverly kneeled beside her chair, pulled her close, and held her. "I'm sorry you had to find out this way." She glared at Lionel.

"I have to interview her," Lionel said, moving to the other side of the table.

"All I asked was that you let me break the news to her."

"I thought you had." Lionel picked up the chair, brought it over to Faith's mother, and stepped back toward the door.

Faith pulled free of the hug and dried her eyes with the back of her bandage. "What happened to Dr. Melding?"

Faith's mother sat down and sighed. "Poor Leesa opened the office this morning and found him. She's absolutely traumatized by the whole situation."

"She's still at the hospital," Lionel said. "They're treating her for shock."

"She was catatonic when I saw her," Faith's mother added.

"What happened?" Faith asked again, more urgently.

Faith's mother squeezed her arm. "Someone broke into the office. He was stabbed to death."

"He was *murdered?*" Faith's head spun like she'd just stepped off a Tilt-A-Whirl. "Why am I here?" She held onto her mother's arm and focused on a spot on the table, trying to get her balance back.

Her mother raised an eyebrow.

"We're speaking to everyone who was in his office yesterday. It's standard procedure," Lionel said. "You saw him at eleven?"

Faith nodded.

"Was anyone else there?"

"No. Just Leesa."

"We typically schedule a few minutes between appointments so that patients don't see each other," Faith's mother explained.

"How did Dr. Melding seem? Did he appear nervous or concerned about anything?"

"I'm sure Faith is going to say Dr. Melding seemed completely professional. If something was bothering Alex, he certainly wouldn't confide in a patient," Faith's mother said.

"No, he wouldn't, but his behavior is pertinent." Lionel scratched the stubble on his chin hard enough to leave red tracks. "Please let Faith answer the questions, Beverly." He looked down at Faith. "How did your appointment with Dr. Melding go?"

How did it go? I swore, yelled, knocked over a chair, and stormed out of his office.

"It was . . . a rough session. Yesterday was a hard day for me. Dr. Melding was thinking about switching my meds."

"Are you having problems with your medication?" Lionel asked. "Psychiatric medication?"

"Her medication doesn't need to be adjusted," Faith's mother said.

"But Dr. Melding thought it did?" Lionel asked.

Faith's mother squeezed Faith's hand. "Maybe this is too much for you right now. You're getting confused, honey."

"Was anyone in the office when you left?" Lionel continued.

"No. Just Leesa."

"Did you notice anyone outside? Was anyone hanging around the building?"

"No."

"How was Dr. Melding when you left?"

Faith pictured herself standing in his doorway and swearing at him, the clatter of framed diplomas as she slammed the door. She felt her eyes welling up again.

Faith's mother wrapped her arm around Faith's shoulders. "Shh . . . Let's get you home."

"What happened to your hand?" Lionel asked.

"I cut it," Faith said.

Her mother's eyes narrowed.

"It's not bad," Faith added.

"How'd you cut it?" Lionel asked.

"Making a sandwich," Faith lied.

Her mother pulled her close. "Shh," she whispered. Her voice dropped even lower. "Stop talking—now."

Faith closed her mouth.

Her mother kept one arm around Faith's shoulders as she spoke to the detective. "I'm taking her to my house. If you have more questions, let's discuss them in a less emotionally stressful environment."

"Certainly." Lionel cleared his throat. "Beverly, I need the rest of the client list." He put his hand on the door handle but didn't open the door.

"Lionel, please understand that there are confidentiality issues. You have to provide a court order. If not, I could lose my license."

"I'm getting one," Lionel said, his voice gruff.

Faith's mother's arm trembled. "I'm not trying to be difficult, but Alex would have thought about his patients first. This will be incredibly challenging for them."

"I understand that, Beverly, but his patients' *safety* could be at stake, too. You said that there had been a credible threat made against him. If you could just tell me who made it, that would be a start."

"I want to tell you, Lionel, and I will, but I can't until I hear from my lawyer. Now please—let me take care of my daughter."

Lionel jerked the door open.

Faith's mother escorted her out of the police station. On the way out, Faith caught sight of Tommy, but he was standing among a group of other policemen and didn't notice her.

Her mother didn't say a word all the way to the car, but the minute they were both inside her white BMW, she started to cry.

"Mom? Are you okay?"

Her mother grabbed a tissue and pressed it to her face. Her body shook with sobs.

Faith placed her hand on her shoulder. "It'll be okay, Mom."

Her mother nodded.

"Do you want me to drive?" Faith asked.

Her mother shook her head, blew her nose, and sat up straight. "No. I'm all right. I just . . . I couldn't reach you. All last night. I called and called."

Faith saw the deep circles under her red-rimmed eyes. Her mother looked like she hadn't slept at all. "I'm so sorry. I . . . I didn't know anything until Lionel picked me up."

Her mother started the car. "Let's just get you home. Where's your car? We can pick it up and you can follow me."

34

Faith sat at the kitchen table, watching her mother pace the floor. Thad stood leaning against the marble countertop, sipping a vodka and orange juice. He took a long gulp, snatched the bottle of vodka, and added more in one practiced motion.

Her mother picked up her phone, dialed again, then hung up in disgust. "You'd think with all the money we pay him, he'd pick up the damn phone. How can you go hiking and not take a phone?"

"Even a lawyer gets a day off. He probably didn't take a phone on purpose."

"He should be reachable in an emergency." Faith's mother closed her eyes and crossed her arms. "I'm sorry." She exhaled and looked down at Faith. "I should be thinking about you. We need to talk."

"Why don't I make everyone something to eat first," Thad said. "I think both of you need to relax."

Faith's mother pressed her lips together and rolled her eyes.

Faith was used to this scenario. Her mother was a type-A personality whose motto was "Damn the torpedoes and full speed ahead," while Thad had a much more laid-back style. But right now, Faith was on her mother's side. She wanted to wring Thad's neck. He *knew*. Sara-Jane had told him that her father hadn't been unfaithful. He knew, and he had said nothing. Faith's good hand balled into a fist.

"You know I'm right," Thad said to Faith's mother. He started to pull sandwich fixings from the refrigerator. "Why don't you change?"

"Because I might be called back over there."

Thad set packages of ham, turkey, and cheese down on the countertop. "If that happens, change back. You might as well be comfortable until then."

Faith's mother rolled her eyes again, but kissed his cheek and said, "That's an excellent idea."

"I knew you'd agree." Thad smiled without showing teeth and rocked back on his heels. He waited until Faith's mother left the kitchen, then locked eyes with Faith. "I have to ask you something important."

Faith waited.

"White or wheat?" Thad smiled, his hazel eyes sparkling.

"Completely not appropriate for the situation."

"Come on. I'm just trying to lighten things up. This whole deal is so surreal. How are you handling everything?"

Faith took a sip of her water. "Fine."

"Under the circumstances, it's okay not to be fine." Thad started making her sandwich.

Faith spun her phone on the table like a top. *I shouldn't call Tommy, but he's the only cop I trust.*

"What happened to your hand?" Thad asked.

"I cut it." Faith sat up straight. "Making a sandwich."

"Guess you're not helping with *this* then." Thad brought the sandwich over. "Can I do anything else for you?"

Faith stared down at the sandwich. She didn't like Thad. All her therapists said it was because of her father issues, but they were wrong. Faith simply hadn't wanted to let anyone worm their way into her heart. Not even her mother's new husband.

Long ago, Faith's mother had talked to Faith about guarding her heart. She said there were boys out there who would hurt her. She talked about herself and her own experience. And, ironically enough, the boy who had broken *her* heart—was Thad, in college. They fell in love, but he broke up with her. And now, here they were together again. Married.

Maybe that was another reason Faith disliked him. He'd hurt her mother when he dumped her in college. Who was to say he wouldn't do it again? Why should she trust him? "Why did you dump my mother?" she blurted out.

Thad dropped the mayonnaise. Good thing it was a plastic jar. "Why did I what? What are you asking?"

"In college. My mother said you dumped her and broke her heart."

"I did." Thad picked up the mayonnaise jar. "I was stupid. Your grandmother hated me. Well, hate might not be strong enough. *Loathed.*" He stretched out the word, and Faith could almost hear her grandmother saying it. "She thought I was an immature twit who didn't make a shred of effort to better himself." He held up his hands like he was surrendering. "She was right. Your mother and I were about to graduate, and I was just floating. Beverly was concerned about that, too. Again, justifiably. So, to meet their low expectations, I just . . . walked away. I was a fool. Why do you ask?"

"I ran into someone who knows you."

"Who?" Thad leaned against the counter.

"Sara-Jane Bradley. She said she gave you a note to give to my mom."

"You talked to that—" His mouth clamped shut and his nostrils flared. "Yeah, she came here. A couple of times. She even came with some minister's wife so I wouldn't toss her out on her ear." He made a face like he'd eaten something sour. "You didn't speak to that woman, I hope?"

"She gave you a letter. Why didn't you give it to my mother?"

Thad's anger softened, and he cast a nervous glance toward the doorway. "I can't believe you're even asking me that. Faith, I know you think your mother has her act together because she's your mom and an all-star therapist, but she's human. She hurts. She loved your father. They were high school sweethearts. Can you imagine waking up one morning and finding out that you were in love with a . . . " His voice trailed off.

"A what?" Faith shifted in her seat.

Thad shook his head. "I promised myself that I'd never say anything bad about your father."

"Why didn't you promise that you'd tell my mother and me the truth?" Faith's voice rose.

"What are you talking about? I've always been truthful to both of you."

"My father never slept with Sara-Jane. She recanted the whole thing."

Thad blinked rapidly. "Is that what she's saying now?"

"Didn't you read her letter?"

"No. I threw it in the trash—where it and that woman both belong. She's ruined so many lives I didn't want to hear anything she had to say." Thad stood up straight. "Do you believe her?"

Faith rubbed her leg with her good hand. Thad's explanation made some sense. "Sort of. But I talked to Mrs. Foster's sister, too. They both say that my dad didn't cheat on my mom."

Thad looked up at the ceiling, then back at Faith. "I'm sorry. I just thought it was some ploy for sympathy. I guess I should have read that letter. I should tell your mother. Or you should. She deserves to know."

At the sound of Beverly's heels in the hallway, they both turned. She hadn't changed her outfit. There was a familiar look of pity and resolve on her face as she marched over and crouched down in front of Faith's chair. She searched Faith's face with tear-glistening eyes. She reached out and squeezed Faith's left hand. "After you left Alex's office yesterday, he called me."

Faith waited for more, but her mother just rubbed Faith's cheek as a tear ran down her own. "Yeah?" Faith said finally. "What did he say?"

Her mother remained silent. She reached over and started to unwrap Faith's bandage.

"What are you doing?"

"I need to see your hand."

"What? Why?" Faith tried to pull her hand back, but her mother held her wrist. "Mom, you're hurting me."

Her mother kept unwrapping the bandage until the bloody gauze over the knuckle was visible. Her face went even paler. "How do you cut your knuckle making a sandwich?" Her mother's voice was low and even.

Faith started wrapping her hand back up. "I punched a mirror. In the cabin. I kinda trashed the place."

"Faith."

"I'm serious. I went out to the cabin. Someone had been there, they'd had some party . . . and I just went nuts."

Faith's mother stood up and crossed her arms. "Alex said you had an issue with him at your last session."

"He wanted to change my meds. He was going to throw me back in Brookdale." Faith cradled her hurt hand. "So what? I *do* hope you're not suggesting that I murdered my therapist, Mom. Have I ever hurt anyone?"

"Yes, Wendy Belcher."

"Oh, yeah, poor friggin' Wendy. I was thirteen and she told me Dad deserved to die because he was a cheating man slut, so I punched her in the head a couple of times. Boo-hoo."

"What about the therapist you stabbed?" her mother asked.

Thad gasped.

"That therapist groped me." Faith looked at Thad. "I guess you're the only one who hasn't read her book. It's in chapter 11."

Faith's mother reached for her hand, but Faith pulled it away.

"I'm sorry, honey, but you have to see how this looks."

"How does it look, Mom? Like your sad little crazy daughter lost it and stabbed your partner to death? I hate to disappoint you, but I didn't do it."

"I think everyone needs to take a step back," Thad said.

Faith glared at him.

Thad held up a hand like he was directing traffic. "I believe you, Faith. But your mother is right, this looks bad. Think about it from the police department's perspective. You argued with the murder victim the day he was killed."

"And the police have read my book, so they're aware that you did stab one of your therapists before," Faith's mother added.

"In the leg," Faith pointed out.

"I'm shocked they didn't detain you," Thad said.

"They don't know that she had a heated exchange with Alex." Faith's mother stood up. "I never told them."

"Leesa knows," Faith said.

"How?" her mother asked.

"She came into the room. When we . . . I knocked over a chair."

Faith's mother lowered her head. "It was that bad?"

"I gave him the finger and stormed out. I pushed the stupid chair over. I didn't throw it across the room. I was ticked off, but I didn't kill him."

"Why didn't Leesa tell the police?" Thad asked.

"Because she's being treated for shock at Mercy Hospital," said Faith's mother. "But once Lionel hears . . . " She started pacing again. "Was anyone with you at the cabin?"

"No . . ."

"Faith. Do you understand that you need an alibi? Think."

"Tommy picked me up after."

Faith's mother exhaled. "Oh, thank goodness."

"But I can't say I was with him," Faith added.

"What are you talking about? Of course, you're going to say you were with Tommy. It's the truth, right?"

"He covered for me about trashing the cabin. He's covered for me a lot, and I don't want him to get into trouble. He's already in trouble for trying to help me."

"Lionel is going to think you killed Dr. Melding. You'd be *my* prime suspect. Motive, opportunity, and access." Faith's mother ticked off each word on her fingers. "Faith, this is as bad as it gets. Damn it. I'm calling Marty again." She picked up her phone and pressed redial. "The police shouldn't even be looking at you anyway. One of Alex's former patients has been threatening him."

"You have to tell the police that," Thad said.

"I did, but they want a name."

"Then give them the name!" Thad said, his voice rising.

"It's not that simple. They have to get a warrant or I'm liable. That's why I need to— Hello?" She covered the phone and mouthed *voicemail.*

"Marty. It's Beverly again. This is so far past the critical stage I can't even begin to tell you. I need you to write up something so I can provide the police with the name of the former patient who was threatening Dr. Melding. Please call me as soon as you get this." She reached for the disconnect button, but put the phone back to her ear. "Oh—the patient's name is Woods. Jeffrey Woods."

I guarantee you need a drink." Thad headed for the cabinet. "One Long Beach Iced Tea, coming up."

Beverly pressed her lips together and tilted her head toward Faith. "No thank you. I'm going to go lie down." She stopped in the doorway. "Faith, your room's all made up."

Faith nodded, but her mother's words barely registered.

Jeffrey Woods was a patient of Dr. Melding.

Thad waited until Faith's mother left the room and then whispered, "You're okay if I fix her a little something, right? I think she really needs it, but I wouldn't want to be a bad example, you know?"

"I don't care," Faith muttered, staring at the floor, counting tiles.

It's all my fault.

Thad poured a shot of rum and drank it himself. "It's going to work out, Faith. Marty's the best lawyer I know." He poured a second shot of rum and began to make a Long Beach Iced Tea.

If only I'd figured out earlier what that man really said in the woods, Dr. Melding would be alive. It's my fault.

"If anyone can fix this, Marty can. Don't worry about a thing," Thad said.

"I'm not worried," Faith lied.

Thad wiped down the butter knife with a napkin and proceeded to stir his drink with it, the ice cubes clinking against the glass. "There's my girl." Thad winked, picked up the glass, and left the kitchen.

Marty can't fix this. Only I can.

Faith picked up her mother's keys and flipped through them until she found the one she was looking for—the little brass key.

The key to the gun safe.

***

Faith looked beyond the trees at the run-down duplex. She'd parked behind the house so she could use the woods for cover, careful to stop between the pools of light cast by the streetlights, which had just turned on. Her phone buzzed in her pocket— again. Her mother had to be in a panic right now, but it couldn't be helped. Faith had slipped out while she was lying down. She would never understand why Faith had to do this.

She cradled the gun in her lap. She'd rather have the cowboy gun, but this one was much lighter, which was probably for the best. Her hands were trembling—she didn't know if it was because of fear, anger, or needing a drink.

She doubted she could fire a gun with her left hand. She unwrapped her bandage and then rewrapped it tightly. Firing with her right hand would tear out her stitches, but she didn't care.

She'd been watching Woods's house for almost fifteen minutes and had yet to see anyone move inside. An old red pickup truck was parked outside the two-door garage and there was TV light from a window at the rear of the house.

It was time. She opened the door without hesitation. She'd already waited ten years; she wasn't going to wait any longer.

Faith pressed the gun against her leg as she crept through the trees toward the house. The closer she got, the more crushing the weight on her chest felt. By the time she reached the house, her breath was coming in shallow gulps.

Before going inside, there was one thing she needed to check. She crept to the garage and peeked in the dirty window. The old Crown Vic was partially covered by a tarp.

Faith's heart leapt like a fish.

She returned to the back of the house and peered through the window lit by the TV. She could see the TV clearly, mounted on the opposite wall; she could even see the action movie that was playing. In front of it, facing away from Faith, was a couch, with the top of a man's head visible at one end, and his feet in socks sticking out at the other end.

Faith ducked down. She was breathing in little puffs and her head was starting to spin.

I could shoot him in the head from here. He wouldn't see me.

But she *wanted* Woods to see her. No. She needed to see *him*. She had to look him in the face and tell him what he had taken from her. Then she'd ask him who the other man at the cabin was.

Then she'd blow Rat Face's head off.

Faith walked softly and slowly on the balls of her feet to the back door, sticking to the shadows cast by the pitched roof. The kitchen door was open with only the screen door closed. Faith peered through it into a dirty kitchen. Plates and bottles covered the counter, and the table looked like a dumping ground for anything Woods had in his hands when he came home. A yellow toolbox crushed some papers beneath it, a jacket with an A&R

Construction logo was tossed over a chair, and a pair of heavily scuffed work boots sat on the floor beneath it.

Faith opened the screen door quietly and slipped inside.

The TV blared from the other room, filling the air with the sounds of machine-gun fire and explosions. *Woods must have an expensive sound system.* This thought fueled her anger even more. Woods had a truck, a TV, a house . . . a life.

Kim had none of those things. Neither did Anna, or Mrs. Foster, or even Faith's father.

Neither did Faith.

She ground her teeth and crossed the kitchen into the even messier TV room. A wide leather chair had a block of wood in place of a missing leg. Whiskey bottles, beer cans, and trash littered the coffee table. One of the bottles was tipped over, its contents dripping onto the floor. Faith was behind the couch, so Woods couldn't see her—but she could see the top of his greasy head.

More gunfire from the TV made Faith jump. A little voice inside her screamed something, but Faith didn't listen. It didn't matter what it said. The rat-faced man lay on a platter in front of her.

He's a dead man.

Faith crept forward and pressed the gun against Woods's temple.

And then she stopped.

She gazed at the face that haunted her for ten years: pointy nose, weak chin, bad teeth—Rat Face. But his face was splattered in blood and his eyes were wide open and a deathly pale gray. A long, deep cut ran across his throat. Blood soaked his shirt and a knife stuck straight out of his chest, pinning to his body one of Faith's wanted posters. His glassy eyes stared blankly, and his mouth was unnaturally pulled back in a sick grin like someone had posed him.

Jeffrey Woods was already dead.

Faith gagged. She started to turn away, then froze, her eyes fixing on the knife. The black plastic handle with a divot melted into one side, where she had set it down against the burner of the stove before Robert tossed it into the sink.

Faith had just found her missing steak knife.

Faith drew in a long breath to scream, just as the sound of sirens filled the air and blue light pulsed through the windows.

Faith swore and ran for the back door.

She didn't know where she was going, but the voice in her head was yelling at her to run, and this time she listened. She slipped out the back door, ducked low, and raced to the woods behind the house. Blue light spilled into the backyard, and her shadow stretched across the grass. She ran into the shadow of the trees and to her hidden car just as two police cruisers skidded to a stop in the driveway.

***

The air vent obviously wasn't a very good hiding place for the new gun, but in her tiny apartment, where else? As she replaced the grate, she noticed her left hand was covered in blood, but it wasn't hers. She must have touched the couch when she put the gun against Woods's temple.

Her head snapped up. She thought she could hear sirens in the distance. She listened carefully. Yes, definitely sirens. And they were coming this way.

"No, no, no." She ran into the bathroom and tried to scrub the blood off her left hand. Her soaked bandage turned a disgusting muddy pink.

The sirens stopped right outside her apartment.

Faith started ripping the bloody wrappings off her hand. The stitches throbbed as she pulled at the tape, but she managed to tear it off. She yanked opened the medicine cabinet and grabbed the extra bandages that Jay had given her.

Someone pounded on the door.

Faith grabbed the Ace bandage and wrapped her hand.

The banging came again.

Faith eyed the little window in the bathroom. Could she shimmy through it?

"Faith!" Detective Walker shouted. "Are you in there? Faith!"

Faith pulled a clean shirt over her head.

"This is the police! Open the door or I'm breaking it down!" Lionel yelled.

"One second!" Faith called. She ran across the floor and opened the front door.

Lionel stood in the doorway, his shirt soaked in sweat. "Are you okay?" he roared.

Faith took a step back and nodded.

"What the hell's the matter with you? I've been pounding at the door. I almost kicked it in."

"I was in the bathroom changing my bandage." Faith held up her hand. "I'm not feeling well."

Lionel stepped inside. "We need to talk. Take a seat." He pointed to the chair.

"What's this about?" Faith asked. She didn't sit.

"Hold on." He took out his phone and dialed. After a minute, he spoke. "Frank? She's here. She's okay. Lock down the scene, and I'll be back as soon as I can. How long? Okay. Thanks." He hung up. "Could I have a glass of water?"

Faith was about to tell him to get his own water, but then thought of the knife block next to the sink. The knife block with the missing knife. Only Henry knew about that.

"Yeah, sure, be right back."

Lionel pulled out the stool while Faith went to the kitchen area, grabbed a glass with her left hand, and slid the knife block behind the toaster with her right.

After she handed Lionel the water, he pointed to the chair. "Sit."

Faith sat.

Lionel drank half the water, then set the glass on the table. "I think we found the man you saw when you got back to town. He owns a brown Crown Vic, and he matches the description you provided."

Faith waited for the detective to continue, but he was studying her face, gauging her reaction. "Great!" Faith blurted out, a little too excited. "I mean, you arrested him, right?"

"He's dead."

Disbelief, confusion, shake your head.

"I needed to make sure you were safe. Does the name Jeffrey Woods mean anything to you?"

"No."

"We're putting together some pictures. In a couple of hours, I'm going to need you to come in for a photo lineup."

"What? Why?"

"If you're right about what happened that night, and your father wasn't the killer, then that means the killer is still out there—and it could be that he killed Woods. Tying up loose ends maybe."

Faith cast a nervous glance at the door. *I'm a loose end.*

Lionel stood. "I'd like to take you to the police station. For your own protection."

Faith looked down at her feet to buy time and her eyes widened. There was a big bloodstain on the toe of her white sneaker. She tucked her bloody shoe behind her other leg. "I don't want to go to the police station again." She hadn't forgotten Henry's warning—she couldn't trust the police.

"It's for your own safety."

"The only person who needs to go to the police station is the killer, not me." Her anger and suspicion were rising. Lionel had arrested Woods years ago, so he knew what he looked like. And then he'd seen the police sketch of Rat Face that was based on Faith's description—a sketch that was pretty darn accurate, it turned out. So why had he never made the connection?

"Six people have been murdered in the last ten years in this town," Lionel said. "You're the only person connected to every one of them. You're in danger, Faith."

Faith shook her head again.

Lionel scratched the side of his jaw. "I can't force you to come to the station, but you shouldn't be here alone."

"I'll go to my mother's," Faith said.

Lionel appeared to consider this for a moment, then nodded. There was something different about the way he was looking at her now. "Your mother didn't happen to mention Jeffrey Woods, did she?"

"What? What would my mother know about him?"

"Woods was a former patient of Dr. Melding. Did she ever say anything about him?"

"No. Never."

"Okay. Will you promise you'll go directly to your mother's? I have to go. Officer Williams is right outside. He'll take you over to your mother's when you're ready."

"Yes, I promise I will."

"Good. I'll pick you up from there in a couple of hours and bring you down for the photo lineup."

When the door closed behind Lionel, Faith leaned against the wall. Her world was spinning and she was struggling to hold onto her sanity. This was a whole different level of bad, and she couldn't see any way out of it.

Faith checked her messages yet again: her mother, Nyah, Robert, Rachel, Tommy, and Thad had all phoned—but nothing from Henry.

"Damn it, I need you!" Faith shouted.

She ripped the closet open. She needed to change her shoes because of the blood. She grabbed her running shoes and made a face. *Great. What's this gloop? Did something spill—*

Faith dropped the shoes. They were covered in blood.

How—? She grabbed the closet door handle to steady herself, winced, and switched to her left hand. She stared at the shoes on her feet with the splash of blood on them and then the running shoes.

This can't be happening. Someone was framing her.

Backing away from the bloody sneakers, she looked around the room and her eyes landed on the air vent. She ran to the vent, grabbed the gun, and headed for the bathroom. She stuck her head out the window and groaned. It looked impossible. Her apartment was on the second floor. The window below hers had an air conditioner in it. *But that's still a long way down.*

Faith opened the window and slid out. She held onto the windowsill with her forearms resting on the wood, glanced down, and dropped.

She landed on the air conditioner. Glass broke and metal shrieked as the frame of the window bent under her weight and then the whole unit tilted down. She hit the ground hard, her legs bending so deeply that her chin struck her kneecaps, clacking her teeth together.

She fell back on her butt and fought down a scream as her hurt hand hit the ground. Wiping the tears from her eyes, she got to her feet and hurried away.

***

She was pounding the wood with everything her left hand had to give, but Tommy took forever to answer the door. When he finally yanked it open, he was in a towel with soap still in his hair.

"Faith! What's wrong?"

"Everything," she blurted, pushing her way in. "They found Rat Face."

"What? Where?"

"He's dead. Tommy, I'm in trouble. Big trouble." Faith told him everything she knew. Everything. She didn't leave out a single detail this time—even Henry.

"Why didn't you tell me all this before?"

"I saw how much trouble you were in already because of me. Besides, Henry was looking into it. But I can't get hold of her, and now I'm worried about her too. What if they killed her?"

"I didn't even know the feds were involved," Tommy said. "I guess that's not surprising. I'm the low man on the totem pole."

"We need to reach her. I think Lionel may be involved in all this. Not in a good way."

"Detective Walker? No way. He might not look it, but the guy's squeaky clean. Completely by the book."

"He arrested Woods years ago. Why didn't he recognize him from my sketch?"

"People look different. Maybe the guy gained or lost weight." Tommy ran his hand through his wet hair and looked at the bubbles on his fingers. "Look, let me rinse off, then I'll call my delegate. She has to know some lawyers."

"You think I need a lawyer?"

"No, I think you need a really *good* lawyer. Hold on, okay?" Tommy went back into the bathroom, and the shower turned on.

Faith knew Tommy was right. This looked bad. Really, really bad. While she waited, she walked into Tommy's bedroom and studied the wall of pictures and clippings. *Ten years' worth of searching.* She focused mostly on the pictures of Kim. Many of them had nothing to do with the investigation, as far as she could tell; they were just happy photos. Kim laughing. Kim smiling. *He still loves her.*

Faith stopped at a photo of Kim playing soccer, racing down the field, a look of determination on her face. In the background, a group of people watching from the sideline had been circled with a red pen. Faith looked closer. One of the men circled was . . . Thad.

Why would Thad have been at Kim's soccer game?

Faith snatched the photo off the wall and banged on the bathroom door.

"Are you in my bedroom?" Tommy's roar seemed to bounce off the bathroom tiles. The shower turned off immediately, and a moment later the door opened. Tommy had pulled on a pair of jeans and was struggling to get a T-shirt over his still-wet torso. "You shouldn't have come in here," he said, his eyes flicking to the wall.

"I'm sorry. I saw it all when I slept over anyway. Look," Faith said. "I get what you're doing. It's fine. It's . . . I'm glad you're doing it. I just wanted to know." She held up the photo. "What is this?"

Tommy stared at the picture and his eyes hardened. "A couple of months ago, I was looking back over some old photos and noticed that. Quite the coincidence."

"Did you ask Thad about it? He didn't even live in this state then."

"He said he was on a business trip and was visiting a friend. He chalked it up to fate."

"What do you think?"

Tommy took the picture and pinned it back up on the wall. "I don't know." His voice was distant. "That's why it's up there. Can you wait in the living room?"

As she closed the bedroom door behind her, Faith realized that Henry was definitely wrong about Tommy. If there was a bad cop on the force, it wasn't Tommy. He was looking for the killer, too.

Henry isn't the only one who was wrong about Tommy, said a voice in Faith's head. *So were you.*

For ten years, Faith had blamed Tommy for what had happened that night. For lying to Kim, for causing her to go to the cabin in the first place. *But it wasn't his fault. He loved Kim. He was going to propose to her. He—*

Faith stared down at the coffee table and almost lost her balance. Lying on Tommy's coffee table was a gold watch with an old leather band. Her hand shaking, Faith picked up the watch and turned it over to see if there was an inscription on the back.

Time for Fishin'.

She sank to her knees.

Her father's watch. Her father was wearing it that night.

***

Tommy walked into the living room, towel-drying his hair. Faith pointed her gun at his chest.

"Faith . . . " His voice laced with fear, Tommy dropped the towel.

Faith gritted her teeth. Her breath came in staggered, halting puffs. Her hand shook.

"What's going on, Faith?"

"Put your hands behind your head and get on your knees."

"Faith—"

"Do it now, or I shoot you in the groin." She pointed the gun at his crotch.

Tommy interlaced his fingers behind his head and knelt.

"Look on the table," Faith said.

"Faith—"

"LOOK ON THE TABLE!" she screamed.

Tommy nodded. "It's your dad's watch."

"He had it with him at the lake. You took it as some kinda sick trophy. That's what they do."

"No." Tommy started to move his hands, and Faith raised the gun to his chest. "Faith, listen. Your father gave me the watch that morning. At your house."

"You're lying."

"I'm not lying. Your father was an old-fashioned guy. I respected him. He did a lot with me, and I just knew . . . "

"Spit it out, Tommy, or I'll blow your brains out."

"I knew your dad wanted me to ask him before I asked Kim. I was getting my paycheck that night and was going to pick up the ring the next day. I thought I'd propose at the bonfire, so I went to your house that morning and I asked if I . . . "

Faith watched his tears splash onto the carpet, then soak in.

"Your dad didn't say anything at first. I got worried—I figured it was a no. But then he held out the watch. He said—" Tommy choked back a sob. "He said . . . his father gave it to him and told him to give it to his . . . " His voice broke. "To his son."

"You're lying."

Tommy looked Faith in the eye. Tears were streaming down his cheeks. "If you think I could have hurt one hair on your sister's head, then take the safety off and pull the trigger. You'd be doing me a favor. Please, shoot me."

He looked like a wounded animal yearning for the sweet relief of death.

She backed up toward the door.

Tommy started to lower his hands.

"Don't." Faith's hand trembled. She clicked the safety off. "Wait until I'm gone."

"Faith, you're so wrong."

"Shut up." Faith's hand shook as she turned the knob. "I want to believe you. But I just don't know what to believe anymore."

38

Faith knew she had to go somewhere but . . . where? She lay curled up on the floor near her bed. The police detail that Lionel had stationed outside had left. She didn't feel safe in her apartment, even with the lights off and the blinds closed. She'd believed the nightmare of her life would get better once she found Rat Face. *But now Dr. Melding is dead, too. If only—*

A knock on the door snapped Faith out of her thoughts. She didn't move.

"Faith?" It was Robert's voice.

Faith's phone buzzed in her pocket. She ignored that, too.

"Hello?" Robert called again.

She didn't move until she heard Robert trudge back down the stairs. Faith just couldn't deal with him or anyone else right now. She needed to think of a way out of this nightmare. A killer was out there and was after her now, but where could she hide?

Her phone buzzed again. It was her mother. She'd already sent about a million texts. Most were short, some were longer, but they all said basically the same thing: *Come home, we can work it out.* She read the last one again. *Let's talk. It's for the best.*

Faith banged the back of her head against the floor. *It's for the best.* That's what her mother had said before she had her locked up. She was about to get locked up again. Best case, she'd get sent back to Brookdale. More likely jail.

Faith ignored the texts. What she needed right now was to talk to Henry, and if Henry wasn't going to come to her, she would track her down. She dialed information.

An operator answered. "What number?"

"The FBI in Boston."

"What department?"

"Um, law enforcement."

After a moment, a new voice answered. "FBI, how may I direct your call?"

"I need to speak to Agent Henryka Vasilyeva. It's an emergency."

"One moment."

The hold music was electric piano. Faith tapped her head against the floor again.

"Can you please spell the name?" the receptionist asked.

Faith spelled it out.

"I'm not seeing it."

"Is there anyone with something close to that name? Maybe I'm spelling it wrong."

"I'm sorry, but we have no one here named anything like that."

Faith sat up. "No. You're wrong. She covers the state park in Marshfield."

"One moment."

Faith exhaled. Her heart felt like it was misfiring. After another brief hold, a man came on the line. "FBI. This is George Sutton. This line is being recorded."

Faith ground her teeth. "I'm looking for Henryka Vasilyeva. She covers the state park in Marshfield. She's a federal agent."

"I'm sorry, miss, but I'm not familiar with any agent named Vasilyeva, and I cover Marshfield. Is there something I can help you with?"

She hung up the phone—then burst into tears. She kicked her legs and pounded her fists on the floor, like a child throwing a tantrum. *Am I losing my mind?*

She had to get out of there. She didn't know whom to trust, but one thing was clear: she needed to run. *Someone killed Woods and Melding and they're framing me for it. But who? Is Henry part of it?*

Faith pulled out her duffel bag, shoved in a few clothes and some toiletries, and headed out the door. She threw her bag in the trunk, got in the driver's seat, and awkwardly turned the key with her left hand.

Nothing happened. Not a click, not an electrical buzz. Nothing.

"No, no, no."

She turned the key again. The car just sat there.

Faith got out of the car and slammed the door. She turned in a circle and pressed her left hand against her head. She swore again and kicked the front tire.

"Just a wild guess, but your car won't start?"

Faith jumped.

It was Hunter. His red Camaro was parked right where it had been the first night she saw him. He gave a little wave as he crossed the street.

"Need a jump?" he said with a smile. "Faith, right?"

Faith's heart sped up and she took a step back. Her purse was on the front seat and her gun was inside. She eyed Hunter suspiciously. "I'm fine."

"Are you sure? Your face is bright red."

"Yeah, I'm just . . . upset about my car." Best not to tell him that she was running from the police, a murderer, and her mother, all to avoid jail, death, or a mental institution—that she might be going insane, and that she really had to wonder why the hell he kept turning up outside her apartment.

"It's probably just the battery." Hunter pointed to the driver's seat. "Get in and I'll give you a jump."

While Hunter returned to his car, Faith yanked open the door and grabbed her purse. She kept the gun inside, but as her fingers closed on the grip she decided she could trust Hunter enough from a distance. She popped the hood on the Camry.

Hunter pulled up in front and hooked up his jumper cables. "Don't start it just yet. Let it get some juice."

Faith drummed her fingers on the steering wheel.

"You need to relax." Hunter stepped over the cables dropped between the cars and started walking toward her door.

Faith's left hand tightened around the gun still in her purse. "I wouldn't come too close. I think I have the flu."

Hunter shrugged. "I got my flu shot." He took one step closer but still kept an acceptable distance. "It looks like you're not having the best evening."

"That's the understatement of the year."

"Really?" Hunter gave an expectant smile. "Why?"

"It's a long story. Maybe another time."

"Fair enough," Hunter said. "Actually, I'm kinda glad your car wouldn't start. I mean, I'm sorry it happened. The truth is, I wanted to ask for your number the last time I saw you."

"Right now, my life is pretty complicated. I don't think it's a good idea."

"Life's messy. I get it. I'm just thinking dinner. Nothing long-term. Not that I'm opposed to that." He grinned again. "What happened to your hand? Did you hurt it fighting off all the guys asking you out?"

Faith's lips pressed together.

"Sorry. Lame joke."

She smiled.

"See, I can make you smile. All I'm asking for is one date. I'll even provide references."

"References?" Faith shook her head. "I'm sorry and I don't want to be rude, but I have to go. Can I try to start it now?"

His smile drooped but didn't disappear entirely. "Give it a try."

Faith said a quick, silent prayer and turned the key. The engine sputtered and started. "Yes."

"One second. Let me get the cables."

As Hunter walked around to the front of the car, Faith drummed her fingers against the steering wheel. Now she could go. Where, she didn't know, but she'd drive until she was safe and come up with some kind of plan. She set her purse down on the seat beside her.

Hunter shut her hood and walked up to her window. "I'd let the car run for a while before you shut it off. That way it will build up a charge again. If not, it might not start next time."

"I will. Thank you so much. You have no idea . . . " Faith's words trailed off. *A&R Construction.* The logo on Hunter's shirt. *That's where Woods worked.* Suddenly, she could barely breathe. Hunter was with those construction workers at the bar the first night she met him, when she bought him one of those fancy beers. Why hadn't she made the connection before?

Oh, dear God.

Rat Face's accomplice. The man who butchered Kim right in front of her.

"You okay?" Hunter asked. "Because you don't look so good."

"I'm fine," Faith said, trying to sound calm as she reached out for her purse.

But Hunter moved with the speed of a cat. His left hand grabbed the door and his right fist smashed Faith right in the face. Lights sparkled, and her head wobbled like a prizefighter about to fall to the canvas.

Please, God. Please, God.

She jammed her foot down on the gas and the engine revved, but the car didn't move. It was still in park.

Hunter put his large hand on the back of her head. "Actually . . . " He looked like a child peeling back the wrapper of his birthday present—a smile widened across his face and his eyes brightened. "You're anything but fine." He slammed her head into the steering wheel, and everything went black.

When Faith opened her eyes again, everything was still black. Her wrists and ankles were strapped to a chair. There was some kind of hood over her head, and something plastic had been shoved into her mouth. She tried to scream.

Her vocal cords strained and her lips burned; her eye and one whole side of her head throbbed where Hunter had hit her. It was hard to breathe underneath the hood, especially with the gag in her mouth. She forced herself to take shallower breaths through her nose. Her heart was pounding in her ears, but she heard the footsteps. They stopped right behind her chair.

Her neck snapped back as someone ripped the hood off her head. Bright overhead lights blinded her, but Faith tilted her head down and blinked rapidly, forcing herself not to close her eyes. She needed to see where she was.

She was sitting at a long, polished dark-wood dinner table in a formal living room. The walls were covered in ivory-and-gold damask wallpaper, and a crystal chandelier hung overhead. But Faith got only a glimpse before the lights went out.

God help me . . . please.

The person started walking away. Faith turned her head toward the sound and caught a glimpse of Hunter passing through a swinging door into a kitchen. The door swung back and forth three times before it closed, a faint line of light sneaking out along the edges.

Faith blinked, letting her eyes adjust to the dark. A bit of brown light seeped in through heavy shades on the windows. Leather straps secured not only her forearms to the chair but her biceps as well. She couldn't see her legs but felt similar straps around her ankles and shins. A thinner leather band was pulled tightly around her chest, pinning her to the seat like a prisoner about to be electrocuted.

Faith couldn't move, but she started to shake when she heard Hunter humming. The sound drifted in softly from the kitchen. She couldn't make out the tune—until the door opened again. In his hands, he carried a birthday cake, the candlelight bouncing off the ceiling and bathing his face in a macabre glow.

As Hunter sang "Happy Birthday," Faith fought back tears and clamped down hard on the plastic bit until she felt something snap, either the bit or her teeth—she didn't care. She wouldn't give him the satisfaction of seeing her cry. She clenched her jaw harder.

Hunter's face stretched into a wide grin as he set the cake down in front of her. Large pink letters spelled out *Happy Birthday, Faith.* Like torches at some demonic ritual, the candle flames danced in Hunter's wild eyes, revealing the kind of madness that Faith feared most—the evil-crazy kind that will kill you.

When he finished the song, he clapped. "I know this is *your* birthday, but it's really *my* special day now, too, isn't it? So I think

I'd better be the one making the wish." Hunter laughed, closed his eyes, and blew out the candles.

The darkness was brief before he flicked on the light.

"I'm breaking a personal rule here, but this is just too good not to remember." He walked behind Faith and pointed to a shelf beside the door. "See that little thing by the vase? That's a video camera. Smile, Faith. Give a little wave." Hunter let out a demented, rolling laugh. "Oh, that's right, you can't!"

Hunter leaned down and gave her a kiss on her cheek. Then he put his lips so close to her ear she could feel his hot breath.

"Happy birthday, Spitfire," he whispered.

The words wrenched pain from deep inside her. She tried to fight back the tears, but they streamed down her cheeks. *Spitfire.* That's what her father had always called her.

"I knew it." Hunter clapped his hands together. "I knew I could get you to cry. You were fighting it, right? Right? But guess what? I peeked at your card ten years ago. I did. That's what dear old Dad called you, right? Spitfire?"

He sat on the table beside the cake, swinging his legs like a happy kid, stuck his finger in a pink flower, and licked the frosting from his finger. "Do you like chocolate or vanilla? I didn't know, so I got a half-and-half. But you can't eat like that."

He reached behind her head and undid her gag. Faith thrust her head forward to bite his throat, but he pulled back and her jaws snapped the air.

He hopped down from the table. "Damn. You almost got me. You *are* a spitfire, aren't you?"

Faith opened her mouth to scream.

There was a brief flash as Hunter ripped a giant hunting knife from its sheath and held it up. It had to be at least a foot long. The metal caught the lights and gleamed as Hunter slowly ran two fingertips down the length of the serrated blade.

"It's party time, Faith!" Hunter sprang toward her and slapped the flat side of the knife blade against her throat.

Stunned by the mock execution, Faith let out an involuntary yelp.

"Shhh," he whispered softly. "This is a surprise party. If you yell, you'll spoil the surprise." Hunter laughed and tossed his arms wide. "I mean, what other killer does all this? I bet you thought you'd be in my dark, scary basement sitting under a bare light bulb with water dripping and a rat chewing on a skull, right? Instead I'm serving you birthday cake in my gorgeous dining room."

He pranced over to the window and peeked out. "Do you like my house? It's a wonderful neighborhood." He lifted back the curtain just a bit so Faith could see part of the road and a streetlight. "My neighbor's outside. Want to take a guess who it is? Come on. No? I'll give you a freebie. It's Robert! The handsome, flower-delivering survivors' group leader. He's out there talking to Sean, my other neighbor. Sean's a cop."

Hunter hurried back to Faith's chair and got as close to her face as he dared. "Scream, and they might hear you." He raised one hand. "But if you do, I'll take your tongue."

Faith took a deep breath, her eyes darting to the drapes, trying to see outside.

Hunter's brown eyes widened. He was quivering with excitement.

She didn't know if he was telling the truth or not. Either way, she wasn't taking the bait. She looked at the floor and exhaled.

Hunter laughed. "You blinked. I was hoping that you'd scream."

Faith's eyes smoldered with ice-blue hatred.

Hunter turned the knife in his hand, lightly touching its sharp tip against her throat for a second before dragging it slowly up toward her face, softly, so as not to break the skin. "There are lots of ways I can kill you, Faith. Don't make me choose agonizingly slow. Not on your birthday."

Faith spit on the floor.

Hunter snarled and lifted the knife high. "Fine! Fast it is!" he roared, then plunged the knife down into the cake. "I'm guessing you're a vanilla girl."

Hunter cut a piece for himself. He ate the cake right off the table, using the knife as a fork, like a pirate. When he licked his lips and smiled, his teeth were pink with frosting.

"You really are a party pooper, Faith. Come on. Did anyone *else* remember your birthday? Hell, I bet *you* forgot. Or I bet you wish you did."

Faith didn't answer.

"Not talking? I didn't cut out your tongue yet, did I?" Hunter chuckled. "I know what will cheer you up. Wait until you see what I got for you." Hunter disappeared once more through the door behind her.

When Hunter returned, he was pushing a girl's pink bike.

A strangled cry escaped her tightening throat and hot, wet tears erupted.

"Oh, you're priceless. I knew you'd love it. You have no idea how hard it was holding onto this little surprise for ten long years. But I couldn't resist. I even kept the card. I have to admit that I opened it, but it's new for you." Hunter opened the card. *"Your mother and I can't wait to see you zipping around the lake with Anna. Happy birthday, Spitfire."* He tossed the card onto the table. "Do you want to ride it? Come on."

Faith stared down at her father's handwriting on the card on the table. Hunter had dealt a lethal blow to her spirit. Her chin dropped to her chest. Her mind was going numb, the void inside her growing and swallowing whatever was left of herself. Fear had won. He had won. She was dying.

"What am I going to do with you, Spitfire?" Hunter put the tip of the hunting knife under her chin and pushed up. Faith had no choice but to lift her head and look into his eyes. "I'm saving your best present for last," he said. "It's a killer surprise. I mean, what's a party without friends?"

Faith's eyes widened, and she shook her head.

"Oh," Hunter squeezed her cheek, "not your friends. But that would be a wonderful idea. Hmmm . . . the problem is, you don't have many. I suppose I could go pick up a couple of people from your 'survivors' group." He made air quotes around the word *survivor*. "But then they'd have to change the name of the group." He made a slicing motion across his neck and snorted.

Faith couldn't absorb any more. She was in complete overload. Her head wobbled. She was trying to speak but her lips couldn't form the words. *Not another death.*

"Don't worry. *Your* friends aren't coming over. This is *my* friend. And guess what? It's someone you know, too.

"Of course, it's not good old 'Rat Face.' How I loved that nickname of yours. Very appropriate, too. Yeah, I'm the one who killed him. I'm sure you figured out that much. Are you mad that you didn't get to do it yourself?"

When Faith didn't say anything, Hunter grabbed the hair on top of her head and jerked it up and down.

"Oh, don't feel bad, I made sure he suffered—a lot. Poor Woods. He didn't understand the game. But me, I like the sport of it all. Which is why you're here. This is all part of the game. I thought, before we continue, you might have a few questions for me. Perhaps you'd like to hear the details of how I killed your father, your sister, your best friend, and her mom?" He held his hand up to his ear and waited.

She tried to look anywhere but at him; her gaze darted up to the chandelier and down to the table leg until she settled for squeezing her eyes shut.

"I'll take that as a yes." Hunter stood and began pacing. "Look at me!" He slammed his hand down on the table, and Faith's eyes snapped back open. Hunter raised his index finger like a professor making a crucial point to the class. "See, your dad was special to me. He was my first. I found out that killing people is like eating potato chips—you have one, and you just can't stop. But that first one was so very special."

Sweat rolled down her back. Her face felt like she was standing too close to a fire, but she didn't think the temperature in the room had changed.

"Special, but quick. Too quick. You see, I was going to have some fun with your dad, but then your friend came over and so did her mom. That was okay, though. I saved the real fun for the ladies." Hunter's eyes glazed over.

Faith sagged forward against her bonds, wishing desperately she could cover her ears and block out the words. She was burning up now, and with each breath she felt like she was choking.

"And when you and your sister showed up . . . hot diggidy dog, an after-party! It's too bad you were so fast. Like a scared little rabbit—whoosh—you took off into the brush. Of course . . . I think it all worked out for the best." He smiled.

There was a bookshelf on the back wall and she tried to count the books, but she couldn't focus with her chest pumping like a jackhammer.

Hunter wagged his finger at Faith. "I figured you would never set foot in Marshfield again, but boy, was I wrong. Your return was when the fun really started. Did you know I bet Woods a hundred bucks that I could drive you crazy? And it was so easy. Move your car, move the photo. Follow you around. I'd barely gotten started and you were jumping at shadows. Too bad Woods can't pay up."

She shut her eyes, and images flew by like petals in the wind: the hallway at the school, the magician on top of the truck in the parking lot looking down at her with a twisted grin, the open vent in her apartment, her bloody sneakers . . . She felt like she was drowning as she gulped in air.

Hunter rushed to her chair. "Breathe," he said softly. "Shh . . . Deep breaths. Think of butterflies, puppies, kittens." He slapped her hard across the face. "Just cut it out already."

Someone knocked on the back door. Hunter picked the hood off the floor.

"Sounds like my friend is here," Hunter said. "My client, really. It's the person who hired me to kill your father. If it weren't for my friend, I might never have discovered my true calling. I just can't wait for you two to meet! Well," he laughed, "meet *again*, that is, seeing as you already know each other."

Hunter pulled the hood over her head. "And then we'll move on to the grand finale." Faith felt the knife against her neck. "Don't worry," he cooed. "I won't rush it."

Hunter's footsteps moved toward the kitchen. As soon as the door closed behind him she pulled madly at her restraints. She felt as though her arms would snap, but the restraints didn't give an inch. She felt warm blood running down her fingers beneath the bandage.

A door opened—maybe the back door to the house. In the kitchen, Hunter laughed.

Faith tried to rock the chair over. Maybe if it fell, something would break, or she could somehow get some leverage. But her feet didn't even touch the floor, and tied as tightly as she was, she could barely get the chair to rock at all, much less create enough momentum to tip it over.

The door opened, and multiple footsteps approached. They stopped right behind her.

Faith started to pray.

"Are you excited, Faith? This is the big moment. The big reveal." Hunter's voice rang with excitement.

Please, God.

Someone put their hand down on her head. Fingers grasped the hood.

Please, God. Please help me.

A gunshot thundered. Faith gasped.

Something heavy fell against her shoulder, then landed on the floor with a thud. A sharp blow at the base of her skull knocked Faith's head forward, and she slipped into oblivion.

40

Saturday, April 14

Faith felt something wet against her mouth. Her lips were stuck together like she'd drunk syrup, but it wasn't sweet. It tasted rusty. One eye fluttered open. She was lying in a pool of the sticky stuff.

Blood.

She scrambled away until her back hit the dining room wall. Her parched throat clamped shut, leaving her unable to breathe let alone scream.

She stared at the pooling blood and tried to remember. The blood wasn't hers. It was Hunter's. The pool had radiated out from his dead body, on the floor behind the chair she had been tied to. The back of his head was blown off.

Faith stared at the man who had taken so much from her. It was clear he was dead, but from her racing heart to the hair standing up on the nape of her neck, her body's signals all screamed one thing: *Run!*

Faith shook her head like a swimmer trying to clear her vision after breaking the surface of the water. Nothing made sense. Hunter was dead, lying in a pool of blood, but everything else about the room seemed . . . orderly. The chair she'd been tied to was pushed in at the head of the table and there were no restraints in sight. The cake was gone. So was the bicycle. It was as if the sick party had never taken place.

The room felt like it shifted once again when she saw what was lying partway under the table, a mere three feet in front of her: her father's cowboy gun. The one that had disappeared from the vent in her apartment.

I'm losing my mind. I'm really losing my mind.

Faith scrambled to her feet and stumbled into the kitchen, her hand leaving a bloody smear on the door as she pushed it open. Through the window, she could see the rosy sunrise beginning. How long had she been unconscious? She yanked the back door open and staggered out into the backyard. The house next door was Robert's house. That was definitely his Jeep parked in the driveway. Robert lived right next door, just as Hunter had said. Faith ran across the damp grass, toward the back of Robert's house.

She pulled open the screen and pounded on the wooden door, leaving a smear of blood with each thump.

When Robert opened the door, she tumbled into his kitchen. "Please help me."

"Faith! What happened? Where are you bleeding?"

She stared blankly. "It's not my blood."

He grabbed both her shoulders. "Faith, look at me." His voice sounded far away. "What happened to you?"

"It's not my blood. It's his."

Robert grabbed his phone from the counter. "I'm calling 911."

"He's dead," Faith said.

Robert's fingers stopped moving. "Who's dead?"

"My sister's killer. He found me. He lives next door."

Robert swallowed. "You're saying that the person who killed your sister is my neighbor?"

"Was," Faith muttered. She stared down at the blood on her hands. She held her arms out, keeping her hands far away from herself as she rushed over to the sink and turned the faucet on, frantically wiping off the blood.

Robert stood there looking stunned. "Are you sure he's dead?"

"He got shot in the head. He's dead."

Robert jerked his thumb in the direction of Hunter's house. "The guy with the red Camaro?"

"He's in the dining room."

"Don't do anything," Robert said. "I'll be right back." He went outside and shut the door behind him.

Faith removed her blood-soaked Ace bandage and tossed it in the trash. Then she grabbed the faucet—it was the kind that you could pull out—and stuck her head underneath it. As the cold water ran over her head, she felt the tender lump at the base of her skull and winced. She hung her head down and watched the red water swirling down the drain.

After a few minutes, she turned off the water and wrung out her hair. She blotted her hair with a kitchen towel and then wrapped it around her hand. She stood there staring into the sink, watching water drip off a spoon and down the drain.

Robert touched her back. "Faith?"

She jumped, turned around, and searched his face. His lips were tightly pressed together and his skin was pale. He was breathing through his nose and the muscles in his jaw were clenched. He took her by the elbow and led her to a chair.

"You need to tell me what happened. He attacked you? That's why you shot him?"

Faith shook her head. "I didn't shoot him. I think his friend did. Hunter tied me up in his dining room. He had this birthday cake with my name in pink frosting. Someone else came in and shot him."

Robert took a deep breath. The look on his face said it all.

"I know I sound crazy, but it really happened. It happened, Robert." Faith grabbed his hand and put it on the back of her sore head. "Feel that bump? That's where the shooter whacked me and knocked me out. Hunter's been following me. Moving my car. Moving stuff in my apartment."

"His name's not Hunter. It's Cory Norton."

"He must have given me a fake name, then. But he's the guy who killed my father. I'm sure of it. He had the birthday present my dad never had the chance to give me. It was a bike."

Robert got up and poured her a glass of water from the refrigerator. She drank it like someone rescued in the desert. He poured two more before she held up her hand. Then she told him everything, from seeing the rat-faced man driving outside the bar to Dr. Melding being murdered. The cabin. Woods. Henry. Hunter. Everything.

When she was done, Robert got up, walked over to the window, and stood staring out at the yard.

"Say something," Faith said.

Robert turned around. "We can't call the police. Not right now."

"You're the Boy Scout, and you don't want me to go to the cops?"

"You need to talk to a lawyer. What you're saying sounds . . . "

"Crazy?" Faith put her head in her hands.

"Actually, no. It sounds like you did . . . all of it. You sound guilty."

"Do you think I did it?"

"No."

"Why not? You don't know." Faith could feel hot tears running down her cheeks. "Maybe *I* don't know. Maybe I've gone mad. If I was crazy, would I know it?"

"Faith. Don't. Don't question yourself. Look, I know a lawyer. We can go talk to him. Just give me a couple of minutes."

She nodded and he rushed out of the kitchen. She waited until she heard him walking up the stairs before she took out her phone and quickly dialed. "Tommy? Tommy, I didn't do it."

"Faith, where are you?"

"I didn't do it, Tommy. Not any of it."

"Faith, the fingerprints came back from Woods's house. They're yours."

"I know."

"Where are you?"

"I'm going to go talk to a lawyer."

"No! Look, come in. I can protect you."

"Tommy, listen, the two guys that you saw at the cabin, Woods was one of them. The other guy's dead, but someone's helping him. They framed me."

"Tell me where you are, and I can help you."

"I'm getting a ride to the lawyer's office now and—"

"With who? You just said that someone was helping them. Listen to me. If you don't trust me, find a cop. Stay away from Robert. Don't go there. Don't go anywhere with him."

"Tommy—"

"I'm serious, Faith. He's not who you think he is."

"Robert's nice, Tommy."

"You don't know him. His real name is Keith Perry. He moved here from Oklahoma. He's not a survivor."

"What are you talking about? His fiancée was attacked. He was tied up." Faith was whispering now.

"Yeah, and Robert untied himself and killed the two men who attacked her. He stabbed them, Faith. He's a killer. He spent a year in an institution afterward."

Faith shook her head to undo what she'd just heard. "But . . . that's self-defense."

"He still snapped and killed them. And he's been following you. I saw him at your apartment last night. One of your neighbors says they saw him before that, too."

Faith hung up. She'd been a fool to come here. Hunter's neighbor!

There was no one she could trust.

She was out the back door and well into the woods behind Robert's house when she heard him yelling, "Faith! Faith!"

She ran faster than she'd ever run before.

Faith pulled the briars out of her pant leg, a thorn pricking her thumb. She sucked on it as she stood on the gravel along the shoulder of the road, then dialed her mother with her left hand. She had to make it to her mother's. There was nowhere else to go.

The call went straight to voicemail. She even tried Thad, but couldn't reach him, either. That meant she'd have to walk—in clothes that were soaked and spattered with blood. She checked her reflection in her phone and cringed; she looked like a boxer who'd gone ten rounds and lost. Her eye was black and blue and terribly swollen. She kept her head down and tried to keep to side roads, hoping no one would be concerned enough by her condition to call the cops.

"Faith?"

Faith was passing through a residential area—no doubt freaking out the neighborhood watch—but she hadn't expected someone to call her by name. She looked over and saw Mrs. Henderson standing just outside the front door of a postcard-perfect cottage.

"Faith!" Mrs. Henderson waved her over.

Faith wasn't sure whether to run toward or away from this unlikely angel of mercy, but her legs took her up the steps before she could hesitate, and Mrs. Henderson's eyes widened. "Oh, my poor girl, you look a fright. Come in, come in. What happened?"

"I'm okay. I just . . ." The last thing she wanted was to get Mrs. Henderson caught up in everything, but she needed her help. She couldn't tell her the truth. Not yet. "I fell off my bike. I'm all right. It looks worse than it is. Can you please give me a ride across town?"

"Of course I will." Mrs. Henderson looked back into the house. "But I have some muffins in the oven. Can it wait for just a bit? They only have fifteen minutes left."

Faith nodded. "Sure. Thank you," she said warily.

Mrs. Henderson held the door open, and Faith walked inside. It was like stepping into a different world. The place was immaculate, bright, and cheerful. The smell of warm cinnamon permeated the air. Faith felt like a foreign body, infecting the space.

"Why don't you come into the bathroom, where I can take a good look at you," Mrs. Henderson said. "I used to be a nurse."

"Really, I'm okay."

Mrs. Henderson tsked. "Nonsense. That was a nasty fall. You need some ice for that eye, and you shouldn't leave those cuts untreated. We have time before the muffins are ready anyway." She led Faith into the bathroom, where she pulled out several washcloths and a bottle of antiseptic. "Just wait here a moment." She handed Faith the washcloth and headed down the hall.

The mirror showed Faith her matted hair, swollen purple-brown eye, and a long, thin scratch running from her neck up the side of her bruised face.

Mrs. Henderson reappeared with a white top in her hands and another cloth wrapped around a bag of ice. "This will be too big for you, but you can't go around looking like something the cat dragged in." She set the shirt down on the hamper and picked up a fresh washcloth. "Let's take a look at that hand of yours."

"I'm fine, Mrs. Henderson."

"Fiddlesticks." The old woman waited patiently until Faith held out her hand.

The lukewarm water felt good on Faith's battered skin, and Mrs. Henderson worked gently to clean the wound.

"You pulled out a stitch," she said, peering over her glasses and frowning. "The others should hold, but it wouldn't hurt to go back in and get another. Although I do hear they use glue nowadays. Can you imagine that?"

"Were you a real nurse?"

Mrs. Henderson chuckled. "You mean a medical nurse? Yes. Until I moved here. I miss it."

"Why did you stop?"

"My son. After he was killed, I just couldn't do it anymore. I was in pediatrics. My boy was only seven when it happened."

"What happened to your son?" Faith blurted out. "I'm sorry. You don't have to answer that."

Mrs. Henderson put fresh gauze on Faith's hand. "We were at the grocery store. It was back before people locked the doors—back when you told the kids to come home when the streetlights came on. My boy went to the men's room, but he never came out." She made a noise, a sad little hum. "He was stabbed to death. After that, every time I saw a young boy, it hurt so. That's when I moved out here." She wrapped an Ace bandage around the gauze.

A bell chimed in the kitchen.

"The muffins are ready. And I think you are, too." Mrs. Henderson smiled. "Put the ice on that eye. You come on out when you're ready, and I'll get you some aspirin for that nasty bump on your head."

When Mrs. Henderson left, Faith changed into the clean top. It was too big, but it was so soft that Faith didn't ever want to take it off. She opted to hold the bag of ice on the back of her head; it hurt worse than her face. By the time she walked into the kitchen, Mrs. Henderson had set two muffins on plates and was pouring Faith a glass of milk.

The small kitchen was tidy, its flowered wallpaper dated but cheery. A cuckoo clock ticked loudly above a round table with three chairs.

"I really can't, Mrs. Henderson. Thank you, but I just need that ride."

"Oh, yes, I'll take you right after we finish the muffins. I wasn't done sharing my story yet." She handed Faith the milk and two aspirin. "Where was I?" Mrs. Henderson asked.

"You just talked about why you moved here." Faith took a bite of warm muffin.

"That's right. Thank you. Well, back then that sort of thing didn't happen. It was all over the news. Day in and day out. There was no escaping it. So I packed up my things and moved here. I needed a fresh start. It's worked out. My son likes it here."

Faith froze with her mouth full of muffin. For a while there, she had forgotten how crazy Mrs. Henderson was. "Your son?" she mumbled.

Mrs. Henderson nodded. "He needed a new start, too. He took his brother's death so hard."

Faith felt the color rise in her cheeks. *I'm an idiot.* It never occurred to her that Mrs. Henderson had two boys.

"No matter what I said to him, he felt responsible for Leon's death. They both went to the men's room together that day, but Leon needed more time, so his brother left."

Mrs. Henderson got up and fetched a photo from a small shelf near the refrigerator, then handed it to Faith. Two little boys with their arms wrapped around each other's shoulders wore matching cowboy hats, boots, and huge grins. On their puffed-out chests were golden sheriff stars.

"Did they ever catch the man who killed him?" Faith asked.

Mrs. Henderson pointed to the boy on the left. "That's Leon."

"He's a handsome boy," Faith said, trying to be polite.

"He's got his father's hair. His brother got mine. Red as Rudolph's nose." She chuckled as she put the picture back on the shelf. "They were best friends, those two." She picked up a teapot from the stove, filled a cup on the counter, and wound a white kitchen timer to two minutes. "They never caught the man who took Leon from us." Her shoulders slumped. "No one even saw him except Lionel. I think that's why he became a policeman."

Faith started coughing.

"Take smaller bites, dear."

"Your son's name is Lionel? And he's a policeman here in town?" Faith's heart started ticking as fast as the timer.

"He's not a policeman now." Mrs. Henderson smiled proudly, and Faith started to relax. "He's a detective."

Faith leapt to her feet. "Lionel Walker is your son?"

"Well, yes, didn't you know? I changed our last name to Henderson, my maiden name, when we moved because of all the publicity, but when Lionel turned eighteen, he changed it back to Walker, to remember his brother. He's always watched out for you, Faith. You need to trust him."

Trust him? Lionel always loved my mother. He should have recognized Woods. Did he want my father dead?

Faith eyed the door. "I really have to go. Can we leave now?"

Mrs. Henderson pointed at the clock. "Why don't we wait and talk to Lionel? He checks in on me every morning at this time."

Faith ran out the back door, down the concrete path that wrapped around the house, and smashed straight into Lionel Walker coming around the corner.

"Faith!" Mrs. Henderson called out.

Walker grabbed Faith's wrist, spun her around so her back was to him, and grabbed her other elbow. "Mom, are you okay?"

Mrs. Henderson leaned out the back door and waved. "I'm fine. Fine. I got worried when Faith ran out, but she must have seen you coming. She's eager for a ride."

"That must be it," Lionel said. To Faith, he whispered fiercely, "Behave yourself around my mother." His hands tightened on her wrist and lifted up slightly.

"Would you mind giving her a lift, Lionel?"

"Not at all. No problem, Mom." He pulled Faith partway around and started pushing her toward his car.

Faith thought about screaming, but what would Mrs. Henderson do? Call the police on her own son?

From around the corner and already out of sight, Mrs. Henderson called out, "Would you like a muffin for the road?"

"I'm all set, Mom. I'll call you later." He pushed Faith over to his car and opened the driver-side door. "Slide across."

"I'm not going to run."

"Slide in, or I'm putting you in cuffs."

Faith moved over to the passenger seat and Lionel got in right behind her, locking the doors as he did. He started the car and gunned it out of the driveway.

"Put your seat belt on."

Faith didn't move until Lionel put his hands on his cuffs.

Faith put the belt on with her left hand, but scooted forward so she could block his view as she reached for the door handle with her right. She winced as she flexed her fingers beneath the bandage, and managed to get hold of the lever with the tips of two fingers. "Let me go."

Lionel looked at her like she had three heads. "Are you kidding me? You've got trouble, kid."

"Please, just let me out," Faith said.

"How about you answer some of my questions before you make any demands." Lionel turned onto Harrison Avenue and sped up.

"This is the wrong way. This is—" Faith's foot started tapping like it had a mind of its own. She knew the road and they were driving in the opposite direction of the police station. "Where are you taking me?"

"That's what I've been trying to tell you. I don't think you're safe in Marshfield."

"What are you talking about?"

"I'm taking you over to Darrington until I figure something out. There's a cop over there that I trust, but for now you need to trust *me*."

Faith planted her feet flat on the floor. *He's always watched out for you, Faith. You need to trust him.*

Watched out for her? Or just *watched* her? Like he'd always watched her mother?

The sedan raced up to a stop sign. Faith's thumb hovered over the seat belt release and she tried not to make a face as she pulled the door handle back just to the point where she felt resistance.

But Lionel flew past the stop sign without even slowing.

"Let me out!" Faith shouted.

"Calm down or I swear I'll put you in cuffs."

Faith slid as close to the door and as far away from him as she could. She stared at the pavement rushing past her and her stomach tightened.

Lionel's voice softened. "I'm sorry. I just want to keep you safe."

Faith's eyes locked on the Taser on his belt. She knew he had a gun in a shoulder holster—she'd seen it under his jacket several times. But the Taser on his belt was on her side.

"Please, Detective Walker, let me go. I'll disappear. I won't tell anyone." Faith turned toward the door as she spoke and started unwrapping her bandage.

"Tell anyone what? What the hell are you talking about, kid? You don't for one second think that I'm behind this? You've got to be kidding me. You and me, we're a lot alike."

Faith shook her head and let the Ace bandage fall between the door and the seat. "I know about your brother. You're the only one who saw the killer." Faith was surprised she could move, let alone think, but she had a plan. She wasn't about to go quietly to wherever he was taking her. She flexed her right hand and fresh blood appeared on the gauze still covering it, but without the Ace bandage in the way, in spite of the tape and gauze, she could move her fingers and grip something.

"You talked to my mother?" Something about his voice made Faith glance over her shoulder. His gaze pinned her in place. Intensity bordering on rage darkened his face. "That's why I'm doing this. They never found my brother's killer. I live with that, but I'll be damned if you have to. I know your pain, Faith. I know what it's like to wake up with that being your first thought every day. I'm on your side. You're the connection to all of this. You're the only one who's part of all these murders."

That little voice in her head was screaming at her to shut up, but the words tumbled out: "That's a lie. *You're* connected to all the murders, too."

"That bump on your head must have knocked a screw loose."

The car flew past another stop sign. One more turn and they would hit the main road out of town and be in the hills.

Faith grabbed the Taser in Lionel's holster. Pain shot up her arm as her stitches tore. Screaming, she ripped it out of the holster and pointed it at him. "How do you know I have a lump on my head?"

"Are you crazy?!" Lionel roared. "Put that thing down!"

"The only way you could know about my head is if it was *you* who hit me."

"What? My mother texted me. She said you were hurt and bleeding in her bathroom. Now point that thing away from me and I'll explain."

"Stop the car or—"

Lionel lunged for the Taser. The car swerved across the road, but he managed to grab her hand.

Faith jerked backward, but he wouldn't let go.

Lionel squeezed her hand, and a pop followed by an electric crackle mixed with Faith's scream as the Taser fired and embedded twin bars in Lionel's side. His body went rigid when the current raced through his muscles, and his leg jammed down on the gas. The car accelerated sharply. Faith grabbed the steering wheel, but the car was already veering off the road, racing across a lawn, toward the woods and an enormous elm tree.

Lionel made a growling sound, his eyes filled with fear.

Faith shoved his leg, knocking his foot off the gas.

The car bucked like a wild horse as the lawn ended and it drove into the brush.

Branches broke over the hood, Lionel jammed on the brake, and then . . . a deafening bang.

Faith coughed and opened her eyes. Her left eye burned, so she shut it again. She felt the left side of her face. It was wet and sticky. Her fingers followed the wet part up to her hairline, where she found a gash that was steadily bleeding. Her ribs felt like they were on fire.

The sedan had hit the elm tree. Both airbags had deployed. That explained the bang. Her ears were still ringing. She looked over at Lionel. Blood ran down his face, and his head leaned against the window. She couldn't tell if he was still breathing.

Faith unsnapped her seat belt and pushed on her door, groaning. It wouldn't budge. The window was shattered; little squares of glass covered her lap and the seat. Trying not to put any pressure on her ribs, she climbed out, the pain piercing as she scraped against bits of broken glass. Tumbling out of the car, she landed in a heap on her side. Cradling her right hand, she struggled to her feet. Her left knee throbbed.

A loud hiss followed by a cloud of steam poured out from beneath the hood. Faith limped away from the wreck and out to the road. It was deserted. She knew where she was, and where she had to go. These were her woods. She had played here as a child whenever she visited her grandmother; she and Kim used to ride their bikes on the back trails. Her mother's house was less than a mile away. Closer if she cut behind the elementary school.

Faith limped as fast as she could. She needed to get to her mother.

***

"Mom! Mom!" Faith burst through the back door.

Footsteps echoed down the stairs. Thad ran down the hallway and stopped when he saw her.

"Thad, where's my mom?"

Thad's hair was all mashed down on one side like he'd just woken up. His eyes were bloodshot, and he swayed in place. *He's drunk.*

"She's going out of her mind looking for you." Thad's hand shook as he took out his phone. "I'm calling an ambulance. You're bleeding."

"No. Call my mother. I have to speak to her."

Thad hit speed dial and led Faith into the bathroom. "Beverly. Beverly, she's here. Come home." He turned back to Faith. "I got her voicemail."

"Please text her."

Thad's hands continued to shake. "Faith, this is bad. So bad," he slurred. He reeked of whiskey, and his nose was cherry-red. "But we'll work it out. Everything will work out." He opened the medicine cabinet and began yanking the contents out and onto the counter.

"Thad. Thad, stop. Lionel Walker hired Hunter and Woods to kill my father."

"What? Faith, you're not making any sense. Your mother has known Lionel since elementary school."

"No. He's the one. Woods had a record. Lionel arrested him. Lionel worked all the murders. His brother was killed. I thought his mother was crazy—"

"Faith, slow down. You're talking about Detective Lionel Walker? Your mom told me they used to call him Choo-Choo. He was the chubby kid everyone picked on. He's no killer."

"Yes, he is. But I think I killed him."

Thad appeared to sober up instantly. "You mean you *want* to kill him."

Faith shook her head. "No. He was taking me out of town. I Tasered him, and he drove into a tree. He might still be alive. I couldn't tell when I got out of the car."

"Wait . . . just . . . wait here." Thad grabbed the doorframe for support, then stumbled down the hall.

Faith slumped against the wall. She looked across the sea of bottles strewn on the counter for aspirin, but there was none. She knew her mother had a prescription for Percocet for her back pain, though; Faith had often pilfered tablets in the days before Brookdale.

She lifted bottle after bottle, examining the labels. Then she stopped, staring at one particular label.

This can't be right.

Faith reread the label, but she was certain. *Drioxavalyn.* She stormed down the hallway searching for Thad. His voice came from the kitchen.

"You have to get back here," he was saying. "She's lost it. Call whoever you need to, but she needs to be locked up. No, I won't calm down. You should see her. She's something right out of a horror movie. She killed Lionel—" He stopped as Faith entered the kitchen. "Come back now," he finished quietly, then clicked the phone off. He gave Faith a forced smile. "I reached your mother."

"So I heard." Faith held up the pill bottle. "And I found this."

Thad squinted. "What is that?"

"Drioxavalyn. And it's made out to you."

"So?" Thad waved a hand dismissively, then jolted like someone punched him the gut. "I mean . . . no. It's made out to me, but—"

"You have Fabry disease. Kim had it, but not me or my mother." Faith stared at Thad like she'd never seen him before. "You're Kim's father."

Thad paused, then his shoulders fell. "We were going to tell you. But after what happened at the cabin—"

"You knew *before*?" Faith's eyes burned. "Wait—you knew after Kim got tested. That's why you were at Kim's soccer game."

"Tommy told you? He had no right—"

"*You* had no right. You should have told Kim. You should have told me!"

"No one knew Kim was mine until she was in high school. Not until she got sick."

"Did my father know?" Faith took a step forward.

Thad held up a hand like he was warding off an approaching dog. "Yes. But he wanted to try to make it work with your mother. That's what I thought was best, too," he added quickly. "There was you to consider, too, of course."

Faith screamed and threw the pill bottle at him. It smacked him in the face, and he stumbled back into the counter.

Faith's chest hurt. Her head spun. *No . . . Lionel said I was in danger. He didn't want to bring me here . . .*

"You were already in Marshfield when my father was killed." She stepped back.

"Whoa, whoa. You think *I* killed them? No. That's crazy. You're crazy."

"Lionel said it wasn't over. I thought he hired Woods and Hunter to do it, but it wasn't him, was it? You didn't want your daughter being raised by another man. You believed you'd made a mistake by leaving my mother."

"Faith, that's insane. Your mother . . . " Thad shook his head like a dog after a bath. A look of horror dawned on his face. "Oh, no. Faith, we need to get out of here." He lunged forward and grabbed Faith's arm.

Faith screamed from the pain in her ribs as he yanked her forward. They both fell against the kitchen counter.

"Let go!" Faith shrieked.

"Faith, listen." Thad grabbed her wrist. "Please—"

She grabbed at the counter and her hand found a bottle of whiskey. She gripped it tight and swung it hard into Thad's temple, screaming as the remaining stitches tore out of her hand and Thad crumpled like a marionette cut from its strings.

She stood there panting, staring down at Thad, lying in a heap at her feet, when the front door of the house burst open. Footsteps stomped down the hall. "Faith!"

"Mom!" Faith called back, but she didn't move; her feet felt cemented in place.

Her mother rushed into the kitchen and gasped. "Faith . . . what have you done?"

"He attacked me."

Faith's mother ran over and knelt down beside Thad. He groaned, but his eyes remained closed. Faith's mother took out her phone. "I need an ambulance at 512 Sycamore." She stood up and stepped away, turning toward the doorway and putting her back to Faith. "My daughter has suffered a breakdown. She attacked my husband. I'm afraid for my own life." She hung up the phone and turned around. She was holding the gun that Faith had taken from the gun case yesterday.

The last time Faith had seen that gun, it was in her purse before Hunter carjacked her.

"It didn't have to be this way, Faith."

A strange calm descended on Faith. Her scattered mind, battered by such a storm of assaults, quieted like she'd moved into the eye of the tempest. It all clicked into place. Her very own mother was the mastermind. This realization should have broken her, should have sent her screaming to the nearest nuthouse, but instead it gave her clarity. At last she knew the truth.

"You ruined everything," Faith's mother said.

Faith chuckled.

"You find this funny?"

"Yeah. All this time I thought I inherited my crazy from Dad. But I was wrong. I got it from you."

"Shut up. You've done enough."

"Me? No. It all makes sense. Woods was Dr. Melding's patient, but *you* hired him."

"I guess you inherited your intelligence from me. But I didn't have to *hire* them. Cory—the one you call Hunter—was very malleable. He did everything quite willingly."

"You had him kill Dr. Melding because Dr. Melding asked you about the Fabry disease. You didn't want anyone to know that Kim wasn't Dad's daughter. That would make the perfect mom a suspect."

"Right again. But as a bonus, it was also an excellent opportunity to get you sent away permanently on murder charges."

"It all makes sick sense now. You're the one who broke into my apartment. And you had keys to my car."

"I also knew to check the floor vent. When you were a teenager, you used to hide your cigarettes behind the vent in your room."

"Why didn't you just kill me?" Faith asked.

"Kill you?" Her mother rolled her eyes like that was a ridiculous suggestion. "I didn't want you dead. Do you have any idea how many books I've sold? My publishers are all over me for a sequel. It would have been best if we could have maintained your cycle of delinquency and consequences. You go to the mental hospital, get out and do something atrocious, and get sent back in. That stunt in Greenville Notch put me back on the bestseller chart. All this is going to make me a fortune." Her mother's smile made Faith's stomach turn.

Her mother's ring clicked on the side of the gun as her finger tapped the trigger.

Faith went rigid, expecting the gun to fire at any moment. She didn't know whether to laugh or cry—or scream.

Faith's mother looked down at Thad and gestured with the gun. "Move away from him."

"Him?" Faith said. "Is that why you did all this? For *him*?"

"That's how it was supposed to be. Thad, me, and our precious Kim. I didn't hate you, but you weren't part of that. I needed it to be perfect. You and your father were a mistake I never should have made, but Kim was my baby with the man I truly loved. Don't you understand? Thad never should have broken up with me, and if I kept you, you would be a reminder of that."

"All that crap about you having no feelings for me was just bull. You *did* have feelings for me—they were just all hate! You wanted me to go with Dad. You wanted me to be there that night so I'd get killed."

"That was the plan. You should have gone."

"What about the Fosters? Dad wasn't having an affair with her?"

"Of course not. Even after finding out Kim wasn't his daughter, he'd never leave me. He thought we could go back to being a happy family, but how could I, knowing that Thad and I had made something as perfect as Kim? Anna and Jessica went to help with the surprise party. They wanted to have a combined one for Emily. I tried to tell Jessica not to go, but . . . " Faith's mother shrugged. "That gave me a perfect cover, so I let fate take its course. Now, move away from Thad."

"Was he worth it?"

"Yes," she hissed.

The word pierced Faith's heart like a bullet. She dropped down beside Thad and yanked him up in front of her, using him as a human shield. "Then you won't risk killing him, will you?"

"Let him go!"

Faith grabbed Thad's hair and jerked his head back. "Go ahead and shoot me, you psycho monster! Dad said you couldn't hit the broad side of a barn. I bet you'll miss me and blow Thad's precious face off."

Faith's mother stepped forward, the gun shaking in her hand.

The broken top of the whiskey bottle lay on the floor next to Faith; she grabbed it and pressed the jagged edge to Thad's throat. "If you take one step closer, I'll gut him like a fish, and there goes your second chance with Mr. Wonderful."

Faith's mother's head twitched. "Let him go."

"Not a chance."

The front door smashed open, the echo bouncing down the hallway. "Police!" someone yelled, and outside sirens blared, coming closer.

"Oh, that's right." Faith smiled. "Thanks for calling the cops."

"You little witch!" Faith's mother shrieked.

"Freeze!" Lionel Walker limped into the kitchen with his gun drawn, blood running down the side of his face.

"Lionel!" Faith's mother's voice rose high. "Thank God you're here. Faith's lost her mind. She thinks Thad killed Kimmy."

"Drop it," Walker ordered.

"Shoot her!" Faith's mother shouted, the corners of her mouth curling up. "She's going to kill Thad!"

But Lionel didn't turn his gun on Faith; he kept it pointed at her mother. "Drop the gun, Beverly. I know it was you."

"What? Don't be stupider than you already are. Faith killed them. She killed them all."

"Save it. My partner just called me. He found Cory Norton's body. And Cory had a hell of a hidden camera system. He recorded the whole thing, including you putting a bullet in the back of his head."

Faith's mother's hand shook. "It's a lie. All of it." She glared at Faith. "This is all *your* fault."

"Drop it, or I'll shoot." Lionel's eyebrows arched.

"Marshfield, PD!" someone yelled from the front hallway.

"Back here, Officer Carson," Lionel called out. "One suspect with a gun." His head was shaking and his lips were pulled back over his teeth like he was in pain. "Please, Beverly, drop the damn gun."

Faith's mother scoffed. "You love me, Lionel. You'll never pull the trigger."

"But *I* can't stand you." Tommy ran into the kitchen from the hallway and aimed his gun at Faith's mother. "You killed Kim. I'd love to blow your head right off."

Faith stared at her mother's scowling face and fear sliced through her like a thousand little cuts, sending adrenaline coursing through her system. Her mother had her gun aimed at Faith, but Faith wasn't afraid for her own life. In spite of all her mother had done, Faith didn't want her mother to die. The image of them sitting on the steps of the cabin and counting fireflies flickered in her mind. She could almost hear her mother's laugh and feel her wrap her arm around her shoulders.

"Mom." Faith's voice cracked. "Please put the gun down."

Faith's mother raised the gun and aimed at Faith's head.

Seven shots rang out.

Lionel shot once.

Tommy opened up.

Faith's mother fell back and landed on the tile with a thud.

Faith pulled the broken glass away from Thad's throat and gently lowered his head while she watched her mother's blood slowly mix with the pool of whiskey.

Sunday, April 15

Propped up in her hospital bed, Faith wasn't sure how many hours she'd been staring at the blank TV. She shifted her weight, adjusting the pillows under her bulky knee brace. A morphine drip hung at the left side of the bed. She wasn't about to pass up getting as much painkiller as she could, so she pressed the button a couple of times . . . just in case. Right now, her body was numb, but that wasn't the pain she wanted to kill.

A quiet tap on the door, and Rachel stood there, holding a basket covered in napkins in one hand and a canvas tote bag in the other. "The nurse said you might be up for a visitor. Is it okay?"

Faith pressed the morphine button again as if she could hurry it along, like someone pushing the "up" button over and over while waiting for the elevator. A visitor was the last thing she needed, but when she looked at Anna's aunt clutching the basket like a beggar girl, she couldn't bring herself to say no and nodded groggily.

Rachel pulled a chair next to the bed, set the bag on the floor, and placed the basket next to Faith's lunch, which sat untouched on the bedside table.

"Muffins and cookies." Rachel lifted the corner of the napkin covering the basket. "They're from Jane."

Faith stared at Rachel for a long moment. There was no need to ask if Rachel knew what had happened. Tears ran down Rachel's face, and from her red-rimmed eyes Faith suspected she'd been crying for a while.

Rachel reached into the bag and pulled out a book. Faith glanced at the cover: *Surviving Loss*. She was about to tell Rachel she didn't want it, until she noticed the worn edges and dog-eared pages.

"It helped me." Rachel set it next to the basket. She reached back into her bag, but stopped.

Faith waited as Rachel sat there, leaning forward, one arm extended, the other hand on her leg. Rachel seemed to be debating with herself about taking whatever it was out of the bag. After a moment, she pulled out a picture frame and clutched it against her chest, the photo facing Rachel.

"After I lost them," Rachel said, "I tried to force myself not to even think about Jessica and Anna because it hurt so much." She gazed down into her lap. She took in a long breath and exhaled slowly. "But I found that what really helped me was remembering them. Remembering the good." She moved the basket onto the counter and placed the photo on the table so Faith could see it.

The picture was of Faith, her father, Kim, Mrs. Foster, Anna, and Emily at the dock on the lake. They were all holding up fishing poles with large fish on the end . . . well, everyone except her dad, who had a tiny sunfish because he'd spent all his time helping everyone else.

Faith laughed.

"I don't know if you remember, but that was Anna's birthday," Rachel said. "Her dad got called out to California, so your father took all the girls fishing. Anna's mom brought me along. I took the picture."

"I remember." Faith's voice broke.

Rachel kept talking about the outing. She ran down everything they did—how Anna almost tipped over the boat while reeling in her fish, and Emily started a splashing war, and Mrs. Foster realized she'd packed three extra sandwiches and Faith's dad ate them all. Faith stared at the photo and embraced every memory sparked by the words.

Rachel visited for almost an hour. She didn't preach or talk about pain, hurt, and loss; it was only about love. When she was done, she picked up her bag and gazed down at Faith. "Please let me know if I can do anything for you."

Faith glanced at the photo and closed her eyes. "Do you believe in Heaven?"

"Yes."

"What's stopping you from going?" Faith's eyes flicked open.

Rachel didn't seem shocked by the question. From the look on her face, Faith assumed Rachel had asked herself that many times. "I'm needed here."

"What if you're not?"

Rachel switched hands with the bag. "Everyone's needed." Faith shook her head.

"You might not realize it," Rachel said, "but you just helped me much more than I helped you."

Faith pointed to the photograph. "You forgot it."

"Why don't you hold onto it?" Rachel stepped back close to the bed. "But I did forget one thing. Would you mind if I prayed with you before I leave?"

Faith reached for the morphine drip, but Rachel must have thought Faith was agreeing and took Faith's hand in hers.

"Dear Lord, you know our pain. You wept over the loss of your friend and those you love like we have. Thank you for Faith. Please help her through this. In Jesus's name, Amen."

Faith had expected Rachel to go on and on, praying for healing and peace and serenity, so the simple prayer caught her off-guard. As she looked up at Rachel, she remembered what Jane had said about her: *She's real. A survivor. She's one of us.*

"Thanks for the picture," Faith said.

"Thank you for remembering them with me." Rachel wiped another tear away, and she left.

Faith watched Rachel pass the nurses' station and saw Robert talking with the nurse on duty. He noticed Faith and nearly dropped the flowers in his hands.

The nurse approached Faith's room and quietly asked, "Are you up for one more visitor?"

Faith nodded.

The nurse stepped aside as Robert walked in. He stayed next to the door and set the glass vase of daisies on the counter next to the sink. "I was just dropping this off. Your friend, the policeman, talked to me. He told me what he said when you came to my house and why you ran. I should have been more straightforward with you. I just wanted to help, but I also didn't want to push, and it ended up coming off like I was following you."

"I know you were trying to help me." Faith reached out for the morphine drip and clicked three times. She'd already apologized to Lionel for almost killing him, so she figured this would be easy, but her temples were starting to throb. "I'm sorry I showed up on your doorstep like that and then took off. It's just . . . I didn't know who I could trust."

"I should have told you my whole story. I can also see how my actions would have made you suspicious. I explained to Tommy I wasn't, like, stalking-following you, I just . . . I was worried about you. But I can imagine you wouldn't want to be around me."

"That's not true."

Robert's hands started looking for a place to land, and he finally stuck both into his armpits and crossed his arms. "Tommy told you what I did?"

Faith nodded. "It was self-defense, right?"

Robert exhaled and looked at the ceiling, his eyes shifting from tile to tile. His lips moved, but he didn't say anything.

"Are you counting ceiling tiles?" Faith asked.

Robert's hands went back into overdrive. "Sorry. It's a coping mechanism. I . . . Yes. The technical answer to your question is yes, but the fact remains that—" He glanced over his shoulder to the busy nurses' desk and stepped closer to the bed. "It was self-defense, but I still took two people's lives. I have issues with that."

Faith put her left hand behind her head. The morphine machine hummed and sunlight spread through her system. "I like you better knowing you don't have it all together."

The corner of his mouth ticked up. "Do you need anything?"

Faith glanced at the morphine machine and raised an eyebrow. "I might need a ride to a meeting when they let me out. Unless they let me take this thing with me." She grinned and held up the button.

Robert winced. "Hospital medication can be a big trigger. If you want, I can tell them to try to find an alternative—"

"If you even think about telling them to take my smile-making machine away, I'll hit you with a crutch."

Robert chuckled.

Faith tipped her head toward the visitor's chair. "Sit down."

"Really?"

Faith thought of several snarky replies, but one look at Robert's nervous expression and she just nodded.

He sat down and grabbed both arms of the chair. "Do you know when you're being released? I know I sound like a broken record, but you should come up with a sobriety plan."

Faith turned her head to look at him. She had a plan for when she was released. It wasn't a sobriety plan, and it wasn't anything she could tell him, or anyone else for that matter. But it was something she knew she would do if they ever caught the killers.

Sunday, April 22

Faith adjusted the heavy backpack on her shoulder and limped down the gravel path, the bulky brace on her knee squeaking softly with each step, until the little cabin came into view.

She passed the spot where her sister died and kept on walking. Legally, the cabin was now hers, but she couldn't find the key. The cabin door was locked, but she'd come prepared. She pulled a five-pound mini-sledgehammer from her backpack and smashed the lock until the door swung open. She walked inside, crushing broken bits of mirror that still lay strewn across the floor. She laid four flowers in the center of the cabin and bowed her head.

"Your aunt visited me in the hospital, Anna," Faith whispered. "We talked about you and your mom and Emily. I liked that. Rachel said you're happy now. Together. I miss you."

When she opened her eyes, her reflection stared back from the mirror bits on the floor. This time, she didn't flinch. She was glad to have her father's eyes. Somehow, she'd regained her love for him. She even dreamt they'd gone fishing out on the lake.

"I'm sorry, Daddy," she whispered. "I'm so sorry I thought . . . I was wrong. I miss you. I love you so much."

Her legs started to shake and she sank to her knees, her brace clunking on the floor. She pressed her hands flat against the wood, her tears turning the old wood dark and spreading out in a ring.

She didn't know how long she cried, but she wept a cycle of tears like the changing seasons: sadness, anger, pity, pain, and a grief so deep it seemed to come from her soul itself.

Lying on the floor, she remembered the nursery rhyme from her childhood again. But this time, she remembered her father softly singing it to her.

Hush, little girl, rest your head.
Hush, little girl, stay in bed.
The sun and your friends are fast asleep.
Now's not a time to cry and weep.
For in your dreams, there we'll be.
Hurry now, and follow me.

She softly kissed her father's flower, then set it back down, repeating the motion with the others. She wiped the tears away with her shirtsleeve and rose to her feet.

Faith reached into the backpack once more. On the way to the cabin, at the last service station, she'd filled a bottle with gasoline. She poured the gas all around, and dropped the bottle into the corner. Then she went outside, lit a match, and tossed it into the cabin.

Within minutes, the flames were so intense she had to back away. Dark clouds of soot shot upward, but Faith wasn't worried about the fire department coming. She'd gotten a bonfire permit

. . . she just neglected to tell them what she was planning on burning.

As the flames rose higher she took a pistol case out of the backpack, followed by another bottle, this time whiskey, and six shot glasses. She kissed a single rose, laid it on the spot where Kim's body had been found, stepped back, and set the shot glasses down.

A stone in the path caught the light from the fire and glittered. Hope rose in Faith's heart as she dug a finger into the soil, but it wasn't Kim's missing diamond. Just a shard of broken glass.

She closed her eyes, and swayed to the silent symphony that was growing inside her, against the percussive pops and snaps of flames biting through wood, destroying memories. She wasn't crazy, and . . . she wasn't even angry anymore.

I'm free, free of the shadows! Her primal whoops of pain and joy and hope and life echoed across the lake until a breeze blew flames and embers sharply to the west.

She opened her eyes to look across from the cabin, where light and dark played against the old, bent pines. There were a couple more things she had to do before she said good-bye to the cabin.

The dancing shadows and smoke conjured families mourning and laughing and singing together, women holding infants, lovers coupling, sisters, friends, and she knew she was not alone here, and that was a good thing, because she needed someone to share with at this very moment.

Henry appeared beside Faith and watched the flames lap at the sky.

"Finally! Where have you been, Henry? I needed you and you were nowhere to be found!"

"I knew you could handle things. You didn't *really* need me."

"But I *did* need you. Nobody was looking for Rat Face. And I didn't want to talk to the real cops in Dr. Rodgers's office. They wouldn't have believed me, anyway." Faith paused, coming to a realization. "I think that's why I created you."

Henry stood with her hands clasped behind her back, but she seemed pleased.

Faith wiped her nose with her sleeve. "Anyway, thank you for keeping me sane."

Henry was dimming.

"And I know, technically, I shouldn't be talking to you, because you're not real. But I love you, Henry. Even though you wore a business suit to a bonfire."

"I love you, too, Squirt."

Faith clasped her hand over her mouth and squeezed her eyes closed. *Kim.* Faith opened her eyes and there stood her teenage sister, exactly as she remembered her.

"Kim!" The name echoed off the rocks and trees as she whirled the vision in her arms, until the fire and the lake blurred together into a shimmering ring encircling them in gentle warmth, neither hot nor cold.

She stopped when she got dizzy and brought the image closer until she locked on Kim's silvery eyes.

"It hurts to talk to you, but it hurts more *not* to talk to you. I miss you so much, sis. I don't want to be alone."

Kim took a step away but held her hand. "I miss you, too. It's okay to talk to me, but you have to stop living in the past. Come on, did you really think you'd find the diamond just lying here?"

"I hoped."

Kim pointed at the box. "Don't do it."

"I wasn't going to. Not if you showed up here and danced with me by the lake. And you did. I think I just brought it to prove I didn't have to use it. Even here."

"It's not your time." Kim pointed at the burning cabin. "That's going to burn to the ground, but after a while, something's going to grow there. Now, you could leave it to chance and let thorns and weeds grow. Or you could plant something beautiful in the ashes, and help it grow."

"Tommy still loves you."

"I know. You think I don't see things?"

"Yeah. You're my superhero."

"Well, you're *my* superhero, you little badass. Don't forget that. And now you get to do everything I didn't get a chance to do. So do me a favor, stop looking back. Be the girl who lived, and *live*."

Kim was walking away, into the spaces between the pines.

"Please don't go," Faith sobbed.

"I'm never far away. I'm always with you." Kim waved, then turned and disappeared among the trees.

Faith sat alone in the grass with the gun case on her lap for a long time, at peace for the first time in ten years, watching the flames consume the painful memories of the cabin and leave only those she loved, and would always love.

After a while, Faith reached down and picked up the bottle of whiskey. She faced the cabin and lifted the bottle high.

"Here's to the dead!"

And to the survivors.

She tossed the bottle into the flames and limped away, up the trail.

IF YOU LIKED THE GIRL WHO LIVED, YOU'LL LOVE JACK!

The Detective Jack Stratton Mystery-Thriller Series, authored by *Wall Street Journal* bestselling writer Christopher Greyson, has over one million readers and counting. If you'd love to read another page-turning thriller with mystery, humor, and a dash of romance, pick up the next book in the highly acclaimed series today.

Novels featuring Jack Stratton in order:
**AND THEN SHE WAS GONE
GIRL JACKED
JACK KNIFED
JACKS ARE WILD
JACK AND THE GIANT KILLER
DATA JACK
JACK OF HEARTS
JACK FROST**

AND THEN SHE WAS GONE

A hometown hero with a heart of gold, Jack Stratton was raised in a whorehouse by his prostitute mother. Jack seemed destined to become another statistic, but now his life has taken a turn for the better. Determined to escape his past, he's headed for a career in law enforcement. When his foster mother asks him to look into a girl's disappearance, Jack quickly gets drawn into a baffling mystery. As Jack digs deeper, everyone becomes a suspect—including himself. Caught between the criminals and the cops, can Jack discover the truth in time to save the girl? Or will he become the next victim?

GIRL JACKED

Guilt has driven a wedge between Jack and the family he loves. When Jack, now a police officer, hears the news that his foster sister Michelle is missing, it cuts straight to his core. The police think she just took off, but Jack knows Michelle would never leave her loved ones behind—like he did. Forced to confront the demons from his past, Jack must take action, find Michelle, and bring her home... or die trying.

JACK KNIFED

Constant nightmares have forced Jack to seek answers about his rough childhood and the dark secrets hidden there. The mystery surrounding Jack's birth father leads Jack to investigate the twenty-seven-year-old murder case in Hope Falls.

JACKS ARE WILD

When Jack's sexy old flame disappears, no one thinks it's suspicious except Jack and one unbalanced witness. Jack feels in his gut that something is wrong. He knows that Marisa has a past, and if it ever caught up with her—it would be deadly. The trail leads him into all sorts of trouble—landing him smack in the middle of an all-out mob war between the Italian Mafia and the Japanese Yakuza.

JACK AND THE GIANT KILLER

Rogue hero Jack Stratton is back in another action-packed, thrilling adventure. While recovering from a gunshot wound, Jack gets a seemingly harmless private investigation job—locate the owner of a lost dog—Jack begrudgingly assists. Little does he know it will place him directly in the crosshairs of a merciless serial killer.

DATA JACK

In this digital age of hackers, spyware, and cyber terrorism—data is more valuable than gold. Thieves plan to steal the keys to the digital kingdom and with this much money at stake, they'll kill for it. Can Jack and Alice (aka Replacement) stop the pack of ruthless criminals before they can *Data Jack?*

JACK OF HEARTS

When his mother and the members of her neighborhood book club ask him to catch the "Orange Blossom Cove Bandit," a small-time thief who's stealing garden gnomes and peace of mind from their quiet retirement community, how can Jack refuse? The peculiar mystery proves to be more than it appears, and things take a deadly turn. Now, Jack finds it's up to him to stop a crazed killer, save his parents, and win the hand of the girl he loves—but if he survives, will it be Jack who ends up with a broken heart?

JACK FROST

Jack has a new assignment: to investigate the suspicious death of a soundman on the hit TV show *Planet Survival*. Jack goes undercover as a security agent where the show is filming on nearby Mount Minuit. Soon trapped on the treacherous peak by a blizzard, a mysterious killer continues to stalk the cast and crew of *Planet Survival*. What started out as a game is now a deadly competition for survival. As the temperature drops and the body count rises, what will get them first? The mountain or the killer?

————————————

————————————

Epic Fantasy
PURE OF HEART

Orphaned and alone, rogue-teen Dean Walker has learned how to take care of himself on the rough city streets. Unjustly wanted by the police, he takes refuge within the shadows of the city. When Dean stumbles upon an old man being mugged, he tries to help—only to discover that the victim is anything but helpless and far more than he appears. Together with three friends, he sets out on an epic quest where only the pure of heart will prevail.

————————————

————————————

INTRODUCING
THE ADVENTURES OF FINN AND ANNIE

A SPECIAL COLLECTION OF MYSTERIES
EXCLUSIVELY FOR CHRISTOPHER GREYSON'S
LOYAL READERS

Finnian Church chased his boyhood dream of following in his father's law-enforcing footsteps by way of the United States Armed Forces. As soon as he finished his tour of duty, Finn planned to report to the police academy. But the winds of war have a way of changing a man's plans. Finn returned home a decorated war hero, but without a leg. Disillusioned but undaunted, it wasn't long before he discovered a way to keep his ambitions alive and earn a living as an insurance investigator.

Finn finds himself in need of a videographer to document the accident scenes. Into his orderly business and simple life walks Annie Summers. A lovely free spirit and single mother of two, Annie has a physical challenge of her own—she's been completely deaf since childhood.

Finn and Annie find themselves tested and growing in ways they never imagined. Join this unlikely duo as they investigate their way through murder, arson, theft, embezzlement, and maybe even love, seeking to distinguish between truth and lies, scammers and victims.

This FREE special collection of mysteries by *Wall Street Journal* bestselling author CHRISTOPHER GREYSON is available EXCLUSIVELY to loyal readers. Get your FREE first installment ONLY at ChristopherGreyson.com.
Become a Preferred Reader to enjoy additional FREE *Adventures of Finn and Annie*, advanced notifications of book releases, and more.

Don't miss out, visit ChristopherGreyson.com
and JOIN TODAY!

ACKNOWLEDGMENTS

I would like to thank all the wonderful readers out there. It is you who make the literary world what it is today—a place of dreams filled with tales of adventure! To all of you who have spread word of my novels via social media (Facebook and Twitter) and who have taken the time to go back and write a great review, I say THANK YOU! Your efforts keep the characters alive and give me the encouragement and time to keep writing. I can't thank YOU enough.

Word of mouth is crucial for any author to succeed. If you enjoyed the novel, please consider leaving a review at Amazon, even if it is only a line or two; it would make all the difference and I would appreciate it very much.

I would also like to thank my amazing wife for standing beside me every step of the way on this journey. My thanks also go out to Laura and Christopher, my two awesome kids, and my dear mother and the rest of my family. Finally, thank you to my wonderful team: Maia McViney, Maia Sepp, my fantastic editors—David Gatewood of Lone Trout Editing, Faith Williams of The Atwater Group, Charlie Wilson of Landmark Editorial, Anne Cherry, Ann Kroeker—my writing coach and my consultant Dianne Jones, and the unbelievably helpful beta readers!

ABOUT THE AUTHOR

My name is Christopher Greyson, and I am a storyteller.

Since I was a little boy, I have dreamt of what mystery was around the next corner, or what quest lay over the hill. If I couldn't find an adventure, one usually found me, and now I weave those tales into my stories. I am blessed to have written the bestselling Detective Jack Stratton Mystery-Thriller Series. The collection includes *And Then She Was GONE*, *Girl Jacked*, *Jack Knifed*, *Jacks Are Wild*, *Jack and the Giant Killer*, *Data Jack*, *Jack of Hearts*, *Jack Frost*, with *Jack of Diamonds* due later this year. I have also penned the bestselling psychological thriller, *The Girl Who Lived* and a special collection of mysteries, *The Adventures of Finn and Annie*.

My love for tales of mystery and adventure began with my grandfather, a decorated World War I hero. I will never forget being introduced to his friend, a WWI pilot who flew across the skies at the same time as the feared, legendary Red Baron. My love of reading and storytelling eventually led me to write *Pure of Heart*, a young adult fantasy that I released in 2014.

I love to hear from my readers. Please visit ChristopherGreyson.com, where you can become a preferred reader and enjoy additional FREE *Adventures of Finn and Annie*, advanced notifications of book releases and more! Thank you for reading my novels. I hope my stories have brightened your day.

Sincerely,